Elysium's Shadow

Elysium Chronicles: Book One

Matthew Munson

Published by Inspired Quill: September 2017

First Edition

Elysium's Shadow © 2017 by Matthew Munson
Contact the author through his website: www.matthewmunson.co.uk

Editors: Sara-Jayne Slack & Rebecca Hall
Cover Design: Venetia Jackson: vf-jackson.com
Typeset in Minion Pro

Paperback ISBN: 978-1-908600-63-9
eBook ISBN: 978-1-908600-64-6

Printed in the United Kingdom
1 2 3 4 5 6 7 8 9 10

Inspired Quill Publishing, UK
Business Reg. No. 7592847
www.inspired-quill.com

Praise for Matthew Munson

Fall From Grace *is fantastic and unbelievably exciting. I love the way Matthew turns the history of the angels on its head, and the characters are so real I was almost in tears near the end. Simply fantastic.*

– JR Walker, *actor and author*

Great story, good characters. A really refreshing take on the Judeo-Christian mythology which has been done to death recently. But Fall from Grace *has plenty of surprises up its sleeve. As a debut novel, this is a great piece of work.*

– Craig Hallam, *author of Greaveburn*

The storyline is written to keep you on your toes and engaged; I was unable to put this book down. The writing style is easy to read, yet there is a deep plot that keeps you wanting to know more. Worth every penny.

– Oregon Rain, *Top Amazon reviewer*

Dedication

Dedicating a book I care for so much to any one person is tough, so I shan't; this book, the first in a new series, is dedicated to seven people in particular.

Diana, Lynda, Kirk, Chelby, Lynda, Barbara and Helen.

Each of you know why.

6.30pm, 9th April, ICY 418

Island Two, Elysium

JULIE MARTIN BREATHED in, deeply, and savoured the moment. Blain had taken obvious pleasure in putting her in the smallest, most cramped cell his security compound possessed. He hadn't admitted to the gesture being intentional, of course – he'd not said a word to her since her arrest – but she'd had to endure his smug features gleefully watching her as necessary preparations were made to drag her from Island One over to Island Two. Her new home.

These two islands had been Julie's world for the past two years, but didn't form the whole of the Earth-sized planet called Elysium; it was a beautiful world, with a single vast continent they had nicknamed Pangaea dominating a full third of the planet's surface, and an innumerable series of smaller islands – a paltry two of which were colonised by humanity. None of the staff or prisoners ever left the safety of their two islands without heavily-armed guards, and only then to try and find anything that could be considered valuable on nearby islands. Elysium *looked* beautiful, but it was savage, and bristling with predators. Pangaea remained resolutely off-limits to the small band of human residents, and lasers kept the airborne predators far enough away for limited peace of mind.

Her mind was still reeling from all that had happened in just the last few hours, as she stepped down from the shuttle onto the warm dock. Now that she was seeing her new home through different eyes, those of a prisoner, she appreciated how secure it really was. Prisoners didn't even get the run of the entire island, despite the endless seas acting as a far more effective barrier than the wall in front of her ever could. The enormity of what she had done only now hit her.

I'll never see my best friend again.

Her lapse had taken everything away; her reputation, her job, her calling and her *life*. She had stood by and allowed the suppression field – an invisible field capable of pushing down elemental power – to be activated, reducing her abilities to the point of non-existence. Losing them hurt almost as much as losing her friend. In some ways, it hurt *more*. She would never admit that guilty secret to anyone, but her power had been with her since puberty had arrived thirty years ago, and she couldn't remember being anything else.

As the guards communicated with their fellows up in the guard tower, Julie savoured the momentary delay and looked around. While Island Two's dock was half the size of Island One's equivalent, it was nevertheless perfectly serviceable. All of the goods, equipment and personnel that were delivered to Elysium went first to Island One for processing and onward travel.

Prisoners were the one exception. They came directly *here* to the prison island, ensuring Island One was forever unsullied by their presence. Julie, of course, was the exception to *that* exception; the only member of staff, probably in the history of prison worlds, to move from the comfort and security of her staff quarters to the stark and severe world that the prisoners inhabited.

Elysium had been her home ever since the prison had first opened two years previous, and she'd hoped to stay here for a while longer – she was a rare breed; a graduate of the Merlin Institute, working for the Republic as part of a half-hearted programme to try and improve relations between the two sides – but had intended to move on eventually. Not now.

Out of her peripheral vision, she saw men step either side of her. She tensed; the security guards who had accompanied her on the flight were two of Blain's favourites. They were thuggish, only mildly intelligent and no lovers of the power they called magic. She could understand that; not many non-Institute people were. They didn't understand it – of course they didn't, otherwise why would they call it magic? That was for sleight-of-hand card tricks, far beneath the subtle art of elemental control she and her fellow Merlins performed; and the Institute called their power just that. But "elemental control" wasn't very catchy, and the term magic had stuck amongst the general population. The ability to manipulate the elements was a rare art; only a small number of people born with the power. Any human child could be born with the right sequence of activated genes, but scientists still – even after so much research – didn't know the exact sequence, so those born with elemental powers were entirely at the lap of the … Julie hesitated. She wouldn't use the word "gods".

Perhaps "fate" is a better choice of word.

She sighed; pedantry was the least of her worries right now. Human beings often feared what they did not understand, and when an evolutionary quirk had burst those powers out into point five percent of the population, hundreds of years before, the people *with* those powers had been often treated abysmally.

Sadly, things were still difficult between the Institute and the Republic more widely; humanity didn't understand the Institute, and the Institute members struggled to remember what it was like to live without power. A gulf of misunderstanding had split open between them over the years, and proved more difficult as time went on, as each side relied heavily on the other; the Republic needed the Institute for a more creative defence against some of their more unusual enemies, and the Institute needed the Emperors and Empresses to give them political cover to continue with their research and development without interference.

Things had gotten worse under Guinevere's leadership, of course, but no-one was surprised – she made her distrust of the Institute well-known. She had declared, back when she was heir to the Golden Throne, that she would keep the Institute at arm's length when she was in power, and she had apparently been true to her word; she and the Chief Warlock had barely spoken. Or that's what Julie had heard anyway. That did nothing except increase the tension between the two sides; *T'was ever thus*, Julie thought wearily.

Blain's choice of guards, therefore, had made her wonder if the chief of security might have hoped for something to happen to her in the transit time between islands. The guards – Walters and Smith, if she remembered correctly – had been incredibly well-behaved. They had watched her carefully and both had kept their right hands on their nightsticks. The suppression field had done its job well, but the guards obviously still believed that she had some kind of latent power being kept in reserve, to turn them (perhaps) into a frog or a small vase. Of course, she'd certainly thought about it. They would have deserved it.

I even know what to do with the excess matter. But I don't want to get into more trouble – and it's moot anyway with the bloody suppression field engaged. How very prescient of Mr Blain to have had one installed; I knew he didn't trust me.

Each guard grabbed one of her arms, making it clear to her that it was time to move. She bristled at their touch.

I won't be escorted there like some common criminal, she thought stubbornly. *That's one thing I'm not.* None *of the inhabitants here are; I never believed that, even when I was on Island One. I never agreed with imprisoning people purely on the basis of their dissent from the accepted norms, especially when the dissent was peaceful and the norms are so violent.*

She flushed, realising how loose she'd become with her thinking in such short a period of time. She had come into the Prisons Directorate to see what she could learn from people living in the system. She just hadn't expected to be *amongst* them quite so intimately.

But they're all intelligent, resourceful people. I'm no better; they fought against a corrupt system before they were caught, and I respect them. She managed to suppress a guilty smile. *I actually quite like their radical approach.*

She pulled her arms away from their firm grips and glared at each of them in turn; they both tensed, and Smith's hand twitched back towards his nightstick. He seemed to be fighting an urge to pull it out and use it anyway, just for the hell of it.

Walters, for his part, seemed unsure now that Julie had resisted their touch. Walters' indecision spread to Smith, and both men hesitated. They weren't to know that Julie was quite willing to move on; she had made her point. They clearly wanted direction, and she saw two sets of eyes glance back towards the shuttle to seek it.

Julie refused to look. She wouldn't give Blain the satisfaction. He hadn't yet deigned to leave the comfort of the shuttle, and she wondered if he even would; *he* was clearly driving home the point that he was important enough to keep any prisoner waiting – even an ex-colleague. Commander Robert Blain hardly ever left the safe confines of Island One; he had staff to sort out the actual prisoners, leaving him to deal with whatever he chose. Julie had never been entirely sure, in the two years they had worked together, what he *actually* did. He hadn't spent a lot of time in his office or his quarters, but whenever questioned, Blain would merely say that he had enough to keep him busy.

He only got away with it because he and Noble were friends.

Governor Noble. His face floated in her mind's eye again, and through the feeling of vague sickness, a heavy cloak of sorrow and guilt threatened to smother her.

Another movement brought her back to the present moment; Blain had finally decided to leave the shuttle. She looked – she couldn't help but look – and scowled as she saw the insufferable pleasure on his face. His eyes flickered over Walters and Smith for a moment, and then his gaze settled on Julie. He stepped down to the dockside and walked the few steps towards her, making sure his face was turned so that she could see him.

"Are you going to try something?" he asked. "Go on, Julie. I dare you. Try *something*. Let us defend ourselves." He clicked his fingers, like he had only this moment remembered something. "Oh, that's right," he went on, "you can't, can you? I've taken your powers away. You're just like the rest of us now. I've cured you of your ... instability. How does it feel to be properly human for the first time since you hit puberty?"

"Boring," she replied in what she knew came across as a flat monotone. "Bland. Limited. I'm sure I don't need to go on. How do you live in a limited world?"

Blain's face tightened; he clearly hadn't expected to get

a response, not least one that was quite so snappy. He was used to having his authority unchecked; Noble had certainly always been willing to allow that. Julie, however, had never given him an easy ride. Noble had tolerated their disputes because he recognised Julie's elemental powers and was afraid of Blain. Julie also suspected that Noble enjoyed watching them argue.

"I wouldn't be so confident right now," he retorted. "Look around you, Julie. Don't forget where you are." Blain's face settled back into the usual smirk, and Julie instantly bridled. He was *enjoying* himself. The swap programme between the Institute and the Republic was meant to encourage understanding, but Blain hadn't shown anything but bigotry.

Noble was meant to have been his friend! she thought angrily. *But our governor was just a pawn in whatever game our beloved Security Chief was playing. He even convinced the governor to make* him *Deputy over me. I'll never forgive Noble for trusting me so little.*

"I wouldn't ever forget where I am now, nor why I'm here," she replied. "I *want* to remember everything."

Blain nodded, apparently satisfied, but Julie wasn't finished. Her face set hard into a scowl. "I want to remember what Alexis Noble did to his wife. I want to remember the look of terror on Catherine's face as he shot her – his own wife – in the chest with a phase pistol."

"He was defending himself!" Blain barked. "Catherine had systematically lied to her husband since their wedding day. Since *before* their wedding day, in fact. She hid who she was from your own Hunters. They bring in every person with the activated magical – or elemental, if you insist – gene into the Institute, because that's the law, and you people need to be controlled and regulated. But Catherine lied and kept her abilities tightly locked away, and you helped her. She put Alexis' career at risk!"

"She was scared and lonely!" Julie retorted. "And don't you *dare* lecture me about being on the run from the Elemental Hunters, Blain. You know full well that I used to be one. I detected Catherine's latent power as soon as I met her, but she wasn't doing any harm. I was training her to *control* them."

A vein throbbed in Blain's forehead, and his cheeks had flushed red at the ferocity behind Julie's words.

"It's *Acting Governor* Blain to you," he snarled. "Director Wood has named me temporary ruler of this world, and it'll only be a matter of time before he makes the appointment permanent."

"Ruler?" Julie sneered. "You do think highly of yourself, don't you? You're still nothing more than a jumped-up, tin-pot dictator. You won't last five minutes as Governor before Wood sees your true colours and sacks you."

She couldn't bear his supercilious, condescending attitude. However, the two guards, as she saw out of her peripheral vision, had tensed. Walters' hand moved towards the phase pistol in the belt around his waist, but he was watching Blain carefully before making a more overt move.

Blain chuckled, the sound cold and humourless.

"You've clearly given this a lot of thought," he replied,

"but your analysis is completely wrong. After all, you *killed* Governor Noble in cold blood. He was defending Elysium from an unlicensed, potentially dangerous magician. As an ex-Magic Hunter, you must recognise that?"

"I am a graduate of the Merlin Institute. I can control the elements, and so could Catherine. What I did was *not* in cold blood. Noble killed his wife – my friend – for no other reason than he was ashamed of her. She wasn't a threat to anyone; he could see that her powers were so weak they'd barely register on the Institute's scale. Alexis Noble hated practitioners because they were different; he might not have known what Catherine was, but his bigotry made her ashamed of who she was, and I tried to make her see the world differently. When her husband killed her for the crime of being different, then I *had* to act."

"You used *magic* to kill him."

"It's *not* magic, and you know it!" Julie drew in another breath, more ragged this time, and tried to calm herself; Blain was looking for any excuse to do her harm. "It's science; magic is just the word non-Merlin members used when we first discovered what our minds could do. Catherine and I were exploring the capacity of the human brain, not mysticism, and I resent the implication that there was anything improper in that."

"Killing people in any culture is wrong," Blain barked. "I know for a fact it's taboo in yours to kill using your powers."

Julie swallowed hard as shame washed over her; she *had* killed someone. That knowledge would stay with her forever, and hearing Blain tell her what she already knew made it more real somehow.

"We can defend ourselves when needed," she said. "That's what I did this morning. I defended myself against an aggressor after I couldn't protect my friend."

"I imagine that the Merlin Institute would challenge your interpretation of that."

"Then the Merlin Institute is wrong." Julie pressed her lips together, but there was nothing she could do about it now; her words were out, and she had expressed the sentiment that she had been thinking for most of the day. Blain's eyebrows rose as far as they could possibly go up his forehead.

"I would imagine that the Chief Warlock would be *very* interested to know what you've just said. It might put a completely different spin on your career so far." He smiled. "What am I saying?" he went on. "'So far'? I certainly didn't mean to indicate that your career has a future. We both know that you're finished."

Their argument, held on the dock of Island Two against a bright, glowing sun and clear blue sky, with the high walls of the prison compound rising up to show her the future, had a strange sense of unreality about it. Julie shook her head and turned away.

"Take me there," she said, nodding towards the compound. "Let's get this over with."

If Blain said anything else, she didn't hear. The guards allowed her to walk without constraint, up the track towards the prison compound where her new life would begin.

She stepped inside the outer gates – twelve feet tall,

steel-reinforced and impregnable – and turned to face them. All three were staring at her, and Julie knew exactly why. They were waiting for her to do something. They didn't trust the mage, even with the suppression field active.

But I've already made my mistake, she thought. *I can't make any more. I'm going to die here; I'm never going to know freedom again, and all because I killed a murderer.*

4.30pm, 16th April 418

RSS *Merciless* on final approach to Elysium orbit

S PACE WAS COLD and hard; an unforgiving place that career travellers treated with a combination of respect and fear. Jon May – *Governor* Jon May, as he had to keep reminding himself – had observed, with a sense of relief, the Praetorian Guard treating it with exactly the right level of respect and fear throughout the last six days. Despite himself, he liked their attitude towards the savage abrasiveness of space. They were continually grateful for the relative comfort of their ship and the simple pleasures on board: light, heat and food were the main things they were interested in, and everything else, including politics, was secondary.

Despite all that, however, Jon still felt uneasy. He was going stir crazy after just six days, although felt grateful that he didn't get claustrophobic; living in such close quarters with four hundred men and women made him uncomfortable – there wasn't anywhere to spread out. He preferred grass beneath his feet and blue sky above his head, not the rumbling of deck plates and the vacuum of space just beyond the next bulkhead.

The conference room that had been assigned for him to use as an office was silent. The large windows enabled him to stare out into the infinite, inky blackness of space, and he was grateful that there was less of it now that their destination planet loomed into view. He'd first seen it a few hours ago, when the *Merciless* had dropped out of faster-than-light speed to its more-navigable sub-light engines. Now, it commanded his attention. His new home.

A trip like this, to the Outmarches buffer zone, would have taken a full week just a couple of years ago, but now a ship like the *Merciless* – one of the newest warships in the Praetorian Guard's space fleet – could shave a full day off the trip and get him to Elysium that much quicker, thanks to the improvements in FTL engine design.

And I don't want to leave Blain in control of this world longer than absolutely necessary, he thought. *From the rumours I've heard about him, even six days is too much. He's going to resent me for taking the governorship off him, but that's tough.*

But the approach time gave him the opportunity to study Elysium from far above. It was a stunningly beautiful planet that the comms logs, sent back over the two years of the prison's existence, couldn't do justice. He knew that there was a lot of danger on the world – the savagery of its predators, which seemed to be most of the creatures down there, was already legendary. It made the perfect place for a prison world; if a prisoner escaped the high walls of Island Two, where would they go? The oceans were as dangerous as the land, and even shuttles had to follow a particular flight path to avoid the scattering field interfering with its systems.

Although that's one of the mysteries I plan on understanding, May thought. *If McIntyre's right, then someone seeded the planet with a high-energy scattering field that disrupts everything except visual sensors. I want to know who did that, and why.*

It was all damn peculiar, that was for sure, and May was determined to get to the bottom of it.

The swoosh of the doors leading out into the corridor interrupted his thoughts. Usually, he'd be irritated by the interruption, but right now he was glad of it. He'd spent too much time lost in his own thoughts recently; leaving Earth behind had created a strange blend of emotions. His new assignment had come about abruptly, and he was only now adjusting to his new life.

Turning, he saw two familiar faces and one not so familiar. The captain of the *Merciless* had assigned the Governor two security guards. For the most part, they hadn't been needed, but they *had* been able to do the occasional job for him, like now. May had been looking forward to talking with Steven Doy since he'd first come on board.

"Mr Doy, come in," he said, and motioned to one of the seats on the opposite side of the long conference table. "Thank you, gentlemen. Could you wait outside?"

One of the guards – Watson – scowled. "Sir," he said, "our orders from the captain regarding allowing prisoners out of their cells –"

"… are being superseded by mine," May interjected. His tone went steely; he would *not* be argued with. "This is a prison matter. My authority outranks the captain's on this. Please wait outside."

Watson and the other guard, Phillips, exchanged a glance, but they both reluctantly nodded, shot a warning glare at Doy and marched smartly out of the conference room.

Doy watched the guards leave and waited for the doors to close before turning back to May. "That was very brave of you."

"Why?" May retorted. "Because you're a wizard?"

Doy shook his head. "I'm not a wizard."

May frowned. He was comfortable being corrected wherever he was wrong, but he'd studied Doy's file at length before their meeting. That one fact – Doy's status as a failed student of the Merlin Academy – had stood out immediately.

"Well, you're certainly not a mage," he noted. "You have to study for a long time to get promoted to that rank. I do know a *few* things about the Institute."

"Not enough, clearly," Doy said. His tone indicated that he clearly hadn't meant what he'd said as a challenge. "I'm not a wizard because I failed my final exams. I'm not licensed by the Institute, so technically I'm not allowed to channel any power. And you know what the Institute does to non-licensed Merlins. If you don't take the medication they give you – which makes you want to kill yourself, by all accounts, as it suppresses all elemental abilities and most of your personality as well – they'll kill you outright anyway."

"So, why was I brave sending the guards out of the room?"

"Because what's stopping me from jumping across this table and attacking you right now? Who's to say I'm not a complete madman?"

"*Are* you a complete madman?"

Doy hesitated for a moment, then laughed; a deep, throaty sound that seemed completely genuine. "Would I admit it even if I was?"

May relaxed, and judging by the slump in the other man's shoulders, some of his tension had dissipated. He was in his late thirties, and looked older by at least a decade or more, rather than the actual three years. More than anything, he looked tired; his greying hair was thin, and deep worry lines were burned into his forehead. Given the fact he'd finally been caught after almost two decades on the run, it wasn't surprising that he was exhausted. He was slim, had piercing green eyes and radiated intelligence. He also looked very uncomfortable in his orange jumpsuit.

May motioned to the chair opposite. Doy looked surprised, but managed to school his face back into careful neutrality, and sat down. His back remained ramrod straight.

"Actually," Doy went on as he settled down, "I'm surprised you chose to talk to me."

"Why?" May asked.

"Do you even have to ask? I'm a prisoner, and you're

the newly-minted governor of the world I'm going to be spending the rest of my life on."

"Oh, you'd be surprised, Mr Doy. You know I've seen your file?"

Doy chuckled; it was completely devoid of humour this time, as was the smile that drew across his face.

"I'd be surprised if you hadn't," he replied. "You know why I was arrested, then?"

May heard the bitterness in the failed wizard's question. *If I were in his place, would I react any differently?*

"You fled from the scene of a crime and spent the next twenty years in hiding," he said, and had to ignore Doy's flinch. "Your sentence reflects your crime and your years in hiding – and, before you ask, I can't do anything to change your sentence. I'd be lying to you if I said I could, and I suspect you'd see right through me."

Doy seemed surprised by the governor's forthright manner. "I've accepted that I'm going to be here for a very long time," he said slowly, clearly thinking about every word, trying to avoid any signs of a trap. "I wouldn't ask you to do anything about it."

May drummed his fingers on the conference table. He had done the same thing in Wood's office. His meeting with the Director of Prisons and Clara McIntyre had been comparatively short and to the point, but he had left with purpose and reason. All that was a week ago and several hundred light-years away; Jon only had his own judgement now, and he judged Doy to be honest, intelligent and open-minded. Ironic, given the charges against the wizard.

"I'm afraid you're right," Jon replied. "You *will* be here for a long time."

If Doy was upset by that, he hid it well, except for a momentary bobbing of his Adam's apple. He shifted on his chair, then licked his lips.

"Governor," he said after a moment's pause, "may I ask you a question?"

"Please do."

"Down in the holding cells of this magnificent yet terrifying warship, there are twelve prisoners – eleven rebels and a failed elemental practitioner – yet I'm the one you've called up here to this room. Are we just here for a chat?"

May was impressed; the governor would have been happy talking around the subject for another few minutes, but Doy wanted to drive things forward; he wanted to know the facts, and that was promising.

"Why do you think, Mr Doy?"

Doy shrugged. "If I asked the gods, would they be able to tell me either?" he asked. The merest flicker of a smile reappeared on his face. "The other eleven prisoners were all rounded up last week, on Empress Guinevere's first day sitting on the Golden Throne. They were dispatched here that same evening because, I assume, she found them to be more of a threat than her father did." He grimaced. "Although I wonder what real danger they are: free-thinkers, liberals, and scientists are only threats when their areas of speciality are tightly controlled."

Doy's voice tailed off and he pressed his lips together

until they were barely visible in a thin, pale line. His gaze swept down at the table.

"Don't stop now, Mr Doy," May said. "You're just getting to the good bit."

Slowly, Doy raised his eyes and looked slyly at the governor.

"I suppose you're going to tell me that you're a member of the resistance now, are you?" he said quietly. "What are they called? The Sicarii?"

"Yeah, that's them," May replied, "but I've got too many hidden depths without plunging to one which risks my life if Guinevere ever found out."

Doy looked disappointed; perhaps he'd been hoping for that nugget of news to give him some intrigue, but now he had nothing.

"So why me?" he demanded. "If you're not interested in recruiting me to the Sicarii, why are we talking? I'm nobody."

"Oh, I don't know," May replied. "Everyone's somebody. I've seen your file, remember?"

Doy frowned. "What do you mean?"

"After three years of study at the Institute, you were taking your final exams."

"So?"

"The normal Practitioner course is four years. You shaved a year off your studies."

Doy shrugged. For a moment, he looked something akin to a sullen teenager embarrassed by a parent over his accomplishments.

"It didn't do me any good, did it?" he snapped. "I was

young and cocky. I made mistakes in the practical portion of my exam and killed twelve people. The Institute would have locked me up for life if I hadn't run for it."

"And you've been making amends for it ever since."

The failed wizard looked surprised. "What makes you say that?"

"You've got a look about you," May said. "That, and I read the reports. That's why it's taken me so long to invite you here to my … office, such as it is. I wanted to feel like I understood you – as much as I could – before I talked to you. You see, you straddle two worlds. The elemental world you've come from, and the non-magical … err, non-elemental world, where you've been hiding ever since. You understand both, at least to a degree, and that's a valuable trait. Humanity forgets that practitioners are born to human families just as often as practitioner ones; the gene that controls your powers appears randomly. You're humans with an added something, but the Institute keeps you separate and aloof, like you're somehow … alien, and in return, the rest of humanity fears you. Practitioners live in citadels and special communes; it's rare to see one of you living amongst the rest of humanity, so when someone with the gene *does* live alongside humans, it gives them a unique perspective on both sides of the divide."

Doy rolled his eyes. "That's because the Republic and the Institute refuse to trust each other, and haven't done for centuries. We *could* collaborate, but instead we bicker and argue like children constantly searching for the upper hand."

May nodded; he was impressed with Doy's candour. The failed wizard was incisive and apparently unafraid in speaking his mind, despite May being an official representative of the Empress.

Perhaps because he hasn't got anywhere else to go or any further to fall.

"That's been a tradition for so long," May noted, "that I seriously doubt it will vanish any time soon. To be honest, I get the impression that leaders on both sides almost *enjoy* the divisions. It gives them something to complain about, as well as an official scapegoat whenever something goes wrong. But let me reassure you, not *everyone* thinks the same – not all of us non-Merlins mistrust you. There are lots of people who are intrigued by Merlins; we want to get to know you better."

Doy looked at him steadily, with a curious expression.

"Why don't you mistrust Merlins?" he asked bluntly.

"Because my cousin's one," May said calmly, and grinned as he saw Doy's eyes widen. He sat up straight in his seat. "He's forty four or forty five now, I think – he's at least ten years older than me, that much I know. We don't get to see him much; he's off doing his own thing for the Institute working on … whatever he's assigned to do."

"How did your family react when he hit puberty?"

May shrugged, "I don't remember it at the time," he said. "I was just a tiny kid when it happened. There was some … consternation, I think, from my uncle, but he got over it. Now we're proud of having a Merlin in the family; he knows so much, and he's just another person. He's the same as me, just with different active genes. I'm proud of him. So I don't think any differently towards Merlins; you can't, really, when you share DNA."

"I wish more people thought like you," Doy said. "There wouldn't be so much misunderstanding that way."

May made a face, but didn't say anything; there wasn't anything he *could* say to that.

"How do you feel," he went on, "about being in a Republic prison as opposed to a Merlin one? Shouldn't you have been given that courtesy, at least?"

Doy shrugged. He seemed to relax a fraction as he thought about that, and leaned back in his chair. "In an ideal world," he confessed, "but …" His voice tailed off, and he stared into the middle distance for a moment as he thought about his answer. Finally he sighed. "But I wouldn't have fit in there anyway. Merlin prisons are few and far between – we prefer other forms of punishment that you couldn't begin to imagine. In any case, our new Chief Warlock, who's only been in post for about three months and seems to be terrified of Empress Guinevere, caved under pressure from the Republic's illustrious and completely fair-minded leader –" here, Doy's face twisted into an ironic smile before he continued, "– who demanded that I be placed in a prison under *her* control, as a symbol that no-one is above the law when it comes to killing non-Merlins. Like I'm some completely separate species. Elysium was the compromise."

"Sounds like just the leader you want defending your interests."

"The Warlock and the Empress are suitably matched, I think. She demands, and he gives in. A meeting of minds."

May smiled, although the action was tinged with sorrow; Doy's voice revealed his despair. The governor couldn't say anything to make the failed wizard feel better.

"You said a moment ago," he went on, "that you're going to be on Elysium for a very long time. Probably even the rest of your life."

"So?"

"So why not do something productive with your time? Why not continue to make amends for what you did?"

Doy's eyes narrowed. May saw his confusion – and curiosity – in the twitch of his eye and the hunch of his shoulders.

May leaned forward, keeping eye contact. "I need a friend on Island Two," he said. "I need someone to be my eyes and ears over there. I need—"

Doy tensed again. "A spy?" he retorted. "You want me to spy for you?"

"I was going to use the word 'liaison,' but fine – 'spy' works just as well. Listen, you're a unique breed; a failed wizard who's lived amongst humans as an adult. You've experienced humanity in a way most practitioners don't after they hit puberty. Your fellow prisoners will either ignore you, treat you as their best friend or, more likely, tap-dance around you until they think they've worked you out, then treat you as just another prisoner. I want to know everything that's happening over there, and I think you're very well-placed to get the news."

"Why do you care about a prisoner's grapevine?" Doy asked. "It's probably nothing that you can't get from other sources."

"Oh, I don't know about that," May replied. "Information is information, and it's worth hearing twice rather than not at all. I want to hear opinions on everything from the food to the staff."

Doy's eyebrows lifted up. "The staff?" he asked. "Is that what this is all about? You're trying to find something out about … what, the cooking?"

"Spot on," May replied placidly. "We think the chef's poisoning everyone. Don't eat the dumplings, whatever you do."

"You're not going to tell me, are you?"

"Not yet. Maybe soon, but I'm not ready to confide everything I know – especially when you haven't given me an answer."

"Why are you interested in what *prisoners* have got to say? By all accounts, we're all free-thinkers on Elysium. Why should *you* care?"

"Because someone's got to."

Slowly, Doy nodded. "What do you want me to do?"

"Just … listen and ask questions," May replied. "Find out everything you can for me, and try not to stand out too much."

"Well, that shouldn't be difficult for the only person with elemental powers on Elysium."

May blinked, caught off-guard, and a frown immediately crossed Doy's face; he'd clearly picked up on the governor's hesitation.

"What?" he asked.

"You've heard of the Exchange Programme, I presume?"

"The … Yeah, I've heard about it. There aren't many practitioners who actually sign up, from what I remember. It was always considered a fairly pointless exercise. I never thought people would come around to the idea of us just because they worked with one. And most of the Merlins I know were worried about the reactions they might get from the humans they ended up working with. The mistrust amongst *some* –" he made sure to emphasise the point "– meant that it wasn't going to get very far. Why did you ask about it? Is there a Merlin seconded to the prison staff?"

"Up until a week ago, yes," May replied. "Now, however, she's a prisoner. She killed my predecessor."

Doy's jaw fell. "She *killed* a *human?*"

May sighed. "It's a rather long story that I don't fully understand, but I know the facts as recorded on the charge sheet. The Merlin's name is Julie Martin."

Doy visibly paled. "Julie *Martin*?" he repeated. "Are you sure?"

"Perfectly."

Doy's eyes flicked to the padd on the table, then back again to May's face.

"Then you'll understand why I'm reluctant to meet her," Doy went on. "She presumably knows everything that—"

"She knows nothing," May interrupted. "Your addition to the prisoner manifest happened on the same day as her arrest. She never saw the charge sheet." His smile didn't reach his eyes; it felt as tired, suddenly, as the rest of him. "You're in the clear … if you choose not to tell her anything."

Doy swallowed and stared off into the middle distance for a moment, and May continued by asking a question; "Did you ever actually meet her?"

"No," Doy said, and shook his head firmly. "No, we never met. Her reputation precedes her, though. She's one reason that I ran. I was scared of her reaction." He hesitated, licked his lips, and cleared his throat. "Are ..." He cleared his throat again. "Are you sure she doesn't know my history?"

"As sure as I can be," May replied in what he hoped was a reassuring manner. "She won't hear it from me, either."

Doy swallowed and nodded. "Thank you," he said. "Although I'm not quite sure why I've earned that."

"Because we've got to start trusting people somewhere along the line. If you choose to tell her the truth, that's entirely down to you. In any case, a suppression field is in effect. Commander Blain, the security chief, deployed it to control her power." He bit his bottom lip. "By all accounts, she's one of the most powerful Mages in existence. She was certainly an effective Operations Manager for Elysium. Now she's one of you."

May didn't need to be a telepath to read Doy's emotions now; as the Governor had acknowledged Julie's power, Doy's hands were bunched so tightly that his knuckles were almost pure white. May was intrigued. He had imagined that the suppression field would have given him some comfort. Julie's reputation clearly meant a great deal.

As he opened his mouth to say something else, the doors to the conference room swished open to admit Watson. He didn't seem particularly keen to be there; his eyes kept darting from one place to another, then looked almost disappointed that nothing was untoward. His eyes finally fixed on Doy, almost willing him to do something wrong. But Doy remained still, with his gaze now fixed on the table in front of him.

"Sir," Watson said reluctantly, moving his eyes up to the Governor, "the captain says we'll be in orbit in fifteen minutes. The prisoners are being moved to the shuttles now. We're ready for you in the shuttle bay."

May nodded distractedly. "Very well," he said. "Escort the prisoner there now. I'll join you in ten minutes. Thank you, Mr Doy."

Doy nodded. "Thank *you*, Governor."

They made eye contact again, and a moment of understanding passed between them. But then Watson pulled his nightstick from his belt and wielded it, almost lazily, in front of Doy. Taking the hint, Doy rose, turned and left with his head higher than when he entered.

May was left alone in the conference room; giving him a moment to reflect on the conversation in the welcome silence. He took a deep breath, and then smiled as he thought about leaving this ship behind; the air may have been breathable, but the atmosphere on any human-class planet would be far superior. He was looking forward to having grass beneath his feet again.

He turned and looked out of the window. Elysium was getting ever closer, and butterflies of excitement fluttered in his stomach; he was going to make a difference, he was sure of it. There was a mystery to solve, and no-one was going to get in his way.

5.30pm, 16th April 418

Island One, Elysium

ROBERT BLAIN'S CURRENT solitude gave him the opportunity to savour the trappings of the Governor's office one last time. For the last week, he had enjoyed the change of scenery from the space – half the size and not as comfortable – that he occupied as security chief, and he resented being forced out.

Located on the 11th floor of Island One's Tower, from where all the prison planet's operations were coordinated, the Governor's office – *his* for the past six days – was a rectangular space, with windows facing each other on the two longer sides, and walls, covered by landscape paintings, on the other two; neither he nor Noble had been particularly inclined to personalise the office any more than absolutely necessary. A large, solid-timbered desk filled the middle of the room; Blain had kept it in exactly the same position as his predecessor, set so he could see the large bay window on one long wall and the entrance to the office on one of the shorter sides. He liked to see who was approaching.

The only other furniture in the room were two sofas and a low coffee table; Blain disliked the implied informality, and had refused to use that corner.

When Elysium had been established, despite being in the running, he had chosen the lesser rank of security chief over the Governorship, believing that it would give him more time to work on his projects. Having managed the planet for the last six days, he could see that he had been wrong; he could have balanced the two.

I could have continued in the Governor's role, he thought, *if Wood had given me the chance. But instead, he's assigned some "high-flyer" to come here and get his wings before bouncing off to a bigger and better posting. Still, I'm his second-in-command by default and, once Guinevere has settled in and I've completed final testing, I'll soon move up the greasy pole faster than this ... interloper.*

He watched through the window as two shuttles emerged from the cloud cover and began their final descent towards the islands. Traffic Control, on the 12th and upper-most floor in the Tower, coordinated all traffic on and off the planet, using a narrow band of approved flight paths. The scattering field caused too much interference for vessels to be flying everywhere without strict regulation from the Control Room on the top floor.

One shuttle, obviously holding the twelve prisoners, banked and headed the short distance to Island Two. The other shuttle, holding the six new guards on personnel rotation, and Elysium's exalted new Governor, started on a course for Island One.

Blain watched their descent without expression. His shoulders were rigid with tension, but he didn't try to relax; there was no point. He wouldn't react until he had met the Governor and assessed his weaknesses. Only then would he feel more level and calm.

Traffic Control are too good at their job to hope that something will happen to that shuttle. Pity.

Guinevere had had no reason to refuse May the position of Governor, Blain knew; he was too well-qualified, despite the self-pitying time off he'd taken after the death of his sister. Blain had always been dismissive of the whole "grief" phenomenon; death was, after all, a natural part of living, and so it surely made sense to accept it.

And the expression "dead men's shoes" surely has to mean something, doesn't it?

The shuttles themselves were going to remain on Elysium; the *Merciless* were giving them to the prison to supplement the existing complement of six, divided equally between the two islands. It was unlikely they would ever need to use eight shuttles at once, but given that the number of prisoners had now risen to 577, Blain knew that it was always worthwhile to play it safe.

Although I'm not sure the Merciless *would see it like that*, he thought. *The Praetorian Guard resent having to risk detection by the Rixxians every month to supply us, but there's no way we could ever become self-sustaining. This planet is too dangerous, even for the bunch of ingrates and thought criminals that live here.*

The shuttle on course for Island One, a bulky eight-seater, banked a few degrees to the left, clearly getting instructions from Traffic Control to avoid a current from the scattering field. He blinked, realising that he was merely putting off the inevitable by watching their descent, and shook his head.

Well, if I'm not wanted here, then I'll go somewhere that I am. My old job is waiting for me. If the new governor wants anything, he can come and find me. I've got work to do.

Without a backward glance, he walked out of the office, through the small antechamber where the Governor's personal assistant would usually be seated, and stepped into the lift. It began its descent through the Tower, the tall rectangular HQ of the Governor and his team. But Blain was now entirely focused on his *proper* office, located on level two.

As Blain entered the small, boxy space belonging to the chief of security, he locked the door and sat behind his desk. He ran a hand through his salt-and-pepper hair. It had been dark brown at one point, but now the grey had won; unsurprising, given that he was in his early fifties and had lived a full life.

Now it's time to get back to the important *things around here.*

✦　✦　✦

LEGION HAD DETECTED the minds long before realising they were on approaching shuttles. The entity had no need of technology, of course, but the minds intrigued Them. The beings were new to Legion, although they were clearly members of the same species as the previous invaders, and that made them just as guilty.

Anger coursed through Legion like an almost physical burn, as it had every day since Their birth. Legion was ready to take revenge. There were enough minds on this world to choose from.

Since Legion had discovered this colony of humans living on these small islands, two miles off the mainland, They had found their minds curious. The humans were different to the ones They had encountered before. The majority – clad in orange – were open-minded and willing to consider new ideas. The ones in military uniforms, however, seemed to enjoy the power they wielded.

One mind was particularly closed, and particularly familiar. Robert Blain made Legion shiver with fear, and also with rage; so much so that They tried not to think about the man too much during Their observations.

They had discovered another, more powerful mind living on the colony; a female, but with power. She could *channel the matter around her. But her mind was heavily-shielded, and would take some practice to access. The challenge, however, intrigued Legion;* I will have to build up to it.

The gall of Robert Blain to return like nothing had happened was phenomenal; nothing would stop Legion from hurting him and the people he worked for.

Legion had spent the last year – or was it longer? – observing this colony and nothing more, but now it was time to act. Legion had already selected a mind on which to test Their abilities. It was time to make the first jump.

✦   ✦   ✦

ISLAND ONE'S DOCK and harbour, a useful launch point for their heavily-armoured and weaponised fishing fleet (a necessity, given the dangers living beneath the water), was small by most standards, but fine for the amount of cargo that came through it. Peter Northgate was proud that he and his team could cope with anything. He had stolidly fulfilled the role of Dock Master since the colony had been founded. The compact port – landing pads for six shuttles, storage containers for cargo received from the Praetorian Guard's monthly visits, and a docking berth to connect to the shuttles for inspection and recharging – also held a small office for Pete to observe and coordinate the unloading. He hardly used it, preferring to be on the ground and part of the team.

On days like today, with a calm sea, low wind and sunny warmth on his back, he always tried to disappear for a little while and watch the shuttle come in; they were relatively infrequent, so it was a pleasure to see the elegant flights down to the planet – his crew tolerated that quirk of his. There was a useful point on Island One, high enough to give him a good vantage point to enjoy the views of the azure-blue sea and, in the distance, Pangaea just about visible. If he looked behind him, he could see the compound that housed the Tower, living quarters and other staff areas. As the sun lowered towards the horizon, the sunset's reds and oranges became brighter and more vivid.

Northgate nodded with satisfaction as the shuttle landed safely on the pad. Traffic Control had done a good job yet again, and now they'd have some extra food and supplies ten days before their next scheduled drop. They'd also have some prisoners, but he would never get a chance to meet them. His heart sunk treacherously at the thought.

He was curious to meet Noble's replacement. That development had been surprising in itself; everyone had thought Blain would get the job – including Blain himself, or so the rumours had gone.

It's going to be interesting to see how Governor May and our security chief get on.

A consequence of Blain not becoming permanent ruler did mean, however, that Pete didn't have to keep such a close eye on the internal transfer listings that came out every week from HQ. May's leadership spared them from Blain's inevitably awful regime, which meant that Pete felt more comfortable staying.

I bet he's spitting feathers right now.

Heavy footsteps distracted his thoughts; behind him, Reg Patterson pounded up the hill with his thick, soles and big feet. Reg was the other Harbour Master on Elysium, responsible for Island Two, and hadn't ever been light-footed. Reg seemed constantly surprised when people heard him coming. No-one, Pete included, had the heart to tell him that he walked like a ten-tonne elephant.

His weight could charitably be said to be *un*like a ten-tonne elephant, but only by the smallest of degrees.

Whereas Pete was tall and slim (and put away food without gaining weight), Reg was short and round (and put on weight by merely *looking* at food). One of Pete's staff, in an unguarded moment when he thought his boss was out of earshot, commented that, when stood side-by-side, the two men looked like the number ten. Pete had chosen to regally ignore that comment. Inside, he'd roared with laughter.

As his counterpart approached, Pete glanced briefly at him and nodded.

"Reg," he said, trying to sound welcoming without actually feeling it.

"Hello, Peter," Reg replied amiably. "How goes it?"

Pete grunted a response, not trusting himself to saying anything else. He'd found it difficult to like the man, almost from the day Reg had first arrived on Elysium six months ago.

Why did Stan have to retire? Pete wondered, not for the first time. *He was a hundred times better than this ... prat.*

Something about the man rubbed Pete up the wrong way. Perhaps it was the way Reg insisted on called him "Peter." He was the only person who ever did, despite repeated entreaties to shorten it; even Pete's mother dropped the "r" these days.

For the sake of their working relationship, Pete was forced to maintain a polite veneer. He was thankful that they were assigned to different islands, so they didn't have to socialise too often, although they would occasionally travel when larger shipments came in, to ensure everything was dealt with quickly and efficiently.

It would be better if I did it all myself and actually got the credit for it, Pete thought grouchily. *Reg spends half his time hanging around and being nothing more than a carrying case for that stained coffee cup.*

Pete was already counting down the minutes until the shuttle was fully unloaded, then Reg could head back to Island Two and mingle with the new prisoners (*One of them's a murderer, so I hear* – Pete had to stop himself from daydreaming too much about that); to be fair, he doubted Reg would want to talk to the prisoners that much. The fat, stupid Harbour Master would simply continue to be disparaging and insulting about them.

"Any word from Island Two?" he asked.

Reg shrugged. "It's quiet," he replied. "Just another routine day. All the actual cargo is here. Security don't need my help off-loading those twelve pieces of scum."

Pete opened his mouth with a retort, but managed to resist the urge just in time. Island Two was far from "routine", and the prisoners weren't scum. They were clever, intelligent men and women, and each one of them had a story to tell.

If I were there, I'd want to hear those stories.

Was it because they had failed to agree with the prevailing political winds? Were their families too popular or well-known to allow the free thinker a swift death? Had they spoken up against Edgardo or Guinevere? Did they all belong to the Sicarii? Whatever the reason, Guinevere was making her mark already by adding twelve more to the population.

Then, of course, there was Julie Martin. As Operations Manager for Elysium, she had been his superior, and he'd liked her for her calm manner and obvious intellect.

But she's the reason for the suppression field stretching over both islands, as well as a new Governor. He shuddered. *Nasty business.*

Pete knew he would never find working on Island Two boring.

There's got to be more to life than this, he thought wearily. *These prisoners, they've seen more of this republic – and this galaxy – than I can even begin to imagine. I want to know what's out there.*

He couldn't hold back his frustration any longer; he had to say something. "Reg, I can't believe you find Island Two *boring*. Can't you see the potential in your role over there?"

Reg just shrugged. His face was devoid of any curiosity as he looked out at the harbour. "They're just prisoners, Peter," he replied. "Why should I care? This is just a job."

Pete shook his head in annoyance. Reg didn't seem to notice, so Pete turned away and peered down the hill towards the shuttle, where the cargo had started to be unloaded. Putting thoughts of Reg's long-hoped-for retirement day to the back of his mind, he decided it was time to get back to work.

"You seem particularly thoughtful today, Peter," Reg said.

My frustration must really *be showing if he's picked up on it. He's usually not aware of anything outside of the square footage inside his head.*

"It's nothing," Pete said dismissively. "It's just …"

You're doing the job I want! he yelled mentally. *I want to know what they know.*

He sighed again and shook his head. "It's nothing."

Reg took this at face value and shrugged. "Fair enough," he said. "I should get my stuff together. I wouldn't want to miss my taxi, would I?"

Missing you already. "Okay, Reg, I'll see you around."

MAY WATCHED IMPATIENTLY as the door to the shuttle lowered, turning itself into a ramp. Once it was fixed into position, May walked his tall, stocky frame out of the artificial environment and back into clear air. His grey-green eyes squinted against the sun beating down on the island, and he filled his lungs with tangy sea air. The sea itself was visible to his right, just off the edge of the short cliff; it was azure blue, absolutely calm and stunning.

How can anything so beautiful and calm possibly be dangerous?

Abruptly, almost like the world had been reading his thoughts, the waters broke just a few hundred yards from the shoreline, and a lithe, shark-like creature burst out into the bright, sunny sky. May blinked; it wasn't so much the action that surprised him, but the size of the teeth. Although its body had been roughly equivalent to a great white shark on Earth, its incisors stretched out of its mouth – and were double the size of anything the governor had ever seen.

He cleared his throat and looked away; despite the sudden interruption, which none of the harbour staff had batted an eyelid at, a sense of sudden relief overtook him. The pressure in his head had already lessened during these few seconds of being away from all that steel and glass. Praetorian Guard warships were notorious for their lack of home comforts, and May had finally seen that up close. Not having so many minds all pressed together in such a confined space was joyful. How had his sister lived on a ship full-time?

It had been painful for that reason as well, walking the deck of the *Merciless*; it brought back memories of Sara and, given that the anniversary of her death wasn't far away, the constant nagging of his twin sister's death already bubbled near to the surface. Whilst two years had passed since the *Ulysses* had been destroyed in the event horizon of a black hole, it still felt like yesterday. The sorrow was still raw and vestigial; Sara's death had been so sudden and unexpected. Yes, she served in the Praetorian Guard, and death had been a risk she had to accept, but … *but* …to die in a black hole. As the familiar grief threatened to overwhelm him, May drew in a breath and steadied himself.

Focus! he told himself. *Now is not the time to be thinking about Sara. You need to be strong. She would be so proud of you, taking on a challenge like this.*

He looked up and down the harbour front. It was busy, with people coming and going from the shuttle and various containers scattered around, but no-one was paying *him* any attention.

"Where *is* everyone?" he muttered.

"Governor!"

May turned to the voice, and saw a man half-walking, half-running towards him.

"Good morning, Governor," the man said as he drew up in front of May. "I'm Peter Northgate – Pete Northgate – Harbour Master for Island One. Welcome to Elysium."

"Thank you, Mr Northgate," May replied. "I was starting to think I'd have to find my office by myself."

Northgate flushed. "I apologise, sir," he replied. "I don't know what's happened to Commander Blain and his staff. I assumed he was going to be here to meet you. He's the Chief of Security, and he's been acting as Governor for the past week."

"I know who Blain is," May said, and winced at the sharpness of his voice. He was annoyed, but he knew that it wasn't the Harbour Master's fault. "I … was looking forward to meeting him is all."

Pete looked over his right shoulder and May followed his gaze. The island was fairly flat, so he could make out the sight of the Central Tower half a mile or so away.

I assume Commander Blain has been using the Governor's office for the last few days, May thought. *Well, he's been Acting Governor, so he had every right to the trappings of the title, but now I'm here. If he thinks that he's too grand to meet me, then he'll need to be brought down a peg or two.*

Pete was frowning; he clearly hoped that Blain would suddenly appear and get him out of this awkward situation. His shoulders sagged as he realised that no-one was coming.

"I apologise again," he said, turning back to face May. "You shouldn't have been left here without a welcoming committee."

May waved the man's apologies away. "Don't worry, Pete," he said. "Can you show me to my office? I want to get settled in."

Commander Blain is making a point, he thought. *But I know how to make one too.*

REG HAD COLLECTED everything he needed from the Tower – just his electronic padd and satchel, which he'd brought along more out of habit than for any practical reason – and headed back to the harbour.

It would be such an easy life, working on this island, he thought as he looked around.

He wondered – not for the first time – if he should raise the subject with Peter, but dismissed it almost immediately.

No, he thought. *He likes it here. Pity. I could do with a change. I don't like being close to all those thought-criminals over there, being tainted by association.*

Julie Martin's arrival had just made things worse, as would the second magician. He was vaguely conscious that other words were meant to be used as "correct" terms for the people within the Institute, but he didn't care. It was magic. As far as he was concerned, the island was now a lot more dangerous, and he hated the thought of being stuck with it.

He ambled back to the harbour front, but took his time. He wasn't built for speed, and the shuttle would have to wait for him, wouldn't it?

As his eyes scanned the harbour edge, he noticed one particular technician in the middle of the dock who was acting…odd. That was the only word for it. He was blinking furiously, like he'd just stared into the sun for a moment too long.

More fool him if he did.

The technician seemed fascinated, hungrily taking in every detail through now-wide eyes, like he was seeing everything for the first time.

But he's been here longer than I have, Reg thought. *He'll know the intricacies of the dock better than I do, even with today's important cargo.*

The technician's gaze then fell onto Reg; the Harbour Master shivered as he saw the coldness – *No*, he corrected, *the rage* – in the man's eyes even from the eight or ten feet distance between them.

"George?" he said aloud. "What's wrong?"

The technician didn't react; didn't even blink. He remained rooted to the spot, staring at Reg. The Harbour Master had the strangest feeling that he was being examined like a bizarre, breathing waxwork.

All of sudden, Reg became aware of the silence around them; he and the technician were alone. The three other technicians had moved off to complete various errands, the pilot had already left, and the door to the shuttle was firmly shut.

I could do with some company right about now.

Reg looked back and jumped in surprise; the technician had managed to get right up close to him without making a noise.

"Bloody hell," he breathed. "How did you … I didn't even hear …"

His voice was cut off as the technician's hand snapped forward and covered his mouth.

"You … are senior to … this one," the technician hissed.

Reg frowned as he ran the words through his head. In addition to the odd use of the third person, the technician's speech was slurred and halting, like he was learning – or *re*-learning – how to speak. The fat man nodded and, in response, the technician took his hand away.

"I'm one of the Harbour Masters, yes," Reg said. "You're a technician."

Reminding the technician of his rank gave Reg a sudden bout of confidence and he drew himself up to his full height. All 5'6" of it. Unfortunately, his rotund stomach and the perspiration on his forehead didn't help him project that same confidence, and the technician maintained his intense stare.

George didn't reply; instead, he remained rooted to the spot, and tilted his head to one side, looking with blank fascination at his senior.

"Very well," Reg said. "You're going to the infirmary, while I go and talk to Mr Northgate. Come with me."

Reg jumped as the technician's right hand whipped forward and grabbed his forearm.

The technician's grey eyes flared with a sudden, vivid blue. "You plan to … imprison me."

"Imprison you?" Reg repeated. "In the infirmary? Don't be ridiculous. It might feel like it sometimes with Dr Lee in charge, but it'll help you get better." He scowled. "Are you an unlicensed telepath? You know it's illegal to work if you are."

Reg tried to prise the technician's hand off his arm. He yelped in pain as the same vivid blue that had appeared in his eyes circled the technician's hand and sent an electric shock through Reg's arm.

"You are more use than this one," George said. "You are senior."

Reg continued to try and yank his arm away, but nothing would budge the man's fingers; his grip was vice-like.

"I *will* make use of you," the technician said with finality.

Blue light flashed in front of Reg's eyes and he felt sharp, stabbing pain *everywhere*.

Then the blue light vanished as suddenly as it had flared, and Reg died. His body, however, remained standing. The technician crumpled to the floor, and a small, tight smile touched Reg's lips. A flash of blue light flashed past his eyes, but disappeared in an instant. All was quiet again.

SWEAT POURED OFF Pete's forehead, and more trickled down his back. He gasped for breath as he and Governor May continued on their brisk walk. His lungs were constricted and painful as he tried to suck more oxygen down his throat.

I really need to get back to the gym, he thought. *This is embarrassing. I shouldn't be this unfit.*

May had asked to go the "long way" to the Tower, in order to tour the island in the rapidly disappearing sunlight, and the only circuitous route Pete knew took in most of the island. Thirty-five minutes later, and still ten minutes from their destination, the harbour master was sincerely regretting it.

Pete had started with the docks and storage facilities, then passed through the Visitor's Centre, which was nothing more than a small, glass building on top of the hill where Pete and Reg had so recently sat. That had been an initiative of Noble's, shortly after the colony had been opened, to impress any visitors that came to Elysium.

The only problem, Pete thought, *is that there aren't many visitors willing to come to a prison planet in the back of beyond. Just another one of Noble's vain follies.*

Just beyond the barely-used building was a long path leading to the main compound, along which Pete now led the new governor. The iconic Tower was already visible – it could be seen from pretty much anywhere on this tiny island – and apart from that, there wasn't necessarily much to look at; the rest of the buildings were squat, bulky affairs that housed living quarters, infirmary, a canteen, a library with texts "approved" by the Empress' propaganda teams, a recreation room, and a smaller "classified building" for "questioning".

I'm sure Guinevere will make use of that facility.

Edgardo did.

"Have you been here since this place opened, Pete?"

"Hmm?"

Pete blinked, abruptly realising the casualness of his reply. He flushed with embarrassment.

"Sorry, Governor, I –"

May smiled, looking genuinely amused. "Don't worry. I was just asking if you'd been here since the beginning."

Pete breathed out as his tension disappeared. "Yes, I have. I travelled here on the Prisons Directorate ships with Governor Noble and the others. Well, except Commander Blain, of course. He arrived here first. This place has grown beyond … well, anything I expected, that's for sure."

"I'll bet," May said. "What –"

He stopped as a strange cacophony of sound made him look back towards the Visitor's Centre that they'd only just put behind them.

"What the hell was that?" Pete muttered. He squinted and raised a hand to shield his eyes from the evening sunlight.

"What's happening?" May asked. "I'm not sure," Pete replied. "It sounds like an argument. I'll go and –"

A sudden, savage burst of energy erupted from the centre, and a shock wave knocked both men to the ground. Pete felt the *heat* wash over him in a wave, and he gasped with the dual pain of that and the awkward landing on his backside. Fire burned his right arm as he shielded his face from the blast.

As the flames receded, he pushed himself up to a

sitting position, blinking tears from his eyes. He winced as a shooting pain ran up his back; it didn't feel like he'd broken anything, but his coccyx and hips screamed. His ears rang from the explosion and everything around him seemed muffled; he could hear voices in the distance, but couldn't make out the words. His head felt like it was packed with cotton wool.

Where's the Governor?

He turned his head, carefully, and saw May a short distance away, lying face down on the gravel.

"Sir?" he croaked, but May didn't move.

Forcing himself to his knees, he leaned forward and rested his hands on the gravel path as he retched. After a few seconds, he began to feel more composed. Pushing himself upright again and onto his feet, he squinted against the sun to look at the Visitor's Centre. Or, to be more precise, what was left of it. The Centre was a shattered wreck; its large floor-to-ceiling windows were blown out, scattering shards of glass over a huge radius, and a couple of the steel beams, which had previously supported the structure, were warped almost beyond recognition. Behind him, May moaned, and Pete turned slowly to avoid any dizziness. He pressed the emergency alert clipped to his tool belt; he was pretty confident that security teams would already be on their way after *that*, but he wanted to make sure they knew *where* to come – along with the right support.

"Governor," he croaked, "stay still. A medical unit will be here shortly."

May half-muttered something in response, but it was

too quiet and indistinct to penetrate Pete's slowly-clearing brain. He blinked hard as something new appeared in his field of vision; a figure was walking towards him up the path from the Visitor's Centre.

"Reg?"

His fellow Harbour Master paused a few steps away from him, and Pete frowned as he realised his colleague's face had changed from the usual slack-jawed boredom he always wore to one of cold calculation.

"What happened back there?"

Pete felt a chill shudder through his spine. Reg didn't reply; instead, he maintained his cold, steady gaze, looking over Pete like he was nothing but a piece of meat.

"Reg?" Pete whispered. "Talk to me."

"You are not senior to this one," Reg said in a harsh, flat monotone, then cocked his head to one side. "Unacceptable. I seek power."

His eyes then moved to May, who was moaning in pain and still only half-conscious.

Where the hell is the medical team?! Pete wondered. *What if he's got brain damage?*

Reg was studying the Governor, and looked confused; he clearly didn't recognise him.

"Identify him," he said.

"That's Governor May," Pete replied. "He got off the shuttle half an hour ago. Reg, he's hurt. He needs a doctor *now.*"

If Reg was upset or worried, then he didn't show it. Instead, he stared blandly at May's prone body.

"I do not know him. I cannot sense his mind whilst

trapped inside this body." Reg's gaze returned to fix on Pete. "I have memories of *you*, however."

Pete had no clue what Reg was talking about; the fat man's tone was scaring him.

"What happened in the Visitors' Centre?" he asked, trying to deflect his counterpart's worryingly-direct attention.

"I was searching for a senior officer to this body," Reg replied without emotion. "The humans there tried to resist me. They failed."

"What's going on?"

May's voice cut between them as he came round at last; he sounded woozy, but was conscious enough to know something was still very wrong.

"This is Reg Patterson, sir," Pete said without turning round. "He's my counterpart over on Island Two. He's … not well at the moment."

"You are the ruler here?" Reg asked. "You are ultimately accountable?"

"'Accountable' to whom?" May asked through gritted teeth. "Not to you!"

Reg hesitated; for the first time since he had approached them, he looked uncertain.

"You are not … ultimately accountable?" he asked slowly.

"For this world, yes!" May exclaimed hotly. "For the Republic? No, of course not!"

Reg's face grew darker. "Then I must reach these people who *are* ultimately responsible," he said. "For that, I will need your body. Surrender yourself."

Pete struggled to follow what was going on; he turned to look at May, who had pushed himself onto his back, but hadn't yet sat up. He had a nasty gash on his forehead, which bled freely. Pete inched towards him.

"Sir, that's a bad cut you've got," he said. "You should lay still until—"

"I don't think so," May retorted. He raised his voice. "There's something you need to know about me, Mr Patterson. I don't surrender to anyone."

"Sir," Pete interjected, "I wouldn't recommend antagonising him while he's like this; I can't vouch for him. He's usually placid."

May scowled at him. "He's already antagonised, don't you think?"

A sudden movement caught his eye; as Pete turned to look, his heart jumped into his throat. Reg had raised his arm to aim a small laser pistol at the two men.

"Reg!" he said, more sharply than he'd intended. He cleared his throat and, in a more controlled voice, said; "What the hell are you playing at?"

"I need to attract the one who is ultimately accountable," Reg replied. "Only they can answer for what has been done here. Perhaps this will attract them to this world."

"You think killing me will bring the empress *here?*" May asked incredulously. "You're wrong; she won't *care* if I die. I'm just one part in a bigger puzzle."

"Then I will continue killing until she does."

Pete felt time slow as he saw Reg's finger begin to close on the pistol's trigger. Without thinking, he lunged forwards and collided with Reg, forcing both of them onto the ground. He was cushioned by Reg's bulk, and heard a great "oooof" escape his lips; he'd been badly winded by the fall.

The utility knife, subtly taken from his waistband, buried itself into Reg's chest. Pete felt the laser burn through his side.

Funny, he thought dispassionately, *shouldn't I feel angry? Shouldn't it hurt?*

He glanced down and, as he felt his own strength slip away, he saw the life fade from Reg's eyes too – and then a final sob escaped Pete's lips. *I wish …*

Pete's body slumped over Reg's large frame.

May's chest felt heavy and breathless from a combination of adrenaline, fear and pain. As the adrenaline began to fade, however, the throbbing in his head intensified. Lowering himself to lie flat again, he couldn't contain the sorrow that flooded through him at Pete's death, and he let out a sob of his own.

The edges of his vision began to darken; he realised he was losing consciousness again. He fought against it; *There's no way in hell I'm doing* that *again!*

Something caught his eye; turning his head towards the two corpses, he thought he saw Reg's face blur for a moment. *What the hells …?*

He blinked to clear his vision, but it didn't work. The air in front of Reg's face *had* taken on a blurred quality, distorting everything behind it.

I'm seeing things, May decided. *The pain's making me hallucinate.*

As the formless energy began to move away from Reg's head, May became aware of alarmed shouts coming from behind him.

Ah, he thought woozily, *the medics are here. Or is that a security team?*

The blurry piece of air moved towards him, and May began to sense something; a consciousness at the edge of his own, gently exploring and probing. The amorphous being was trying to get into his mind. Was that even possible? Could that ... that *thing* actually be *conscious?* He felt rage and pain and anger. A name also came to him ...

"Legion," he muttered. "Who are you?"

The being didn't respond; it just kept moving towards him.

THE PRICKLING OF his senses stepped up a gear, and May ground his teeth again. He'd been trained to resist just this sort of thing; although it had always been assumed that the attack would be from another person, but that didn't matter now. Legion was weak and fragile after being forced from Reg's body. May could exploit that to repel it.

"Leave me alone!" he protested "Whatever you want, you won't get it from me."

In a surge of panicked emotion he sat up and, with nothing but his mind, *pushed* the entity away from him and towards the people coming towards him; there was a man dressed in security uniform red, and the others had operations uniforms – green and black. There were three of those, and had presumably been on a shift change when the explosion happened; they all looked shell-shocked, but were staring at May – none of them seemed to have registered Legion's presence. The entity vanished. May sat upright with one hand on the ground to steady himself, and opened his mouth to ask the staff what it was, but something stopped him. It didn't feel right; he didn't want to set the wrong example. One of the operations staff knelt down beside him and opened the box she'd been carrying. May flinched away as she reached towards him, but relaxed when he saw the red cross on the box, and let her gently dab at the cut on his forehead. It would do until he could see a proper medic; although that might be a while.

"Sir?" the guard said. "Are you alright?"

May swallowed against the dryness in his throat. "Yes, I'm fine. Reg attacked me. I don't know why."

He moved tentatively, taking a moment as his vision swam, then looked down at the two bodies lying in the dirt and swallowed again. Pete Northgate had sacrificed himself for the governor, and there wasn't any way he could thank the man for that.

"I want them treated them with respect," he said to the guard. "Have their bodies taken to the medical bay. We'll arrange a funeral for them after a full investigation. In the meantime, escort me to the Tower. Someone call ahead. I want Commander Blain waiting for me in my office."

As he walked away, shaking off any help so he could walk alone, he glanced back over his shoulder. The sky – still bright, but with the hint of sunset beginning to take shape – remained still and calm. There weren't any amorphous blobs of energy floating anywhere. Where had it gone?

THEY WALKED TO the base of the Tower, where May thanked the guard for the escort, then dismissed them. May wanted to savour the experience of entering his new office for the first time without an armed guard. He didn't entirely know why, but it felt right.

The journey up in the lift was quick and silent, and the outer office – where his assistant, whom he had spoken to over the comm from the *Merciless,* would sit – was thankfully empty.

Lights came on automatically as he entered his office; the views out the window were spectacular. The office itself was pretty decent as well. He had half-expected Blain to have trashed it before leaving it behind – or, at the very least, to have sabotaged something. Instead, it was immaculate, and May wondered if he hadn't – even to a small degree – misjudged the chief of security. Then he remembered the scraps of information that McIntyre had discovered about him.

Maybe not.

He crossed the office with quick, easy steps and sat in the chair – *his* chair – and nodded approvingly at its comfort. The door chime sounded, interrupting his meditation.

Aha, he thought. *Here we go. Well, let's get this over with.*

"Come," he called.

The doors slid open to admit his visitor. The Praetorian Guard uniform, with the gold commander's braid around his cuffs, was sharply at odds with the rest of the staff's drab Prison uniforms – browns and deep greens. May was conscious that he was in civilian garb (ripped and scuffed from the explosion), but refused to apologise for it. Civilians ruled over the military, so it didn't matter what he was wearing, although he doubted Blain would agree with him on that point.

"Commander Blain." May said, standing to greet him. "Good to meet you."

"And you," Blain replied. He stopped in front of the governor's desk and shook May's proffered hand. The security chief's eyes flickered briefly to the cut on May's head; he knew that he should go to the infirmary and get it checked out, but this was more immediate – and far more important. May felt surprisingly fine aside from the cut; he imagined that the adrenaline coursing through his system meant he'd suffer for it later. "I'm glad to see you're well. I was surprised to hear of Reg's attack. It was completely out of character for him."

"So I've been told."

May thought of Pete Northgate, and wondered if Blain was going to mention him, but the security chief didn't seem to have given him a second thought. He motioned for Blain to sit, and had to grudgingly admire the man for the way he kept his focus and hadn't yet looked round the office.

"I'd hoped to meet you when I arrived on Elysium an hour ago," May said, "but Peter Northgate – the Harbour Master who just died saving my life – explained that you've been very busy. Hence you not having time to arrange a welcoming committee for me."

Blain stared at the governor, his grey eyes blazing with sudden annoyance. His shoulders tensed and he leaned back in his chair. He seemed to be daring the new governor to say something more, but May didn't need to; he'd made his point. He touched the cut on his forehead briefly; it still throbbed, but the first aid he'd received had stopped the bleeding.

"What can you tell me about the man who attacked me?" he asked instead.

Blain scowled; he seemed almost disappointed that they wouldn't be arguing any more about the lack of a welcoming committee, but he recovered admirably.

"Reg Patterson was a solid, dependable manager by all accounts. He transferred here from one of the inner colonies. A water world, I'm given to understand. He liked the easy life. All of his psychometric testing came up clean."

"If psychometric testing was that good, wouldn't that do away with police forces entirely?"

Blain ignored the Governor's retort and carried on. "The reports from the Visitors' Centre came through just as you arrived. I've only had the chance to quickly glance at them, but it seems that the staff on duty tried to subdue him, and he fought back rather violently. He seemed quite focused on getting to the two of you. He'd got one two of the plasma guns out of the dock hold, where we keep a small supply should any of the larger avians – well, they're more like winged dinosaurs built from pure cruelty – ever get past the laser cannons. One of those things can easily blow up something larger than the Visitors' Centre if set high enough. Anything that barred his way wouldn't have stood a chance."

"He was only intent on me when he discovered I was senior to Pete Northgate," May noted. "He seemed quite obsessed about that. Seniority, I mean. Was he an ambitious man?"

"Not particularly," Blain replied. "Looking through his service record, he seemed to fall into each job he had, rather than actively seek out promotions."

"What about the things he said?" May prompted. "Reg talked about making someone – the person with ultimate authority – accountable for something. What was he talking about?"

"I'm not sure we'll ever find out. He seemed to be suddenly acting out some sort of fantasy world."

"You're saying he was delusional?"

"You have another opinion?"

May scowled; Blain was stopping just short of an outright challenge, but not by much. The governor wasn't willing to tolerate such open insubordination; he would speak his mind just as bluntly in return.

"There was a strange distortion in front of Reg's face, almost like something had left his body after he died."

Blain's eyebrows shot up, and he grinned. *That*, he clearly found amusing. "You're suggesting you saw his soul?"

"No, of course not," May retorted sharply. "But I know I saw *something*."

"You *were* concussed," Blain said. "Maybe you still

are."

"So you're not taking this seriously? You believe it was the work of a lone gunman living out some sort of fantasy world?"

"Yes, I do."

May struggled to formulate a reasonable response, amazed by Blain's bland answer. *Do you genuinely not care?* he wondered. *Or is this all part of some elaborate act?*

"Doesn't all this seem a bit … odd to you?"

"Not really," Blain replied. "It's an occupational hazard. People seeking to move up the greasy pole and all that."

I've stepped into a parallel universe, May thought, *I must have.*

"You … you don't seem that interested in investigating this attack on the life of your new Governor, Mr Blain."

"I would say that the answer has already presented itself," Blain replied. "He was clearly a lunatic. As for the disturbance in the air … well, I suspect you were seeing things. It happens when you're under pressure."

May had to take a moment to ensure he hadn't misheard; Blain had already closed the book on the attack. The governor desperately wanted to explain his brief mental connection to this Legion character, but he couldn't, at least not with Blain. He didn't trust this man one inch.

"Mr Blain, I want an investigation into this … *incident* that almost left me for dead!"

"Are you absolutely sure, Governor?"

May blinked; what the *hell*? The security chief seemed to pick up on the governor's hesitation and smiled; a vicious little quirk of the lips that seemed to suggest he rather enjoyed his new superior's surprise.

"Sir," he continued, "Governor Noble chose me as Elysium's deputy over Julie Martin because he didn't trust magic, or whatever name they use to describe the things they do. As a result, I am *your* deputy too, and so it's down to me to ensure you consider all sides of an argument. It's not in our interests to have an investigation right now. We are only just recovering from the death of your predecessor after an insane attack by our Operations Manager. To have another attack on our *new* governor, who had only just arrived on the planet, *and* was walking around without any security, will only cast unwanted attention on this world. We need to stay focused on rebuilding Elysium's reputation. We cannot afford any more intrigue, and I know the Empress will agree. Perhaps we should ask her directly if you're unsure?"

May cursed inwardly; he had allowed himself to be led into that trap. He *wanted* the investigation, because he was sure it would show up Blain's shortcomings that he'd already heard about on the grapevine. But, of course, any investigation would have to go through Blain's department, and he would weaken May by going straight to the Empress. May doubted the security chief *wanted* to go to her just yet – at least, not until he was ready to unveil whatever plans he was preparing, and May needed to find out what they involved first; that was at least partly why he was here, after all. May needed to keep all of this far from the Empress' desk for as long as possible. Perhaps there was another way …? He'd have to think about it.

"Can we move on?" Blain asked calmly. If he was aware of May's incredulity – the Governor was sure *some* of it had to be showing on his face – then the security chief wasn't acknowledging it. He seemed eager to talk about other things instead.

"Oh, please do," May said airily. "What's next?"

"Steven Doy," Blain said. "You met with him on the *Merciless*, I understand?"

News travels fast. "I did. So?"

"Can you give me a feel for him?" Blain asked. "Will he be adequately covered by the suppression field?"

"I have no doubt," May replied. "Mr Doy's powers are limited."

"You know why he was sent here, I assume?" Blain asked.

"I do," May replied, "but I don't think he's the violent soul you clearly assume him to be. I got a pretty good read on him when we met on the *Merciless*. He was quite open with me." May didn't want to say anything else on that; he felt for the failed wizard.

Blain smirked. "Hardly the basis for a psychological assessment."

May sighed; he decided to move on. Blain clearly had very firm views.

"I'm keen to get the Operations Manager post filled soon," he said. "It's a key part of the executive, and Julie Martin's … issues aside, I understand she was excellent in the role."

Blain nodded. "Julie was the best you could hope for," he answered, which surprised May: he hadn't expected Blain to be positive about anyone. "The fact she was a Mage was irrelevant, although we certainly benefited from her experience."

"Ideally, I'd like another Merlin graduate in the role."

"Agreed," Blain said. "It would be useful. Your assistant can do the necessary liaison with the Institute's personnel division. However, I will say just one thing. You need to vet any potential candidates *fully*. The half-baked applicants that the Academy will send you first would barely be able defend us against a student with the suppression field on full. Ms Martin is a danger to us, even *with* the field, so the sooner we can get someone to defend us against her, the better."

"I thought you respected her."

"I do. I also understand her anger at the system for locking her up after committing a crime of passion. She's bound to be angry." He paused, then added, "Or we could just get her back, I suppose. But then she'd have to defend us against herself."

May couldn't help but laugh, surprised by Blain's spark of humour. "I look forward to meeting her."

Blain's crossed his legs and scowled, the brief moment of warmth between them gone in a flash.

"I wouldn't recommend that," he replied, "and if you ignore my advice, then have members of my guard present at all times. Whilst I have utter confidence in our suppression field, it wouldn't surprise me if she knew a way around it."

May shook his head. "I *will* meet her," he said. "I will accept protection from your guards, however." He half-smiled, but without any humour. "Perhaps they can recover their reputation at the same time."

"What do you mean?"

"None of your guards came and found me at the Visitors' Centre. If they had, the situation would have turned out very differently. Pete Northgate wouldn't have had to take a laser bolt meant for me. In fact, I still haven't heard from *any* of your rota of guards. If they're as highly trained as you make out, perhaps you can spend some time finding out why they took so long to respond to a security issue of that magnitude. Except you don't think it's *that* important, do you?"

Blain's face froze, clearly insulted, but May didn't give a damn; *I've made my second point of the evening, I think.*

"That will be all for now, Commander," he said calmly, motioning towards the door.

Blain's eyes widened; a dark cloud crossed his face and he balled his hands into fists. He obviously hadn't been expecting the abrupt dismissal, despite their tense conversation. However, he composed his face back into a calmer visage, stood and stalked out of the Governor's office.

May watched him go and shook his head. Whilst it never bothered him to be forceful if he had to, he preferred a collaborative style by and large, and it was difficult for him to start off a relationship so harshly.

But I need to establish my authority, he thought heavily, *especially with Blain.*

A thought that had been nagging away at him suddenly came to the fore. During their entire meeting, Blain hadn't called him "governor" or "sir" once. May sighed.

Looks like I've got a way to go yet.

5.00am, 17th April 418

Island One, Elysium

THE SUN HAD barely risen above the horizon as Blain walked across the compound from the residential block. Rather than making his way to the Tower, he instead made his way to his *other* office.

He stifled a yawn; last night he'd been plagued by dreams of Jon May and his twin sister standing side by side, mocking him.

The May siblings were as bad as one another. Sara had been a meddling fool, and Jon was the same. The genetic stock was clearly a failure and needed to be eradicated from existence. Or perhaps enhanced. Blain smiled at the thought.

He had prowled his quarters like a caged animal for some time before going to bed the previous evening, debating whether or not to contact Guinevere immediately.

Eventually, he'd calmed down as his brain had caught up with his emotions. He knew that he wouldn't be doing himself any favours contacting Guinevere until he was absolutely certain that his creation could carry out tasks exactly as ordered. Once the security chief was happy, *then* he would contact Guinevere and get the glory and recognition that her father had been planning to heap upon him.

I can deal with that interloper until then.

HE RELAXED AS he entered his other world, the underground lab that kept Blain connected to his past and his current scientific research. The engineers who had first hollowed out the space beneath Island One's infirmary had met with accidents towards the end of the prison planet's development a couple of years ago, and Blain had cannily ordered the equipment from different suppliers over the last two years and had them shipped here on different supply runs. So far, it seemed to have worked well. Blain savoured his privacy in what had quickly become a second home. Lab equipment, computer terminals that monitored different parts of his experiments, workbenches, a couple of beds and various storage cupboards were distributed liberally around the large, circular room.

"Rachael, come down here," he called up to the high ceiling, where his latest experiment was flying. "I want to talk to you."

Rachael landed delicately, then unfurled her elegant limbs into a standing position. She was tall and humanoid, but certainly *not* human. Her eyes were yellow with vertical slits, like a cat's, and her skin was a deep green.

She had always seemed uncomfortable wearing many clothes; Blain had insisted upon her wearing a shirt, modified to accommodate her large, white-feathered wings (*Maybe I should try scales* next, he thought), and trousers which she had already ripped down to ragged shorts.

I hope she sees that I'm trying to teach her to be sophisticated. I know she can learn.

"Hello," Rachael greeted him in her calm, lilting voice. "How are you?"

Blain's eyes widened. "I'm fine, thank you. How are you?"

"Well, thank you. I'm stretching my wings as much as the lab allows. It's refreshing."

How are you developing those types of conversational skills so quickly? Blain wondered.

"But you've stayed in the lab as I instructed?"

Rachael nodded. "Of course," she replied. "I've followed your instructions perfectly. Why would I disobey? You want me to wear the shimmer suit when I do leave, and you haven't given it to me yet, so I will not leave. But may I ask a question?"

"Of course."

"You keep me hidden away all the time. Are you ashamed of me? Or perhaps I make you feel uncomfortable in some way?"

"Uncomfortable?" Blain said. "No, you don't make me feel uncomfortable. You do, however, intrigue me. I didn't design you for such rapid development in emotional subtleties."

Rachael looked thoughtful at Blain's question, but didn't reply. If he were being honest, Blain hadn't expected an answer; after all, Rachael didn't have any knowledge of biological engineering. He sighed and walked over to the drinks cabinet in the corner of his lab. He found a moment of calm as he contemplated the choices in front of him; was it too early in the day?

"Did you intend for me to think this way?"

Blain was reaching for the kettle as Rachael asked her question. His hand froze. "No," he admitted. "I didn't intend for you to develop so quickly over so few months."

"Then why am I … experiencing these feelings?" The plaintive edge in Rachael's voice hadn't been there a moment before. "I do not understand them."

I'm not sure I do either, Blain thought.

"I allowed for self-improvement," he said. "You've exceeded my expectations."

"I never had *any* expectations until recently. I was just like the others of my kind."

Blain couldn't answer that, at least without getting into a conversation he wasn't comfortable having with a Fairfield being.

Especially one I've enhanced.

He poured out a measure of whiskey, doubled it, then took a long swig. He savoured the liquid as it burned his throat, then smacked his lips and turned to examine Rachael again. She hadn't moved an inch. Her eyes, sharp and intelligent, were fixed on Blain, and she looked like a coiled spring; even when she was at rest, she was still on edge.

Such a paradox of sentience.

"I have a mission for you," Blain said. "There's something I want you to do for me."

A strange blend of emotions crossed Rachael's face in quick succession; disappointment – clearly at not continuing the conversation they had started – and excitement. She had been agitating to leave the confines of the laboratory for some time, and she was clearly thrilled to finally be given the opportunity.

"What is the mission?" she asked, and the eagerness in her voice was almost childlike. "Tell me. I will not disappoint you."

"I need you to observe Governor May," Blain replied. "I want to know what he's doing, who he's talking to and what he's planning. I can't give this to my team, despite their loyalty to me. Spying on the governor is a serious task, so they will show a certain … compunction that I know you won't. Can you do this for me?"

Rachael nodded. "Of course," he said. "I assume –"

"Yes," Blain retorted quickly. "You'll need the shimmer suit. I've made adjustments based on your comments when you last tried it on."

"Good," Rachael said. Her lips curled. "It was tight in all sorts of horrible places. I didn't like it."

"Well, I've made it better. Get dressed and start your mission. Report to me at sunset."

"I won't let you down … Father."

Blain smiled; he really *had* got her loyalty constructed perfectly.

Interlude

Four Years Ago, RSS *Ulysses*

SARA MAY GLANCED over at Mulholland, wanting reassurance from the calm, measured captain. She found herself glad to be watching the Emperor's televised address – only the third he'd ever done in the four years since he had taken office – with the captain in her ready room.

"And finally," Edgardo was saying, "I must touch on the subject of a terrorist cell that call themselves the Sicarii."

He heaved a sigh, looking like a man who would rather be discussing anything other than this weighty subject.

"The Sicarii may have plagued the Republic for the past few years," he said, "but they are connected to the long history of violent terrorism plaguing our internal security.

"Of late, the Sicarii has had some successes – I won't deny that. They have killed and maimed our citizens, they have destroyed buildings, and stolen money and information, all for the purposeful, abject destruction of our way of life. They are cruel, evil and vindictive.

"*The Praetorian Guard continue to hunt down the leaders and members of the Sicarii, and are bringing them to justice faster than ever before –*"

Mulholland snorted. "For 'Praetorian Guard, read 'Black Watch.'"

"*– and,*" the Emperor continued, "*we will succeed. I will not allow them to fulfil their objective. The Republic is strong, and we will not be weakened. They will be hunted without mercy and punished. We should be rightly proud of the Republic that we have created.*"

The comm link went dead. Both officers stared at the screen for a moment before either contemplated speaking. Sara had been standing behind Mulholland's right shoulder during the broadcast so she could easily watch the screen, but now moved around the desk and sat down opposite the captain.

"Well, that was cheerful, wasn't it?"

Mulholland smiled. "That's one word for it. Talk about ending on a high."

"His script writer should be shot."

"I hear he writes his own scripts."

"That would figure."

"I hear that the Sicarii have got a newspaper now."

"Yeah, I heard that too," Sara replied. "The *Free Enquirer* or *Free Chronicle*, something like that. They're becoming a force to be reckoned with."

"No wonder Edgardo's so worried about them. Have you ever heard of a sitting Emperor making such a public pronouncement on a terrorist threat before?"

"Never. I knew there were other terrorist groups in the past – or freedom fighters, depending on your interpretation – but no Emperor has felt the need to publicly address them. There must be more of a conflict than we thought."

"So what's your *interpretation?*" Mulholland asked. "Terrorist or freedom fighter?"

Sara shifted awkwardly in her seat. "I think the taking of lives is serious," she said carefully. "So is the destruction of property."

"But are those charges Edgardo levelled at the Sicarii true?"

"Captain, are you suggesting that our leaders lie to us?"

"I'm suggesting that everyone lies at some point," Mulholland retorted. "I'm just wondering how much Edgardo is the same."

"One thing's for sure."

"What's that?"

"For as long as we're stuck out here in the Outmarches, listening to two-day old transmissions, we'll never know."

Mulholland chuckled. "Too true. The Sicarii will never be interested in non-aligned space – and we shouldn't be either. It's far too risky, being stationary in the Outmarches for too long. I'm just glad the Rixxians haven't detected us yet."

5.10am, 17th April 418

Island One, Elysium

J ON MAY GASPED and sat bolt upright in bed. His chest
heaved as he gulped oxygen into his lungs, and felt
grateful for the light breeze coming in through the
slightly-open window. He touched his forehead; it still
throbbed from the previous evening, but more than that,
from the intensity of the dream he'd just had.

His eyes darted around the room; everything was
where he'd left it the previous evening. He was on a planet,
not a starship; but the dream had felt so *real*. Many of the
details, however, were fading already, like mist being burnt
away by powerful sunlight.

He remembered the previous Emperor's speech
clearly; he'd watched it in Richard Wood's office, back
when they had both worked for the Interstellar
Communications Board. Had Sara actually viewed it in
her captain's ready room whilst stationed in the
Outmarches?

As he gulped down a few more calming breaths, he

recalled a similar dream he'd had a week ago, while still on Earth. He'd actually *spoken* to his sister in the dream, stood in the heart of Elysium's forests on its single landmass of Pangaea – somewhere that neither of them had been. Jon still hadn't, and Sara had never told him about any adventures on this world.

The strange feeling passed, and he scrubbed a hand across his face. His heart rate had begun to settle, and his breath was far more regular. Glancing at his bedside clock display, his shoulders sagged as he realised that he only had twenty minutes before his alarm went off. He'd never fall asleep again now.

Oh well, he thought. *I might as well get an early start on my first full day as governor.*

He dragged himself out of bed, stumbled into the bathroom and peered into the mirror. He winced as he saw the gash. He'd gone down to the infirmary after his confrontation with Blain the previous night, and one of the doctors had surprised him by stitching it up the old-fashioned way. It seemed that some of the more advanced medical technologies hadn't quite reached the Outmarches. He wasn't surprised that it still hurt: the bruising was vivid and colourful, with yellows and purples merging together.

The doctor had wanted the new governor to spend the night in the infirmary for observation, but May had politely declined. He wanted to spend his first night in his new home in his own bed, not on some hospital gurney. He'd eventually got his own way, although not without a full and frank exchange of views with the chief medical officer, who had eventually, and reluctantly, conceded.

Let's hope today ends better than yesterday. He touched the stitched-up wound again and winced. *I'd like to end up without any more scratches and bruises, thank you very much.*

He turned on the shower and stepped in; he didn't want to take long getting ready. He had things to do – starting with establishing some ground rules with a certain security chief.

+ + +

AS RACHAEL LEFT to begin her assignment, Blain went back above ground and headed for the Tower. He wanted to look at the personnel rotas now that his six additional guards had arrived – *about time too, I've been asking Director Wood about extra resources for months; I need to be taken seriously as chief of security, and I can't be without a decent sized staff* – and working on his plan of action for revealing his project to Guinevere. He needed to present it in *exactly* the right way.

In his office, he peered out the window as he poured himself another drink. He took a sip and sat down at his desk. Images of Jon May, his predecessor Andrew Noble, Julie Martin and Rachael, flying free amongst the clouds, floated in front of his eyes. He squeezed them shut, shaking his head to try and knock the thoughts loose. He didn't have much success.

The door alarm chirruped, thankfully interrupting his thoughts.

"Come in."

Jon May walked in, his shoulders hunched and his eyebrows brought together in a scowl. Blain stood up to half-attention; out of deference to the office, rather than the man. From his peripheral vision, he spotted the half-drained whiskey glass on his desk, and inwardly cursed. He didn't like being caught on the hoof. May glanced at it for a fraction of a second, but didn't comment. Blain wasn't sure whether that made the situation better or worse.

"Is there something I can do for you?" he asked neutrally.

"I'm used to being called by my title, Commander," May shot back, "especially when I afford others the same courtesy. Even if you don't respect me, you should respect the office."

Blain refused to be cowed. "Indeed … Governor," he replied. The title caught in his throat, but there was nothing he could do. For the moment, at least, May held the role, regardless of Blain's feelings on the matter.

"After you left my office last night," May continued, "I stewed on what we'd discussed. I can't work out why the hell you were so quick to close the case on the attack yesterday evening. I couldn't help but wonder if there was anything you were keeping from me. Any unexplained phenomena that could be linked to what happened yesterday."

"Like amorphous blobs floating in mid-air?" Blain snapped.

"Something like that. It may sound odd to you, but I

know what I saw, and I've always been taught to believe what's in front of my eyes – the facts, if you will." May spread his arms wide and, uninvited, sat down in the visitor's chair on the other side of the desk. "I'm fascinated to know your take on what the role of a security chief should be," he went on, half-changing the subject. "Perhaps you could enlighten me."

Blain gritted his teeth, trying to stop his blood from boiling. He clenched and unclenched his fists a couple of times, and forced himself to sit down.

"Governor, you are clearly an educated man," he said carefully, "and I'm sure you don't need me to explain the political confines in which we work."

"We deliver justice here on Elysium," May said, "not politics."

Blain's eyebrows rose half-way up his forehead. "I doubt very much that you're *that* naïve. Emperor Edgardo was perceived as a liberal reformer, at least by today's standards, but he still believed in punishment. Empress Guinevere most certainly *isn't* a liberal reformer, and I suspect she believes in punishment *and* force."

"You may well be right," May conceded. "What are you trying to tell me? That there's no point in investigating *anything* after the prisoners – and staff – are sent here?"

"I'm telling you that prisoners who are sent to Elysium aren't ever expected to leave, except in a body bag – and even then, only if they have influential family knocking at your door to request a proper burial. All of the prisoners here are political refugees and thought criminals from the four corners of the Republic, with a few more hardened criminals like Julie Martin and Steven Doy thrown in for good measure. If a few of them disappear every now and then … well, I'm sure Guinevere won't be too worried about it. It's all a matter of degrees. An amorphous blob, if it exists, might even do us a favour and weed out some of the population."

May's jaw hung open; Blain wasn't surprised. Weak-arsed liberals like the governor always thought he was presenting an unnecessarily harsh line, but he wasn't; it was necessary *and* practical.

And logical. Emotions can't play a part in this sort of decision.

May roused himself. He seemed to be digesting Blain's comments now, although the look on his face told the security chief that he still wasn't very happy about it.

"If you don't care about the prisoners," May said, "then tell me you're at least a little worried about the risks to your own guards if this sort of attack is repeated."

"Yes, that *does* concern me. The rule of law must be maintained."

"How can you maintain the rule of law without finding out what caused Reg to change his personality so dramatically?"

Blain shrugged. "Reg was an isolated case. We're in the Outmarches, in the middle of nowhere, with the Rixxians breathing down our neck. That can send some people insane; Reg was one of them. If it happens to the occasional prisoner, then we'll protect the guards as best we can. I wouldn't worry about it. Governor Noble wouldn't have."

"I'm not Governor Noble!"

Blain interlaced his fingers and released a breath. "I am learning that very quickly."

May looked like he wanted to say something else, but instead stood and strode from Blain's office without a backward glance. A thin smile touched Blain's lips. He stood, picked up his glass and walked back to the cabinet beneath the window.

✦　✦　✦

MAY PROWLED THE six-foot square lift, taking two steps, turning, and moving back to the opposite wall. He was angry with himself more than anything, although his anger with Blain was raging a close second; he'd let his emotions get the better of him down in Blain's office, and that was unlike him. He had risen through the ranks by learning how to be cleverly diplomatic. Cursing, he let out a shaky breath as the lift slowed and opened its doors, releasing him into his outer office.

The sole desk was now occupied by a young man in his early twenties; he had sandy hair, bright blue eyes and a slightly startled look on his face. He clearly hadn't been expecting May quite so early; perhaps rumours of the attack had been exacerbated over the past few hours.

"Hello," May said as he stepped into the room. "I'm Governor May, and you are ..."

He'd seen the assistant's name written down on a report somewhere, and it had managed to completely escape him. If the younger man was offended by his new superior's memory lapse, he didn't show it. In fact, he smiled a broad grin, like he completely understood.

"Joshua Greene, Governor," he said. "Please don't worry. You've got a lot on your mind at the moment, I'm sure."

May nodded. "On that note," he said with a wan smile of his own, "we are in complete agreement, Mr Greene. You worked under both Noble and Blain, didn't you?"

Greene hesitated, then nodded slowly. "Yes, sir. Governor Noble appointed me to the post about a year ago. I hope we can work together even better."

"So do I."

May was good at reading between the lines, and the subtext in Greene's comment intrigued him. He was suddenly looking forward to getting to know his assistant; he wondered how much Greene had picked up in the year he'd been here.

"Is there anything I can do for you, sir?"

"Actually, yes," May replied. "Get Director Wood on a secure channel, please."

As Greene nodded, May strode into his office and sat behind his desk. May sighed and rubbed his eyes. He didn't *like* getting angry; he was able to have rational discussions, and find common ground, with pretty much anyone. Robert Blain, however, had managed to provoke him on their second meeting. That was quite an accomplishment.

Finding a replacement for him has suddenly moved from priority three to priority one.

He had to tread carefully, of course, but *would* work out how to head off whatever plots the security chief had; even if it was to use his drinking against him and suspend him. That way, May could question him under that cover and see if Blain let anything slip about what else he was going here. It was a long shot, but perhaps worth a try.

"Governor?"

Greene's voice came through loud and clear on the intercom, choosing not to interrupt him in person. A gold star already for the tactful assistant; as well as starting work early, he'd read May very well.

"Yes, Mr Greene?"

"I have the Director for you, sir."

"Thank you."

He faced the screen just as Wood appeared on it. May relaxed slightly. It was good to see a friendly face.

"Jon, good morning," Wood said lightly. His smile faltered as he saw the stitched cut on the Governor's forehead. *"Looks like you've been in the wars already."*

May snorted with savage humour. "You could say that," he replied. "We had an … incident last night just after I arrived."

He went over everything, from the lack of a welcoming committee by Blain – clearly designed to make a point – through to the attack by Reg and the strange, formless energy.

"So what's Blain uncovered so far?" Wood asked.

"Nothing."

Wood frowned. *"How long does he expect the investigation to take?"*

"Eternity, I suspect. There *is* no investigation. Blain believes Reg just went mad; end of story, no more enquiries need to be made."

"Jon, please tell me you're kidding."

"I wish I were," May replied, "but it's the honest truth. I can't even suspend or sack him for it; for all I know, he could be absolutely right."

"What are the chances?"

"Not very high, but unless I can prove it …"

"Yeah, I know." Wood shook his head, looking despairingly at the governor through the lens. *"What in the seven hells is he playing at?"*

"You tell me. I wish I knew." Jon looked off into the middle distance for a moment as he tried to marshal his thoughts. "How are things on Earth?"

Wood shrugged. *"Pretty much as we expected, to be honest,"* he replied. *"Guinevere is continuing to make her authority felt. She's completely reversed the few reforms that her father introduced, and she's continuing to round up dissidents that, she says, Edgardo let run around unchecked."*

"That's not surprising. What's her real motive, though?"

"She's searching for the Sicarii," Wood said. *"She wants to kill the entire rebellion."*

"So did Edgardo," May said, rolling his eyes as he remembered the news feeds talking about arrests and imprisonments. "One of the round-ups he did practically filled this place up to bursting. Ninety percent of our prisoners here are Sicarii."

"And yet they're still going," Wood said. He chuckled. *"Still, if it makes the Empress – long may she reign – happy, then who are we to argue?"*

"Indeed."

The two men exchanged a momentary look, pregnant with meaning, but didn't say anything more on the subject. May knew what Wood meant; *Be careful. Keep your head down. Stay out of trouble.*

"So what do you plan to do about this energy … blob you saw last night?" Wood asked, and May was instantly relieved; at least someone was taking him seriously at last.

"I need to tread carefully," he replied. "I want to get to the bottom of it, but not if it just excites Blain to apoplexy – although," he added, "I'm not entirely averse to that for laughs."

"Yeah," Wood said, looking thoughtful. *"If you had an Operations Manager in place, they could have made some discreet enquiries. As it is, you're incredibly short-handed. You just need someone you can trust."*

May agreed with the Director, and he couldn't help but be plagued by a particular thought. He considered the options open to him. Wood was watching him carefully.

"Have you made any contacts amongst the prison population?" he asked.

"I met with Steven Doy yesterday," May replied. "Our failed wizard with the penchant for failed experiments. He's a decent man; if he hadn't done what he had did – accidentally, I should add – then he would have been a very honourable wizard. As it is, he spent the last few years being a fairly honourable fugitive, and now … well, he's got potential, I think."

"Can you trust him?"

May considered it for a moment, then nodded. "I think so."

"What about your other Merlin prisoner?"

"We've not met. I don't know anything about her except the official reports she's written over the past two years, Blain's arrest report, and the little bits Blain told me last night, and I'm not willing to take his word on anything. I want to meet Julie for myself and find out what make her tick."

"Jon, I know it's hard to trust people so quickly, but time's passing. We need to find out what Blain's up to, and I'm curious to know about this energy form as well. Perhaps it's time to take some calculated risks in who you take into your confidence."

May smiled; he was glad to hear the Director say that. "Funnily enough, I was thinking the same. Ironic, really; I'm more willing to trust the murdering mage and failed wizard than a chief of security with very few talents."

Wood returned the smile. *"As least you'll know precisely where you stand with Julie Martin and Steven Doy."*

"Director, would you excuse me?" May said suddenly. "I've got a meeting to arrange."

"Of course, Jon. Happy hunting."

May smiled at his mentor and friend again and terminated the call.

He's right, of course, he thought. *I need to start trusting people. It's earlier than I'd hoped, but it's time to take some calculated risks.*

He pressed a button on the desk and, a moment later, Greene opened the door.

"Something I can do for you, Governor?" he asked.

"Yes," May said. "I need to speak with Steven Doy, right away, and …"

He wanted to instruct Greene to bring along Julie Martin as well, but May was having a rare moment of doubt. Would that cause an even further rift between him and Blain that could provoke the security chief into doing something stupid? Whilst he was lost in his doubt, he didn't lose his observational skills; Greene had hesitated for an almost imperceptible moment, and May was curious to know why.

"Speak your mind, Mr Greene," he urged.

"Might I presume that Commander Blain would be against you recruiting either Merlin resident of Island Two for … extra-curricular activities, such as conducting an investigation into yesterday's attack?"

May's eyebrows rose; Greene hadn't been around yesterday evening for his conversation – *Or should that be argument?* – with Blain, so how the hell did he know?

"I realised that I'd left a book here," Greene explained. "I still like printed books; it's something of an obsession of mine, to be honest. When I arrived, you were talking with Commander Blain and you'd left the door ajar. I … couldn't help but overhear your conversation. The commander stormed out in such a foul mood that he didn't even see me, in the corner of the outer office, and I left before you did; I didn't want to disturb you."

"Or perhaps you were spying?" May said. He wanted to test Greene's reaction to that suggestion, and the assistant looked appalled at the merest thought.

"No, sir!" he protested. "I was curious – of course I was, I'm only human – but I'm no-one's spy. To be honest, I didn't think you'd want to meet your new assistant just when you'd had an argument with your chief of security."

May rolled his eyes. "You're probably right," he noted. "It sounds like you've got a pretty good read on me already."

"I want to prove that I'm more than just the recruit your predecessor selected for the job. I'm not convinced Commander Blain wants what's best for Elysium."

"And you believe I do?"

"I'm willing to take a calculated risk."

Greene smiled at the Governor, and May chuckled; he found himself liking the man, and felt confident that they would be a good working fit.

"So how should I deal with this … delicate situation?" May asked. "How should I meet Julie and Steve without causing a huge row?"

"I don't think that's possible," Greene replied. "Sir, if you want to continue the investigation into this being that you saw last night, you're going to butt heads with your chief of security no matter what. It might be worth just having the meeting and dealing with the consequences."

Easy for you to say, May thought, *but still …*

He couldn't help but be tempted by Greene's argument; he *did* want to meet Julie, and his assistant made a good point – if he and Blain were going to argue, then why not argue about something that mattered?

"I would happily go and fetch Julie Martin personally for you," Greene added. "Some of the guards are friends of mine, and they're not all huge fans of Commander Blain. They wouldn't go running to him if I brought Julie to you for the meeting, so it might buy you enough time to have a proper conversation with her before the inevitable happens."

"Before my security chief finds out, you mean?"

May was impressed; he hadn't been sure if Greene *would* speak his mind, given his youth, but the governor had been proved wrong, and he was glad of it. Greene's Adam's apple bobbed up and down nervously; with his blonde mop of hair, blue eyes and fair complexion, he looked quite delicate.

There's an inner toughness there, however, May realised.

"I take your point," he replied thoughtfully. "I rather suspect you're right. You've got a clever mind, Mr Greene. We'll make a political officer out of you yet."

Greene looked almost offended. "I do hope not, sir."

10.00am, 17th April 418

Island Two, Elysium

STEVEN DOY HAD been known to happily while away hours just watching the world go by and seeing how people interacted. He was people-watching now, in fact; doing it from within the confines of a prison colony made it even more interesting.

The twelve new prisoners had been an object of curiosity amongst the existing prison population, who were – for the most part – starved of hard news and information. There was something of a prison grapevine, but it was somewhat withered; even the traditional enmity between the Merlin Institute and the rest of humanity had been temporarily forgotten, with Doy being quizzed about the state of the galaxy along with the other newcomers.

I didn't realise the information locked away in my head would be quite so valuable, he thought. *I've been asked about everything from Guinevere to news of the Sicarii, and the gory details of Edgardo's death.*

Having spent a long time on the run from the

authorities, Doy didn't know much of anything in great depth; he tended to skim the surface of whatever he needed to just get by. That skim of knowledge from the last few months, however, still interested the inhabitants of Island Two. They had particularly wanted information on old friends and comrades from inside the Sicarii.

Rebellious humans trying to stand up to the Republic, Doy thought with a sense of deep satisfaction.

In the years since he'd first gone on the run, aged just twenty-one, he'd learnt the best places – and the best worlds – to hide on. In all those places, people-watching seemed to be a fairly universal trait of everyone in the Republic … and many of those outside of it, too.

The rectangular, open-plan prison yard provided enough room for the prisoners to exercise and have some privacy in the darker fringes, where the yard met the shadows cast by the walls, should they want it. Although, during the hours they were permitted to be outside, not many seemed to seek out that privacy. They were locked up in their cells for long enough, and seemed determined – dotted as they were around the compound in ever-shifting groups of two, three, four and upwards – to savour human contact for as long as possible. The yard was surrounded on all four sides by a tall, thick wall, wide enough for a guard to walk along and observe the prisoners. There was also a short, squat guard tower in the middle of the yard, which gave a full 360 degrees of vision to anyone inside.

They've really gone overboard with their security, he thought. *As if the planet's natural elements wouldn't be enough to stop any of us escaping or getting to the mainland.*

The walls of this prison were a reflection of the paranoia and mistrust infecting the wider Republic.

As well as the yard, within the wall's perimeter was everything else the prisoners needed – or were told they needed. Dormitories, kitchen, a small infirmary, break room, and laundry services. The break room had been grudgingly agreed to by Governor Noble. Whilst the comfort of prisoners wasn't at the forefront of Noble's mind, the prisoners here were connected – their families might well be important, or they might have money – hence the fact they hadn't been killed, but still needed to be kept out of the way. It was, therefore, an easy enough sop to give them a small room for relaxation for when they had finished whatever tasks they had assigned; preparing the meals, doing the laundry, scrubbing around for any ores in the ground that might prove to be valuable – and was the most attractive work, as it was the only task that got them off their island prison over to one of the other nearby rocks to scrub around for whatever they could find. It wasn't ever much, but if they could send a tiny amount of ore up to the supply ships, then it helped keep them alive for a little bit longer.

It was on the laundry roof that Doy now sat, lost in thought as he watched the world – or as much of it as he could see – go by. The laundry was half-hidden behind the dormitories in a network of small paths, although why the buildings had been placed so close together that they created these alleys was anyone's guess. Doy had already begun looking round, and he had a vague suspicion – they looked older than the age of the prison. Had they originally been built for something else, when security was less of an issue?

I could be completely talking nonsense, he rationalised ... but couldn't help contemplating it nonetheless.

The height of the laundry building allowed Doy the best chance to watch the yard from its roof, unnoticed by the other prisoners. If any vigilant guards had spotted his position, they hadn't considered it an important infringement. Yet. The only reason he'd managed to get up here was thanks to some loose brickwork on one side of the building and a certain confidence he possessed from being Young Free Climbing Champion two years in a row at the Institute.

As well as letting him observe the yard, his hideaway let him see the main gates, which led – via the path prisoners were led up when they arrived – down to the docking berth. He'd already worked out that the flight path for any shuttles coming to Island Two lay on a direct line of sight from the laundry roof; he remembered the flight path that they'd flown in from, and had overheard one of the guards saying that the route was tightly controlled by the Traffic tower. On a clear day, he would be able to see the shuttles coming in.

Which means I'll see what – and who *– comes onto the island first. If information really is as valuable as it seems to be around here, then this spot will be lucrative.*

The crunch of feet on loose gravel reached his ears.

Someone was right by the building; he'd completely missed their approach. He looked down, and his heart stopped as he saw who it was: Julie Martin, ex-Operations Manager and current prisoner. She was looking up at him, a look of amusement and interest on her face.

She was well-known throughout the elemental power community – and beyond – as being one of their most powerful graduates. Doy wished he could have seen her in action; she was said to be an expert in so much Merlin lore. The suppression field put paid to that idea, however, and a part of him was glad. He hadn't been looking forward to this moment for a number of reasons, but he had to face it now. He didn't have much choice.

He climbed a couple of feet down the wall, then kicked away and landed gracefully in front of Julie. She raised an eyebrow, looking vaguely impressed.

"Not many people could do that," she said.

Doy shrugged. "Before I discovered my powers, I was training to be a professional gymnast. My studies cut that career path short, but I still kept my hand in."

Outwardly, he was impressed at how well he was keeping himself together; his shoulders were squared, his voice was level, and he maintained eye contact.

To distract himself from the nerves, he focused on her. He'd noticed two things about Julie in the few hours he'd been here; firstly, she was spoken of with nothing but a mixture of fear and respect by her fellow prisoners. Despite the suppression field and her lack of an amulet – which psi-normal people feared, somewhat justly, as being a powerful amplifier of a Merlin's powers – her fellow prisoners treated her with deference.

And that's not just because of how she ended up here, he thought.

The second thing he'd noticed was that Julie was the only prisoner who had shown no interest whatsoever in Doy, despite their obvious connection.

Oh gods, what if she knows what I've done?

He dug his nails into the palms of his hands, making his brain focus on that discomfort instead of his obsessive, panicked thoughts.

"You're Steven Doy?" she asked.

Doy swallowed. *Stop it!* he told himself. *You're fine. There are more than five hundred people on this island. Someone's name isn't going to stay secret for very long.*

"Yes," he replied. He wanted to ask her about the trace of accent he could detect; it wasn't one he immediately recognised, but he wasn't brave enough to ask.

Julie frowned. "Your name's familiar to me."

"Doy's a fairly common name on the core worlds."

Just tell her, Steven, for god's sake, just get it out in the open! She clearly doesn't know – the Institute have managed to keep it secret from her – so get it out now before she finds out later, and that makes it a hundred, a thousand, times worse.

But he couldn't; his heart was pounding ten to the dozen, and his stomach was doing back-flips.

Julie nodded. "Maybe," she conceded.

"I'm glad to meet you," he said quickly, changing the subject while he still could. "I thought you were ignoring me. I'm glad I was wrong."

"Oh no," Julie said casually, "you're completely right. I *was* ignoring you."

Doy blinked, disarmed by her honesty. "Oh," he said. He stammered for a reasonable reply until his brain switched back into gear. "Why?"

"Because you're a wizard," she replied. "I can't detect a high level of power, but you've got *some*, so you must have studied. One look at your face tells me you don't want to talk about it either, so I'll respect that, but you've got a story to tell, and I want to understand it. Let's go for a walk, Mr Doy."

With some trepidation, Doy followed her along the narrow pathway between the laundry and the infirmary, and watched her closely. She seemed remarkably calm and focused despite her fallen status from Operations Manager to prisoner.

If I'd spent any time on Island Two after being a senior member of the executive, I'd be angry, and I'd want everyone to know it. But she's just calm. I'm not calm, and I've not got her history. He paused. *Although the history I do have is … complicated enough.*

As they walked, Doy took the time to watch her from the corner of his eye. She was shorter than him by three or four inches, and her auburn hair was pulled back into a ponytail. Her green eyes looked thoughtful and reflective as she looked round, and her strong jawline somehow enhanced her natural confidence.

They stepped into the main prison yard, which was the size of a good sized sports field. There were a couple of dozen people, either sitting on benches reading or talking to fellow inmates, or walking – and in a couple of cases jogging – around the perimeter.

"Have you ever wondered why they've erected walls round the camp?" Doy asked. "After all, we're on an island that's so small you could make it to the harbour from here in ten minutes if you ran. Where would you go from there? You've got a choice of the mainland, which is apparently too vicious for words, Island One or the open sea. Surely those are natural perimeters by themselves?"

Julie didn't react; her eyes were grazing across the yard, looking at each inmate. She pointed – although it really didn't matter which way they went, Doy supposed, as they'd get back to where they started from – and said, "Let's take a stroll this way, shall we?"

Doy blinked, then scowled at her retreating back, and had to jog to catch up with her. Julie glanced at him and frowned.

"What's wrong?" she asked.

The reason dawned on him.

"You're deaf."

"Well done," Julie replied, looking impressed, "it takes some people *days* to realise."

Doy was immediately intrigued; *Matt never told me his sister was deaf.*

Doy had grown up in a bilingual home – his father had been born deaf, so he felt comfortable using signed communication – but he had never met a deaf Mage before.

Would you rather me sign? he asked with his hands.

Julie shrugged. "You can if you want," she replied,

"but I wasn't born deaf, so I learnt to speak, lip-read and sign. Just remember to look at me and show basic consideration when talking to me."

"Your speech-reading is perfect," Doy said. "My father never got past the basics."

"Many people don't. They're not given the opportunity and, for those that do, their deafness is often forgotten as a result. I'm sure *you* won't make that mistake."

Doy's mouth twitched in amusement. "Julie, can I ask you a … direct question?"

"You can certainly *ask*."

Despite himself, Doy chuckled. "The suppression field," he said. He paused, and left those three words hanging in the air.

Julie raised an eyebrow. "What about it?"

"Was the generator actually designed to cover both islands?"

"No," Julie replied, "only this one. It was extended to cover Island One after I came here, in case I ever decided to try and break out."

"Do you suppose Blain's realised that, by spreading the field over a wider area, the generator can't guarantee the same level of suppression?"

"That's *Commander* Blain to convicts like you and I, Mr Doy," Julie corrected him, but the look on her face told Doy that she wasn't entirely serious. She shrugged as she considered his question. "He helped design the device that generates the field," she went on, "so I'd hope he understands the physics behind it. However, he's also very confident and very cocky, so I doubt he thinks *anything* he designs has a problem. Despite his position, the intricacies of our powers tend to escape him. He thinks what we possess is a blunt instrument, rather than a fine, discreet source of energy."

Doy smiled. "And you never thought to tell him?"

"It might have slipped my mind. Why do you ask? Do *you* want to tell him?"

"No. I can feel the power there, just behind my eyeballs, but for the first time, I can't access it. I've always been able to access my powers before now, even if I've not officially been meant to use them."

Julie looked surprised. "You accessed your powers even though you didn't qualify?" she said.

Doy nodded hesitantly. The Institute made *that* theory lesson mandatory. "I'm willing to take the risk, admitting it to a Hunter," he said, "and it's not as if I've done it all the time, just when I needed to. The power we have becomes almost … subconscious after a while. It's so natural that you don't even have to *think* about it. I imagine it gets even easier if you're qualified and experienced."

Julie smiled and inclined her head, but didn't say anything, so Doy went on; "Now I'm constantly conscious of it," he continued. "My power's just there, out of reach, but every now and then, I get momentary flashes where it's easier to access."

It's frustrating, he signed, easily slipping back into it.

We're being guarded by people who are ignorant of our ways, Julie replied, signing as well – in her case, so she could keep her words private. *We've remained secretive for generations, so Guinevere, and all of her predecessors, are woefully ignorant of our abilities. By stretching the suppression field, it's given us a small amount of power back. I'd say it's only a tiny percentage of our total powers, but it's there.* She smiled and went on; *I always like to have options. You never know when they could come in useful.*

Doy nodded. *How have you settled in to your new home?* he asked. *It must have been difficult, moving from Island One to Island Two.*

Julie shrugged. She looked away into the middle distance, and Doy felt anxious again. Had he overstepped an invisible boundary? Was she about to get angry?

"Do you know why I was sent here in the first place?" she asked. "You shared the trip here from Earth with our new governor. I imagine he had a lot of stories to regale you with."

Doy shook his head. "He didn't tell me anything," he replied as she looked back round at him. "He didn't betray any secrets, I promise you."

Julie blinked; she clearly hadn't expected that. "That's refreshing," she said. "We have a governor who's not a gossip."

Doy's response was cut off by a sharp *whoop*ing sound. He flinched and put his hands over his ears in reaction to the harsh frequency. Behind Julie. the lights on each side of the main gates, were flashing red in a steady pattern.

He heard Julie saying something, but he couldn't make out what it was. Looking back to her, Doy saw her looking quizzically at him.

"*What?!*" he yelled at her over the noise. He would have signed, but didn't want to take his hands away from his ears. "*What did you say?*"

What's wrong? she signed. *What can you hear?*

"There's a siren going off!" he yelled just as the siren stopped.

"Someone's on their way," Julie said, turning and nodding towards the gates. "That's how they warn prisoners to not get too near the gates. If any of us do, we're stunned with ten thousand volts through our stomach."

"How pleasant."

A mechanical *clunk* sounded, and the gates began to open, allowing through two guards and a younger man in civilian clothing.

Without thinking, Doy signed; *Who's that?*

Josh Greene, she replied. *The Governor's assistant. Nice guy. He reminds me of you a little bit: geeky.*

Doy smiled; he was growing to like Julie, despite his lingering, underlying terror that she would discover the shared connection from their respective pasts. But that was a problem for tomorrow. It was only then that he realised he hadn't told Julie about May's approach to him aboard the ship before he had arrived. He flushed red; *What if that's what this new assistant's come about?* he wondered. *Damn. Have I got time to –*

Suddenly, Greene was right there in front of them. The other prisoners were watching the strange grouping cautiously, but didn't make any moves toward them. They weren't violent, to be fair, but the laser rifles that the guards were carrying helped; it kept everyone at a wary distance.

"Hello, Julie," he said pleasantly. He clearly wasn't fluent in sign, but he enunciated clearly, and waved a hand to indicate "hello." He was trying; Doy wondered if Julie appreciated the gesture or found it annoying.

"Hello, Joshua," she said. "Nice to see you again. I hadn't expected a visit quite so soon."

"Well, I wish I could say it was a visit for pleasure," Greene said, "but I'm afraid I'm here on business. Governor May would like to speak to you –" He glanced briefly at Doy, but then focused again on Julie – "*Just* you for now, Julie."

Julie glanced at Doy herself and, to his surprise, she seemed ready to argue with Greene on that point. Doy quickly shook his head.

"Don't worry about me," he said. "I've got some more people watching to do."

Greene gave him an odd look, but didn't ask any questions. He seemed eager to get moving again, and Julie acceded; she nodded at him.

"Very well," she said. "I'm at the Governor's disposal. Lead on."

Doy watched the two of them leave the compound, immediately intrigued; he would have loved to be a fly on the wall during *this* meeting.

✦　✦　✦

"Julie, how good of you to come."

Julie looked around the office before returning her gaze to Governor May. No-one else aside from the two of them were present; even Josh Greene had gone back to his desk outside the room and shut the door behind him.

I'm a prisoner, she thought. *Shouldn't he be protected by armed guards? I'd have thought Blain would have insisted on being here, for the entertainment value if nothing else.*

"It's nice to be invited," she replied. "It's also nice to be back without security guards leaning over my shoulder."

May smiled. "I figured that you'd be curious enough about this meeting to allow me to live – at least for the time being."

He extended his right hand; without missing a beat, she took it and shook it firmly.

Shaking the hand of a prisoner? she thought. *Governor Noble, the obnoxious little prick that he was, would never have sullied himself with such an act. First impressions count, and May's made a good one. I wonder what his second impression will be, though.*

May motioned for her to sit opposite him, and as she did so, she glanced round the office again, and wasn't surprised to see that the new Governor hadn't changed anything. From the corner of her eye, she noticed that May had sat down as well, and was waiting patiently for her to face him before speaking.

"Incidentally," he said, "is my lip pattern alright for you to follow? I could arrange for an interpreter on the screen if you would rather."

Julie shook her head. "Thank you, Governor, but it's fine. I appreciate the offer, though. Most people wouldn't even bother."

"Then most people are idiots."

Julie smiled; it was a thought she'd often had herself, but it was nice to hear from someone else for a change.

"I was sorry to hear about Northgate and Patterson," she said. "They were good men."

"News *does* travel fast."

"Information is a currency on Elysium."

May nodded, but his face remained frustratingly neutral. Julie relied on facial and body expressions to know what someone was thinking, and he had schooled himself well.

"Governor," she said, "if I might ask – are you related to a *Sara* May?"

May's shifted in his seat.

"Yes," he replied. "Sara was my sister."

Even without the ability to hear his tone of voice, Julie could easily tell what May thought of his sister; pride, first and foremost, and a clear brotherly love flashed across his face. It made her think of her own sibling, Matt, who had been dead for many years; she loved him deeply, and she suspected – no, she *knew* – that May felt the same about his sister.

"She was the executive officer on board the science vessel *Ulysses*," he went on. "They died two years ago when a black hole pulled them into its gravitational field."

"I'm sorry to hear that," Julie said. "I knew of her

connection to Elysium, of course, but hadn't heard that she'd died. We never met; I just knew of her by reputation."

May frowned. "What do you mean, her 'connection' to Elysium?"

"Well, the fact that she and the crew of the *Ulysses* discovered this planet." Julie was thrown. "I … thought it was a matter of public record."

May seemed dumbstruck; his mouth was hanging open as he stared at Julie with flushed emotion in his cheeks.

"Sara … discovered Elysium?" he repeated. "Are you sure about that?"

Julie nodded. "Of course," she said. It was a silly question to ask; her contacts were impeccable. "The *Ulysses* was on a four-year science mission here in the Outmarches, and they discovered Elysium a couple of years into it."

"I didn't know that, but it might explain my dreams," he said, but didn't elaborate further. He heaved a thoughtful sigh, then smiled. "I realise, Julie, that I know next to nothing about the Merlin community; only what the Institute wants us to know. Well, those and whatever rumours fly around the Republic and are probably all untrue."

"We always encourage *all* the rumours," Julie replied. "To be honest, we probably invented most of them ourselves, just to keep people on their toes. Governor, why am I here? You have shown me nothing but respect – you've not even insulted me by calling what I do magic, unlike most people – and now I'd really like to understand why you sent for me."

If May was surprised by her abrupt change of subject, he didn't show it.

"You were arrested for murder?"

Julie hesitated, and May shifted uncomfortably as he realised how blunt he'd been.

"Sorry," he said, "that was a bit –"

"No, it's fine," Julie cut in. "I can't argue with the truth. I *did* kill Governor Noble."

May nodded. "Do you know what else I wanted to ask?" he said. "I mean, before my … tact burnt out."

Julie couldn't help but smile at his self-deprecation, and decided to throw him a rope. "You want to know about the circumstances surrounding the murder of your predecessor."

"Yes," May replied. "I've read the official report, of course, but those things only give half the story. They never touch on the *why*. I want to know *your* side of the situation. You clearly had your reasons."

She released a slow, steady breath and looked off into the middle distance. "I've been here since the beginning, like most of the staff. Alexis Noble hired them all personally, except for the security detail – Commander Blain would never give up that privilege – and me. I requested this assignment, after I was put on the exchange program between the Institute and the Republic. I wanted to meet some freethinkers and troublemakers. I like to think of myself as a bit of a freethinker."

They shared a smile, but Julie then cleared her throat;

realising that she was wandering off the point. "Catherine Noble – his wife – and I developed a friendship during our time here. She became my best friend and was as close to a sister as I'll ever get. Wouldn't you be angry – furious, even – if your best friend was being mistreated and abused by someone she had once trusted? You see, Governor, her husband was a cunning, clever, conniving *bastard* who saw her as nothing but a trophy wife who could further his career by standing by his side and acting like the perfect hostess."

She took a breath, the hot, angry emotions coming back to her in an uncontrollable wave. "Catherine trusted me," she went on, unable to stop herself now, "and in the end, I wasn't able to save her from the darker, more savage parts of her husband's personality. When he discovered a secret that she had kept for years, he killed her. Governor, your predecessor *killed* his wife because she had a *fragment* of powerful ability inside her and had committed the ultimate sin of refusing to submit to the diktat of suppression or death. So Noble took matters into his own hands. He knew that he would never be blamed. Not when generations of the Golden Throne and the Chief Warlock's office sanctioned such actions."

She shook her head. "If all that happened to your best friend," she went on, focusing again on May, "then wouldn't you do *anything* you could to avenge that injustice?"

May's eyes were full of emotion, and in that moment she felt a strange connection.

"Yes," he answered simply.

Julie grimaced. She didn't want to think about that any more. The pain was still too raw. "You never actually answered my question."

"I ..." May cleared his throat. "I seem to have forgotten what it was."

"Why am I here?" she asked again, but this time with a softer edge. "Was it just to find out about my recent past?"

"Not ... entirely," he conceded, "but I *was* curious. I actually wanted to talk to you about something in confidence. I need people I can trust around me right now."

Julie raised an eyebrow, suddenly curious. "What about your chief of security?"

"Would *you* trust him?"

Julie laughed. "Not in a million years," she replied. "He's strong-willed, intelligent and determined. He's also stubborn, authoritarian and angry almost all of the time. Your predecessor was scared of him, although he denied it to his dying day. I loved to torment him as much as I could, and I got away with it because Noble was scared of my powers just as much as he was scared of Blain."

May rolled his eyes. "I've known him for a *single* day, and I realised he was all of those things from the first moment we met. It's nice to know that I'm on the right track."

"I'm not surprised that he's made an impression already."

"Before I came here," the Governor said slowly, not looking directly at Julie, "I ... discovered a few things about Mr Blain."

Julie's interest pricked up. "Oh?"

May's eyes were intense and full of conflicted emotion. "I need to be able to trust someone, Julie," he said, "and I'm choosing to trust you. I hope I'm not wrong."

"I hope you're not either," she said with a wan smile.

"Whilst I didn't know that the *Ulysses* founded this world," he went on, "I *do* know that the scattering field was deliberately seeded two years ago, just before engineers arrived to prepare the planet for the prison complex."

Now that's *interesting*, Julie thought. She leaned back in her chair. *Who could possibly have had the resources to achieve such a wide field?*

"Our beloved Robert Blain once belonged to the Emperor's personal staff," May went on, "although it would seem that it was a private arrangement. Blain's specialism lay in genetic engineering."

Julie's eyes widened. The taboo on genetic engineering reaching across the Republic had been in place for centuries, and even caused the only case of abdication by an Emperor. She knew Blain was radical in some respects, but *that* radical?

And here May is, telling me these confidences like a trusted ally. Why?

"Governor …" she said carefully. "This is astonishing, but what relevance does it have on our discussion?"

"Plenty," May said. "I think you're going to be able to help me piece everything together. Did you know Pete Northgate and Reg Patterson very well?"

"Only a little," Julie conceded. "They reported to me,

so I knew them enough to make sure they were doing their jobs. Pete, I never had any problem with; he was methodical, careful and a decent guy. Reg was a lazy sod, and I was planning to have him transferred off-planet at the next available opportunity."

"Did he know that?"

"No, I hadn't told him," Julie replied, "so it couldn't have driven him to anything, much less murder, if that's what you're thinking. I doubt much could really do *anything* to his mental state, to be honest; he was one of life's coasters."

"Patterson and Northgate aside, has there been anything odd happening recently?"

"Not as far as I know," Julie said. "What are you thinking?"

May shrugged. "Psychic possessions, disembodied beings, that sort of thing."

The Governor's shoulders tense as he used the examples, and Julie could understand why; she'd certainly not been expecting to hear *those* sorts of things mentioned.

"Not that I know about," she replied. "But then again, would I be told even if there was? If Commander Blain knew about anything like that, he'd undoubtedly try and find a way to use it to his advantage rather than tell anyone. If the prisoners ever encountered anything, I'm not sure the Operations Manager would be the first person they'd tell."

"How did you get on with Rob?"

"Oh, we were best of friends," Julie deadpanned.

Julie saw May laugh. "And I'm a two-headed lizard from Proxima Seven."

"*Are* there two-headed lizards on Proxima Seven?"

"There might be. I've never been there. Sara went there a few years back; all she told me was that I should never go in the monsoon season. What do you *really* think of Blain?"

"You've got to watch him. He hates the idea of *anyone* telling him what to do. But on the plus side, if he's working *with* you rather than *against* you, he's a brilliant chief of security."

"Forgive me if that doesn't fill me with confidence," May replied. He turned his head to the window and stared out over Island One. Julie saw his jawline moving, and realised he was still talking.

"I can't hear you!" she snapped. "You have to *look* at me when you're talking!"

May's head whipped back round, his cheeks flushed.

"I'm sorry," he said. "I didn't think."

Julie bit back her first sarcastic response. Wanting to give him the benefit of the doubt, she inclined her head, and May visibly relaxed.

"Thank you," he said. "I was just asking what you thought of Steven Doy?"

"He seems decent enough. He's spying for you, isn't he?"

"What makes you think that?"

"I'm a quick study," she replied. "Don't worry, he's not obvious enough for anyone to notice. Just me."

"Does it bother you that he is?"

"Not particularly," she replied. "I imagined that you would need to recruit *someone* from amongst the prison population, especially with no Operations Manager in place and a Chief of Security as angry as Blain."

May chuckled. "You're right there." He hesitated for a moment, then drew in a breath to speak – but Julie cut him off quickly.

"I won't spy for you, Governor," she said. "That's not in my nature. I'm not cut out for the cloak and dagger lifestyle."

"Good, because I wasn't going to ask you to."

Julie deflated. "Oh," she said, "my apologies. That'll teach me to make assumptions."

"Indeed. Spies have to lurk around in the shadows, and I want you to be more … open than that, to be honest."

Intrigued, Julie leaned forward, cocking her head on one side. "Go on," she urged.

"I believe that Reg Patterson was possessed when he attacked me," May explained. "I saw an energy form escape from his head when he died, and I think it tried to enter my brain. I like to understand the things I see. I want to know what it *is* and what it's *doing* here, and if Commander Blain's involved somehow."

Julie found herself nodding; fascinated by what May had seen, and willing to take his word for it. There were far stranger things in the known galaxy.

"How will you get everyone to agree to work with me?"

"I'll do what I can," May replied. "From what I've

heard already, I suspect a lot of the guards won't be entirely loyal to Blain anyway, and he won't be able to completely override my directions without good reason. He'll probably try to slow you down by telling his followers to take their time, but if I get the word out quickly – and the minute you leave this office, I'll send a message for all the guards to follow your lead– some might be flexible. They'll hopefully respect your abilities and your previous role, if not your current position. Play on that; let them feel you've got an official status in the team again, even if that's not entirely true."

Julie found herself nodding again, impressed by his clarity and attention to detail.

"Agreed," she said. "I'll do it."

"Thank you," May replied. "I've trawled through the species database, but there's nothing like this in there, humanoid or non-humanoid. Find the creature, and I'll look into having your sentence reduced."

"Don't promise something you can't deliver. I've been sentenced to life imprisonment. Guinevere wasn't going to let me go back to the Merlin Institute, and our Chief Warlock is too weak to do anything about that. If Guinevere succeeds in bringing the death penalty back into law, I'm sure I'll be sentenced to that instead."

"You think that'll happen?"

Julie shrugged. "She'll do her best."

May nodded. "Edgardo seemed to be going somewhere with his reforms, and then –"

"And then his daughter kills him off."

May's eyes widened in alarm. "Be careful what you

say," he said. "There's no proof."

"But you've heard the rumours, I assume?"

"Of course. Well, you have my word that I will at least *try* to make representations on your behalf. Also, as a show of good faith, I'll switch off the suppression field while you conduct your investigation. It's the least I can do; a mage with her powers is more useful to me than one without."

Julie's jaw dropped. For a moment, she was convinced she'd misread his mouth.

No, I didn't, she thought. *I'm too good a lip reader for that. But still, better to check.*

"What did you just say?"

May smiled. "I said that I will have the suppression field dropped immediately, as a sign of my gratitude and good faith."

"You're serious. What about Commander Blain?"

"Leave Blain to me."

Julie saw, in that moment, the glint in May's eyes, and it immediately convinced her of his intentions, as well as his willingness to take on the chief of security.

"You're looking forward to the fight, aren't you?" she asked.

"I never back down from a good fight," he replied.

Julie chuckled. "I believe you."

She shook her head and released a slow, steady breath. *Well*, she thought, *I've committed myself now – and look at what I'm getting in return. I think the governor and I are going to get on fine.*

"Thank you, Governor. With your permission, I'd like

to get started."

"By all means. I'll send word round straight away; by the time you get back to the prison, everyone will know."

Julie was almost at the door before she paused and turned back to face May. He was looking at his computer, but turned back as he registered that she had something else to say.

"One final question," she said. "My amulet. Can I get that back for the investigation? Mages work better with them; my power would be greatly enhanced with it."

May gave her a withering look. "Don't push it."

Julie smiled and stepped out into the outer office, closing the door carefully behind her. She nodded to Greene, who nodded and smiled back.

"I hope the meeting was productive?" he asked.

"Yes, it was … enlightening," Julie replied. "He's not how I expected him to be."

"He's going to be an interesting governor, isn't he?"

Julie's reply died in her throat as she suddenly felt something…odd; the hairs on the back of her neck rose and she wheeled around to look towards the empty space in the corner of Greene's office.

What is it? What can I feel?

She wondered if it was be the energy mass the governor had mentioned; if it was, however, there was no sign of it now. She narrowed her eyes, but nothing was visible.

Greene appeared in her peripheral vision, and she turned her head in time to see him say, "What's wrong? What can you see?"

"I don't know," she conceded. "But there was something there."

She turned back and scowled. The corner was just a corner again, and the nape of her neck settled down. How had it – whatever it was – escaped?

RACHAEL TRIED HARD to keep her breath under control. The shimmer suit was meant to shield all those functions – as well as her physical body – from everyone's view, but now that Julie had sensed her, she doubted the shimmer suit's ability to cope against someone able to see beyond the every day.

Father said that the suppression field removed all abilities, she thought, *and yet Julie detected my presence.*

She had managed to step quietly and efficiently past Julie and the human assistant and slip into the lift. A vent covering half of the ceiling led into the lift shaft itself and, quietly, she pushed the vent-grate up and aside, and used a powerful down-thrust of her wings to propel herself upwards into the shaft, landing with feather-precision on the top of the lift. Julie was too busy talking to Greene to notice, and Rachael relaxed when she had moved the grate back into place and, a minute or so later, the lift moved downwards, taking Julie to her destination.

That had been close; too close for comfort. This first mission was more complicated than Rachael had imagined. She flew down the lift shaft and exited onto one of the floors where she knew – thanks to the technical data Blain had implanted in her mind – there were large enough windows in a usually-empty part of the building to let her escape.

I need father's guidance.

✦   ✦   ✦

A SHORT TIME later, Julie had been deposited back on Island Two by one of the shuttle craft and escorted to the prison compound by two guards; she always warranted two, apparently, because of her currently-suppressed power. She smiled to herself and wondered how they would react to the suppression field being lowered.

She paused just inside the compound, to watch as the gate was closed behind her, and then released a slow breath. *This is starting to feel a lot like home already.*

Julie had suffered at the hands of a corrupt man, and her best friend had suffered under a corrupt system. She no longer felt any residual guilt about Noble's death, but she *had* realised that the corruption lay a lot deeper than just the ex-governor of one prison world – it lay with the entire court, from the black poison of the Golden Throne outwards. She felt, in helping Governor May, that she could help to stop the corruption from spreading. At least in one small part of the Republic.

Although disappointed, she understood the governor's decision to not return her amulet. Amulets amplified a Mage's power ten-fold, and every decent Practitioner who had graduated from the Academy had one. Without them, they could expect to be reasonably proficient at telekinesis, matter manipulation, and limited telepathy. *With* an amulet, those powers and more would be greatly increased. Julie wished she understood all the details of how it worked, but the Institute had discovered amulets after humanity's first contact with an alien race – the Hopterians – and their practitioners used objects bonded to them through a surprisingly no-nonsense ritual. Humanity had previously dismissed anyone with powers as witches or simply deluded, but had quickly developed a structured way of studying this new elemental force, before Earth had fallen prey to totalitarianism and imperial fiat. Amulets had become part of Institute culture, even though many practitioners just accepted it as part of their rights when they qualified.

She gradually became conscious of the stares from her fellow prisoners. It was a rare event for a prisoner to be summoned to Island One, and even rarer for them to be returned in one piece. Ignoring them, she scanned the yard and quickly found who she was looking for. Doy was leaning against the wall near the open-air exercise yard, engrossed in a book. That was surprising enough in itself; books hardly existed at all these days, everything saved instead as bits on computer screens, so the sheets of paper in Doy's hands were quite valuable. Intrigued, she walked over to him and peered over his shoulder.

"What're you reading?"

Doy jumped; Julie saw his mouth open wide, and assumed he'd cried out in shock. She always found it amusing – and more than a little ironic – that a deaf person could so easily sneak up on someone who was hearing. The slim, green-coloured book he'd been studying disappeared inside the back pocket of his regulation trousers.

"What *was* that you were reading?" she corrected.

"It's a diary, if you must know," he said, his cheeks flushing red. "An old one, from when I was at the Institute. Governor May was able to get hold of this from prisoner archives; I think he wanted to keep me sweet, so he gave me this just as I was about to get onto the shuttle. My dad was a bit paranoid; he loved diaries, but he hated the concept of his thoughts being recorded onto a computer. He thought they could be hacked." Doy grimaced. "He was probably right, too. So my dad gave me this when I left for the Academy."

"That's brilliant. What a fantastic connection to your father."

"What was it like over there?" Doy asked, clearly wanting to change the subject. "How did it feel going back?"

"It felt … odd," Julie conceded.

What did you think about Governor May? he signed, falling back into old habits from his childhood.

Forthright. He's determined to make this place work. We talked about you.

The colour drained from Doy's face. "I … what … what did you talk about?"

I know that you're working for him – and I don't mind. In fact, I'm rather glad of it.

Doy looked relieved and more worried in the same instant; Julie wouldn't have thought that possible until she saw the mixed emotions cross the failed wizard's face; she wondered what he wasn't telling her.

Why? he asked. *I'm spying for the governor. I thought you'd be furious.*

Julie shook her head. *How many people have asked you about me since I left for Island One?*

Seven, Doy said promptly. *Eight if you accept doubles. Some guy called Alex Finch came back to ask me if you were seeing anyone.*

What did you say to that? she asked in horrified fascination.

I told him you were, but your boyfriend wasn't allowed visitation rights due to being banished from this quadrant for genocide.

Thank you for the save, she said with genuine relief. *Alex Finch is one of the few non-Sicarii here, and his only criterion for a potential date is that they have to have had, at some point in the recent past, a pulse.*

Doy still radiated curiosity. *So why did the governor want to see you?* he prompted.

You've heard about the attack on the governor last night?

Of course.

Blain's refusing to investigate, arguing that Reg Patterson just went mad. The governor also saw an energy mass leave Reg's body just as he died. I'm going to investigate.

Doy looked stunned. *Does that mean you're Operations Manager again?*

No, she replied, continuing to use her hands; this felt much more comfortable in any case, and it was nice to have someone who was entirely fluent. *I think that might be a step too far.*

Then there's a rather big stumbling block in your way. Robert Blain?

Doy nodded. *I've never met the guy, but if the rumours I hear about him are true, then he's one hell of a scary man. Some people believe he's responsible for the attack, and that he engineered the visitor centre explosion to kill off May and get the top job for himself.*

There's a promising career in intelligence for you, if you ever decided to apply.

I think my criminal record would rather hamper my chances, don't you? In any case, how are you going to manage the investigation from here? With no team – okay, except me, and I've pathetically little influence or power to do anything – no amulet, no authority and no abilities for as long as the suppression field is on, you're limited in what you can do.

You're working under a misapprehension.

Doy frowned *What do you mean?*

Julie's smile broadened as she felt the pressure lift from her body; the suppression field had made her feel like she'd been carrying a heavy, thick cloak round her shoulders, but now it had suddenly been taken away. Her powers – telekinesis, enhanced empathic skills, control of the elements, and more – had all been returned to her.

He was true to his word, she thought. *Now I've got to be true to mine.*

She opened her eyes – she hadn't even realised she'd closed them, at least until that moment – and looked for

Doy. He had sunk to his knees in shock; unlike Julie, he hadn't been expecting it. She could see that he was breathing heavily, struggling to contain both his emotions and the power coursing through him.

Kneeling down beside him, she leaned in close to his ear; his eyes were closed, so he couldn't see her hands. "You're in a difficult position," she said, as quietly as she could manage without being able to hear her own pitch. "You received the same amount of training as I did, but you've never received the support that runs throughout a Merlin graduate's life. After a while without them, your powers feel raw and out of control. Am I right?"

Doy nodded. With shaking hands, he signed, *It's more powerful than I remember*, he said. *I've used my powers sparingly, but kept it suppressed for most of my life. The power resurge just now hit me properly for the first time since I've left the Institute, and I can't control it.*

He opened his eyes and stared imploring at the practitioner.

I'll help you, Julie said, *and in return, you help me find out who's behind these murders. Deal?*

Doy nodded. *Deal*, he signed.

Good.

She would have preferred to have taken Doy somewhere more private, but didn't want to run the risk of Doy's powers exploding before they could get anywhere. Placing her left hand on his chest, she closed her eyes and focused.

I won't fail you like I failed Catherine, she promised Doy. *I swear.*

12.30pm, 17th April 418

Island One, Elysium

BLAIN LEANED BACK against the central nexus workstation in his lab, folded his arms across his chest and stared into the middle distance. This space, the very centre of the giant, circular room, held a desk, a workbench, and a currently-empty surgical bed, with four corridors leading off the room every ninety degrees.

His thoughts turned to Rachael. How could they not? This had been the alien's home for so many months whilst Blain had worked on her. Rachael had screamed at him wordlessly; and then, one day, after so many months of work, she had spoken for the first time. He had been trying to stimulate her muscles and stretch their capacity to deal with pain, and she had screamed, "Stop! Please stop! It hurts!" Blain had done so automatically, before realising what had happened; she had *asked* him to shut the device down.

I remember that day so well, Blain thought with fierce pride. *I could have danced all night when she finally gained human-level intelligence. It took so long when we were here before. It was easier this time around, with my refined process.*

Rachael's intelligence had grown exponentially after that. Every day, she had shown new reasoning and creative skills, and all Blain could do was watch with amazement and a fair amount of paternal pride. However, although he would never admit it out loud, a tiny part of Blain was worried; Rachael seemed to be developing personality traits without any consultation to the genetic blueprints that Blain had set down for her.

I wonder where it will end.

His head turned as he heard footsteps echoing down the west corridor. Blain's hand went for the pistol on his belt, but he relaxed as a familiar figure took shape.

"Rachael. I was just thinking about you."

"What were you thinking?"

"About old times," Blain replied. "About how you came to be here in the first place."

"I prefer not to think about that."

Blain frowned. "Why not?"

"Because it was painful, and I was less than I am now. I prefer to think of the future."

"You think about the future?" Blain asked in surprise. "What do you think about?"

Rachael shrugged, her wings heaving behind her. "I think about being more than I am," she replied. Her eyes darted around the room, focusing anywhere but on Blain. "I wonder how I can improve myself."

Blain studied his creation carefully. *How can you be*

thinking about the future? A few months ago, you were barely able to feed yourself. Now you're thinking existentially.

He rubbed his forehead as a headache began to throb above his left temple. "Have you been doing as I asked?"

Rachael nodded. "Yes," she replied. She seemed somehow saddened with the abrupt change in conversation; a droop of the shoulders, a lilt of the voice. "I observed Governor May meeting with Julie Martin."

"Julie Martin?" Blain repeated. "Are you sure?"

"Yes," Rachael replied without hesitation. "You imprinted an image of her in my mind. I will always be able to recognise her."

Why did he meet her so soon? Blain wondered. *I expected him to ignore my advice – he's that arrogant – but why do it now? He's got all the time in the –*

"Of course …" He clicked his fingers. "May's asked her to investigate last night's incident. Is the meeting still going on?"

"No. Julie has returned to the other island."

A loud, whooping alarm cut across their conversation. Blain looked down at the screen in front of him, where an alert flashed angrily.

"He wouldn't *dare!*" he snarled.

He pushed himself up and turned to leave, but Rachael was directly in his path.

"Get the hell out of my way!" he snapped.

Rachael's eyes widened, and she stepped to the side; Blain swept past her without another word and left the laboratory at a run, anger propelling every step.

Rachael watched him go, then peered at the console; she didn't understand the symbols that were being displayed. Glancing around the room again, she shuddered. She didn't want to remain here any longer – and relaxed when she realised that Blain had given her a direct order, to "get out of his way." She decided to do exactly that and explore the islands by herself for the first time. She knew she was interpreting the order rather liberally, but a strange feeling of vague rebellion was swirling round her brain, and she was determined to see how far she could push it. She activated the shimmer suit and left the laboratory.

✦   ✦   ✦

"COMMANDER, YOU CAN*NOT* just barge into the governor's office!"

"Just watch me, you little shit!"

Governor May, sitting in his office and suddenly alert to the noise, sighed. *Well, that peace and quiet was short-lived.*

"Do come in, Rob," he called out. It took all his effort to suppress a grin; the security chief was becoming predictable already.

The doors slid open and Blain stormed in, his hands balled into fists. Greene appeared in the doorway behind, a portable comms unit gripped tightly in his hand. They made eye contact for a moment, and May shook his head – he wanted to hear what Blain had to say. Greene nodded and lowered his hand, allowing the door to close.

"What the *hell* have you done?" Blain snarled. His cheeks were flushed as he leaned menacingly over the desk and stabbed a finger at the governor.

"Mr Blain, have you ever heard of knocking?"

"You've turned the suppression field off!" Blain bellowed. "What are you playing at?"

May focused on the finger being angrily pointed at him. Blain picked up on the unspoken rebuke and lowered his hand.

"The scattering field," May went on, his voice calmer than his internal emotional torrent, "stops Julie from transporting off-world, and her transporting *around* the planet will be inhibited as well. Oh, and in case you've forgotten, Doy is a *failed* wizard."

Although he's still got power, May added in the privacy of his own head.

"And," he added aloud again, "I want to give Julie her powers back while she's investigating something for me, in case she needs them for anything. You can never be too sure, can you?"

"May I ask *what* she's investigating?" Blain snapped.

"Oh, did you not see the message I just sent? You were clearly distracted by the suppression field. Julie will be investigating last night's attack, as well as the energy mass. I'm curious, and I want –"

"There is *nothing* to investigate."

"That's not for you to decide. Do not forget that *I* am the governor on Elysium. You and your teams will cooperate *fully* with Julie. You don't have a choice in this. For as long as I'm governor, I have the right to conduct whatever investigation I want, and if my own chief of security isn't willing to do it, then I'll find someone who is."

Blain growled. "You were right earlier today. You're *nothing* like Governor Noble."

May could no longer hide his smile. He beamed. "Why Rob, that's the nicest thing you've said to me so far."

+ + +

BLAIN STORMED BACK down to his office on the second floor of the Tower, and slammed the door shut behind him. He eyed the drinks cabinet for a moment, but reluctantly decided against it; he needed to keep a clear head now.

Sitting behind his desk, he activated the comm system. The link-ups took a few minutes to connect to the right off-world satellites – *Still, it's far better than it used to be*, he thought. *Instant communication was always impossible here the first time around; we had to wait days for an answer.* Eventually, the screen lit up and a young female administrator appeared on the screen.

"Hello, Commander Blain," she said. *"Whom are you trying to contact?"*

"Director Wood," Blain replied curtly. "It's urgent."

"One moment, please."

The screen went black; Blain leaned back as he waited.

+ + +

UPON HIS EXIT, May had been able to push all thoughts of Blain to the back of his mind, in order to focus on other, more important things, like the effective running of Elysium – without an Operations Manager and with a rather truculent Security Chief, a lot of information flowed through his office.

At least this means no-one can keep anything from me, he thought. *And it means I can be an effective Governor.*

"Sir?"

Greene's voice filtered through his thoughts, and May looked up; his assistant was stood in the doorway between their offices. The governor blinked; he suddenly realised that the comm link had buzzed a couple of times, but he'd been so absorbed in his thoughts that he hadn't taken any notice.

"Yes, Josh?"

"Director Wood on the line for you."

May immediately straightened in his chair, nodded his thanks to Greene – who made a tactful exit – and opened the comm channel. Wood's face reappeared in the same position on the screen as it had a short while ago.

"Back so soon, Richard?" May said with a smile on his face – although a fluttering uncertainty in the pit of his stomach made him wonder why Wood needed to contact him again so quickly. "People really *will* start wondering."

"Sorry for the interruption, Jon," Wood said. He didn't smile in return; instead, worry lines creased the space between his eyebrows. *"I don't intend to be one of these directors who constantly interferes with the way you run your prison, I promise, but I needed to brief you on*

something. Did you have a conversation with Commander Blain this morning?"

May nodded as his heart sank; he should've expected this to have something to do with that damned man. The day wasn't even half-over yet, and already he'd had more than enough of the security chief.

"About twenty minutes ago," he replied. "Blain wasn't particularly thrilled that I'd assigned Julie Martin to an investigation about the attack last night."

"Or shut down the suppression field?"

"How did you know about that?"

"Commander Blain has just been on the comm link to me. He went straight from your office to his and placed the call."

"That conniving, evil –"

"Quite," Wood interjected.

May shook his head. "I'm amazed it's taken him this long to complain about me," he said thoughtfully. "We clashed yesterday evening."

"Then you had a reprieve, and I've only been able to buy you a short one this time," Wood replied. *"I told Blain to give me until tomorrow morning to find out what the hell's going on with our delightful Governor of Elysium. You've got until then to find out what secrets the planet's holding before Blain starts pushing me for a decision – and if I do the right thing and sack him, then he'll only go running to Guinevere."*

"And that's the one thing I'm here to avoid," May said ruefully.

"That's as much time as I could give you," Wood went

on. *"Give Julie a push. Get her to find out what the hell Blain's been playing there. And stop taking time getting comfortable in that chair,"* Wood's voice carried a faint edge of humour, although May knew that he was being serious – *"Elysium can run itself for a day."*

"I will – and I know Julie won't let you down."

The comm link went dead and May sat back; things were getting more serious much faster than he'd anticipated. Only twenty-four hours? He would need to keep a close eye on Blain throughout the rest of the day; Julie needed to be given free rein over the investigation, without interference from the man who thought he should be Governor.

✦　✦　✦

RACHAEL FLEW AWAY from the islands where she had so recently been reborn, as Blain insisted on calling her transformation. Her great wings, one of the elements that made her so different to the rest of her species since her rebirth, propelled her over the vast ocean, and she called out in joy at being able to stretch them properly. For months – or was it longer? She couldn't remember – she had been cooped up in that lab, being improved and upgraded by Blain, and now she was free. At least until Blain summoned her back via the transponder he had built into her brain.

And I intend to make the most of it.

She considered travelling to the mainland, to visit some places that she could still vaguely remember, but decided against it.

What if everything's changed? Or what if everything's stayed exactly the same? I'm not sure that wouldn't be worse.

Surprisingly, she found herself at home in the air. Up here, she wasn't answerable to anyone, or obligated to do anything. It was just *her*. Given that she had never flown before the artificial limbs were forced onto her back, it was bizarre to say that flying felt *right* somehow.

Blain had seemed interested in the fact that May and Julie Martin were speaking; she had found it intriguing, though difficult to follow. Her father had downloaded a lot of information into her consciousness, but emotions were still a complex set of experiences that she needed to properly sort through, and so any subtleties were still a subject she had yet to master.

As she flew, a momentary feeling of familiarity caught her off-balance. She managed to catch herself from falling, and her wings continued their regular, rhythmic beating, but she stopped pushing herself forward and hovered in mid-air.

What was that?

She looked around, trying to put a physical presence to what she had felt, but the air, aside from a few odd white clouds hovering far above, was clear. It had felt … familiar somehow, and had dredged up a sickness in the pit of her stomach. A horrified fascination seized her.

Blain wouldn't help her; something about him had begun to unsettle Rachael, although she instantly felt guilty at that thought. Blain had given so much to create her, after all. She pushed that to the back of her mind for now; she needed answers.

Of course!

The answer was entirely logical: Julie Martin. She had managed to sense Rachael's presence in the anteroom to May's office earlier that day, even when she had been wearing the shimmer suit. She would be a good ally.

2.00pm, 17th April 418

Island Two, Elysium

S AT UP ON the laundry building's roof, the power of the universe flowed through Steven Doy's body. Or, at least, that was how it felt. He and Julie had spent an hour together, helping him to control the power again surging through them, and then he'd needed a break.

The intensity with which it had flowed through him when the suppression field had been lowered caught Doy by surprise. The power had always been there, but he had buried it so deep inside his mind and heart that it had been a *relief* to feel the suppression field; he hadn't needed to worry about it, as the field did the work for him. When the power had returned, he hadn't been ready for it, and it had threatened to overwhelm him. He was grateful that Julie could help him contain it again; he didn't want to accidentally lose control, as he had in his final exams all those years ago.

The logical part of his brain knew that the Merlin Institute would punish him for using his powers without being qualified; the penalties were severe, and they would make him suffer. His heart, however, was exalting in this few hours whilst he was working with Julie.

"Steven? Come down, I need to speak with you!"

Doy looked down over the lip of the roof: Julie stood, with her hands on her hips, looking straight at him.

Impossible! he thought. *How can she see me?*

Despite the logical part of his brain telling him all of those things about prohibited energy use, he'd been unable to resist, and had been trialling camouflage. That was one subject he'd passed with flying colours back at the Institute and, right now, he knew that he was doing a damn good job of it. Jumping down from the roof, he cancelled the spell and scowled at Julie.

"How did you see me?" he demanded. "I was top in my class for camouflage."

"Then I suggest you ask for your money back," she retorted. "I saw straight through you. That, and I took an educated guess you were up there. People are creatures of habit."

"You tricked me!"

"No, you allowed yourself to be tricked," Julie retorted. "You made an assumption, lowered your camouflage and let me see you." She sighed. "There are some things you only learn when you're out in the big wide universe practising your art. Sometimes, the best work we do is nothing more than smoke and mirrors. Add in a few fancy hand movements and a bit of chanting and you're halfway there. That's what humanity *expects* to see most of the time anyway; they don't care that we have much more power than the ability to do tricks by hiding the right card up our sleeve."

"I can't believe that I spent three years at the Institute to just be told that it's all just deception!" Doy snapped. "We could *create* the right card out of thin air!"

"I didn't say that it's *all* make-believe. I've just been doing it a lot longer than you. I know what I'm talking about. Now, can we get on? We need to start talking to people."

Suppressing his embarrassment, Doy followed Julie out into the courtyard and fell into step alongside her. They walked at a leisurely pace; Julie smiled and nodded at the people who were still outside; a lot had gone inside to their cells, to get out of the heat, but many were still around enjoying a few minutes after their lunch before heading back to work. Every prisoner here had some kind of importance to the Republic; usually a significant relative or a heavy financial interest in some industry or other, which had kept them from being executed, and had them given light duties instead of being left to the native fauna.

Julie chatted amiably enough, saying a word here, having a short conversation there. Doy soon realised what she was doing; gathering information and gossip by carefully extracting random facts and hints of feelings towards different matters. It was at a price, of course, but one that Julie seemed happy to pay; a Mage's friendship was a valuable asset, and she gave it with a pat on the shoulder or a chuckle at a joke. After forty minutes or so of apparently aimless strolling, Julie and Doy found themselves by the perimeter wall, out of the way of the blazing sun.

So what have you found? Doy asked. He had tuned out after the first ten minutes, as a lot of the conversations had been murmured and quiet.

Why, Mr Doy, what a suspicious mind you have, she signed back. *I've just been talking to my fellow prisoners and making friends.*

Doy raised an eyebrow, and Julie smiled. *Well, Governor May isn't the only one to have seen this … energy blob,* she went on. *Half a dozen people have seen it, hanging around the island over the last few months.*

Why didn't they report it to the guards?

Julie laughed. "Why do you think?" she asked. "The chief of security won't believe the Governor *himself* when he said what he saw. Why would any of the prisoners here –" she waved her hand around the yard, "be believed any more than the Governor?"

So what *is* it? Doy asked.

No idea, but everyone round here is calling it Legion.

Legion? Doy repeated. *Why?*

Julie shrugged. *Heaven knows, but everyone I've spoken to has called it the same thing. The only explanation they could give is that it felt like the right name to use.*

Intriguing.

Indeed – and right now, I'm completely baffled.

Doy rolled his eyes. "That's just what you want to hear from the woman running the investigation," he said without thinking.

Julie frowned. *Do I detect a note of sarcasm in your tone, Mr Doy?*

"You can't detect *anything* from my tone."

Your body language is insinuating it.

A shadow fell over them. They looked round to see one of the guards standing in front of them, wiping his hands on his uniform. Doy vaguely recognised him as one of the guards who he'd travelled with on the *Merciless*.

"Ms Martin?" he said to Julie, addressing her directly with careful lip patterns – he had clearly been coached.

"Yes," Julie replied simply, and then fell silent as she waited for him to continue.

"I – I'm Guardsman Travers," he said. "I've just seen the message from Governor May. He's said that you're leading the investigation into the attack last night."

"You're right," Julie replied. "Do you know anything about it?"

Travers shook his head. "I arrived too late to see Reg Patterson alive," he said. "We all did – the new guard contingent from the *Merciless.*"

Julie nodded. "You arrived yesterday along with Mr Doy here."

"Yes." Travers glanced at Doy and smiled at him; Doy smiled back; *I clearly don't pose as much of a threat.*

"Ms Martin, I … I'm worried about one of my colleagues," Travers went on. "He's been acting oddly ever since he escorted Governor May to Island One's Tower yesterday."

"Odd how?"

"Just … out of character. I mean, I haven't known Fibbens that long – only the week we were on the ship together, plus a few day's basic training before that, but you get to learn about someone's character fairly quickly, don't you?"

"Yes, I believe so," Julie said.

Doy swallowed and continued looking straight ahead.

"Well, Fibbens spent the rest of yesterday evening quizzing everyone about Governor May, Commander Blain ... all the senior figures, really. We all just assumed that he was curious, you know?"

"And now?" Julie prompted.

"The prisoners think that we don't hear them talk about Legion, but I have already. Some of the guardsmen who've been here longer have seen it, too."

Aha, Doy thought, leaning forward, *now* this *is interesting*.

"Are you suggesting that Legion and Guardsman Fibbens' behaviour are linked somehow?" Julie asked.

"I ... I don't know," Travers conceded. "I don't know what I'm saying, but I know he started behaving oddly after we found Governor May – and when Legion apparently tried to attack him. What if he attacked someone else instead?"

"What if, indeed?" Julie said thoughtfully. "Where's Guardsman Fibbens now?"

"In the Infirmary over on Island One, Ms Martin."

Julie frowned. "What's he doing there?"

"He collapsed about an hour ago. I ... we don't know why. The doctors say he's fallen into a coma."

"Right," Julie said, standing up. "Mr Doy and I will deal with this. Thank you, Guardsman. Leave it with us."

Travers nodded, and walked away across the prison

yard. Doy watched him begin a patrol of the yard itself; focused entirely on groups of three or more prisoners, walking over to each group and forcefully pushing himself into their conversation, looking from one to the next, and checking what they were talking about.

Doy looked at Julie. "Do you think this Legion actually exists?" he said. "Are you sure it's not just some kind of collective hallucination?"

"I've got no idea," Julie conceded. She sighed. "I've got a lot of questions."

"So where do we start?" Doy said. "With the guard? Julie, I'm not sure if you've noticed, but we're prisoners on Island *Two*. Are we really going to risk Commander Blain's wrath by teleporting there, especially now that he'll know what we're up to?"

"You're a little ray of sunshine this morning, aren't you?" Julie said. "I'm not intending to teleport. Fear not, Mr Doy. I have a plan."

"Why am I suddenly feeling very nervous?"

"You'll be perfectly safe. Now, excuse me for a moment. I need to catch up with Guardsman Travers and convince him that it's in his best interests to help us."

Doy watched her leave, and shook his head. He paced back and forth until Julie was out of sight behind the Tower.

He felt a sudden gust of air on the back of his neck and, a moment later the, vibrations of something landing on the ground behind him. Turning, he gasped at the sight.

No-one else had reacted to the green-skinned woman

standing in front of him; they were carrying on their conversations or reading or exercise without so much as glancing over.

"How…how did you…?" he croaked.

"The suppression field has been turned off," the being said. "People with certain perceptive strength can see through my shimmer suit."

"Oh … right." Doy had noticed that the woman wore a one-piece uniform of silvers, golds and blacks that did indeed shimmer in the afternoon sun. But if there was something more unusual about the clothing, he'd obviously missed it.

"Where is the Mage Julie?" the being asked.

"She … Well, she's just gone away for a minute," Doy said. He licked his lips; what else should he say to her? This day had been odd enough already, and while his mind was still trying to keep up with everything else that was going on, he realised that meeting a green-skinned alien was probably the least of his worries. She wasn't trying to kill him, at any rate; that had to be a positive, right? "She won't be long."

The being nodded and shift uncomfortably on her feet; her eyes were darting constantly around the yard, and her wings stretched out a couple of times, like she half-wanted to fly away instead of waiting.

"Who are you?" Doy asked. "What's your name?"

"Rachael."

"I beg your pardon?"

"You asked for my name," Rachael said slowly. "My name is Rachael."

"That's an … unusual name," Doy conceded.

"I was under the impression that Rachael is a common name among your people."

"… true. I didn't realise it was common elsewhere, however."

"I was named by my father."

"Your … father? Was he human?"

"My … adoptive father, yes."

Rachael's mouth opened to say more, but she winced in pain and emitted a low growl from deep in her throat. Doy took a step back in alarm, but quickly realised that the sound hadn't been directed at him. Rachael pinched the wrinkled bridge of her nose with her fingers – a curiously human gesture.

"I … cannot tell you," she croaked.

"What's wrong?" Doy asked.

"I am … not able to tell you his name," Rachael replied.

So it's a he, Doy thought. *Well, that narrows it down, at least.*

"Okay," he said, "I won't force you. Why are you here?"

Rachael shook her head, clearly trying to block out the pain. She looked up at the failed Merlin. "You are investigating the entity on this world that does not possess any physical form," she said, as a statement of fact rather than as a question. "I have been watching you, so I know your task. Have you … sensed anything unusual? A mind that doesn't belong, perhaps?"

Doy hesitated; he wasn't entirely sure how to reply to

this green-skinned, winged being in front of him who had just admitted to spying.

Who's she spying for? Blain? It wouldn't surprise me.

Something about Rachael made Doy trust her, however; there was a depth to her soul and her eyes that Doy liked, and she seemed desperate to understand something without having any other agenda.

"Yes," he said. "I was wondering if it was a parasite of some kind – it seems to be interested entering the minds of powerful people. Do you know anything that might help?"

"Perhaps," Rachael conceded. "I sensed something just now that made me wonder …"

Her voice trailed off, and Doy shifted uncomfortably. He'd met aliens before, of course – the Republic had conquered many worlds in its bloody, violent history – but, by and large, they kept themselves to themselves.

"So *you're* the one I sensed in Governor May's office earlier."

Both heads – one human and white, one alien and green – snapped round towards the sound of the voice. Julie was stood by them, staring with naked curiosity at Rachael.

"Yes," she replied. "I am."

"She's wearing a shimmer suit," Doy said, trying to act like he knew what was going on. "That's what caused her to be hidden."

"I've seen one of those before," Julie admitted, and Doy deflated. "They were well-designed. In a full suppression field, no-one can see you."

"You alarmed me when you seemed to sense me," Rachael admitted. "I hadn't expected that. Your powers were … impressive."

"And now you're here, with the suppression field down," Julie went on. "You must have realised that we would see you. Why are you showing yourself to us?"

"Rachael's sensed Legion," Doy explained.

Julie frowned. "Who's Rachael?"

"I am," Rachael responded without a hint of irony.

"Are you native to this world?" Julie asked, and the being nodded.

"Yes," she said. "The rest of my species live on the mainland. My home is here now."

"What about the scattering field?" Julie asked abruptly. "Did your people create it?"

Rachael grimaced. "No," she replied. "We did not seed the atmosphere with that strange field. My species are not capable of such an action. No-one else is … quite like me."

"Able to fly, you mean?"

"Able to *think* in this way."

"Your species don't have the same level of sentience as you?" Doy asked quietly. "Then how do you?"

Rachael winced again. "I … I cannot say," she croaked and blinked away tears of pain. "I must go," she said. "I … cannot stay here any longer. I will find you again."

"Wait!" Julie protested. "I've got more questions –"

But it was too late; Rachael was already beating her wings and lifting off from the ground; she flew over the wall and was soon out of sight. Doy blew out his cheeks as he turned back to Julie and caught her attention so she could watch his lips.

"Can we go after her?"

Julie shook her head. "No," she said, "not now. We'll find her again. Right now, we don't want to keep Guardsman Travers waiting."

"What are you talking about? Where are we going?"

"Island One, of course. Our new friend is giving us a lift. Come on."

2.30pm, 17th April 418

Island Two over to Island One, Elysium

J ULIE WATCHED THE ground fall away as the shuttle took off vertically. In the early days on Elysium, shuttles had taken off by flying forwards off the runway and over the water, until a couple of nasty accidents with the local sea life had meant two of their shuttles had been dragged down to the briny deep. The Republic had provided Elysium with vertical lift-off shuttles very quickly after that.

The equipment's often more valuable than the people.

She and Doy were sat side-by-side in a small passenger shuttle with just seven seats; the pilot – where Travers was sat – and co-pilot ones up front, and two seats behind her, side-by-side, each with a window to let the inhabitants look out over the scenery. There was a solitary chair at the back of the shuttle, manned by another guard. The small console behind him controlled the roof-mounted laser; no-one took any chances any more. The wildlife on this world had a reputation for attacking anything that moved;

no guard was going anywhere without some sort of defence.

"Rachael could be anywhere by now," Julie said to Doy, whose attention was fixed on the window. "You won't see her out there."

He turned towards her. *Rachael knows more than she told us about Legion.*

She'll find us again, I'm sure of it.

Doy nodded; *I hope so.*

Incidentally, how are we going to talk to Fibbens if he's still unconscious?

I was first in my class at mind-sifting at the Institute.

Doy seemed to falter; his hands lost their natural rhythm. *Only the elite trainees get into mind-sifting.*

Julie shrugged. *I was always a natural.*

I heard some people can sift minds without touch.

With my amulet, I could read someone's mind without touch, but there's a huge ethical dilemma there; should I? Peoples' thoughts are meant to be private. With my amulet, or if I'm touching somehow, I can read minds more strongly – but even then, I'd only do it in the right circumstances. I prefer to be moral about that particular power.

She watched Doy nod nervously and look back to the window. *Most people worry when they meet a mind-sifter, but this is something else,* she thought. *What are you hiding?*

IT WASN'T LONG before they arrived at Island One and were able to leave the shuttle behind to walk the rest of the way. Travers accompanied them into the compound, but then agreed to wait outside the infirmary – a squat, two-story building that smelt, unsurprisingly, of antiseptic. The first floor was mostly administrative, with some high-dependency rooms, and the ground floor was set aside for minor and emergency treatment, operations and research. The guard's room was on the first floor and, as they entered, Julie did a double take.

"He's albino."

Sorry, Doy signed as they looked at each other, *I should have said. I know the Republic consider them pariahs, but Fibbens was ... just another guard. That's certainly how he was treated by everyone, anyway.*

The albino was lying peacefully in bed, covered from the waist down by the bed-sheets and wearing a hospital gown. He was connected to various monitors by wires sticking out from both arms and small, square surgical pads stuck to the sides of his forehead. His face had a faint sheen of sweat. Julie looked over what she could see of his body, but there weren't any marks or scars. His eyes were moving constantly under his eyelids, and his lips moved as though whispering.

Doy attracted her attention. *Should I ... stay outside?*

Steven, she said, sighing, *I wouldn't ever force myself into your mind, I give you my word. I need you here in case he says anything out loud when I'm not looking.*

The albino's face was contorted in pain, and the murmuring hadn't stopped since she and Doy had entered the room. Julie prided herself on being an excellent lip-reader, but she just couldn't make out what he was trying to say – his mouth moved too quickly.

Her fingers lightly touched the albino's face. If he gave any indication that he felt them, he didn't show it – the sheen of sweat continued to reflect a glow from the harsh, overhead light that compensated for the lack of a window, and his murmuring continued.

Closing her eyes to shut out distractions, she began to delicately probe his mind. It was difficult enough to swim against the flow of a person's emotions, thoughts and feelings when they were trying to control the flow in synchronisation with the sifter. But when the subject was unconscious, and their thoughts chaotic and manic, it was like trying to stay ahead of the crest of a huge wave.

Stop fighting me! she told him. *I'm trying to help you – let me through! TALK TO ME!*

"HELP ME!"

She stepped back in shock; she had felt the *vibration* of his shout. She opened her eyes as she felt Fibbens move; he sat up, eyes wide open and his chest heaving like he'd just finished a long run. Doy took a cautious step towards the guard and signed as he spoke, to ensure Julie knew what he was saying.

"Adrian, my name is Steven Doy," he said.

Fibbens didn't respond; instead, his eyelids closed and he slumped backwards on the bed. Julie caught him to make sure he didn't land awkwardly.

"Can you make out what he's muttering?" she asked Doy.

Doy leaned forward, putting his ear closer to Fibbens' mouth. After a moment, he swallowed and straightened, turning his face away from Julie.

"What did he say?" she asked.

Doy didn't reply, so she grabbed his arm and pulled him round. She caught her breath as she saw that his eyes had brimmed with tears.

"He keeps saying 'kill me'," he replied. "'Please kill me before Legion does'."

Julie drew in a breath. "Legion's taken over," she realised. "We need to get it out of Fibbens' head." She sighed. "And I'm going to need my amulet to do it."

JULIE AND DOY agreed to split up; they could cover more ground separately right now. Doy asked Travers to take him to the recreation centre, where the off-duty guards often sat and relaxed, to find out if any of them had seen Legion for themselves – and if they would tell him anything about Blain. That second point was more for his own curiosity than anything else, but he wanted to know why the security chief had refused to conduct the investigation. Was it because he didn't believe there was anything to investigate, or was there any other other reason behind his decision?.

At the same time, Julie cautiously made her way across the compound to the Tower. Although she'd been given official charge of the investigation by the Governor himself, she was still a prisoner. As a result, she knew that guards loyal to Blain would willingly challenge her if they saw her here on Island One. She couldn't afford the loss of time.

She reached the 11th floor without much of a problem – although she'd had to hastily camouflage herself in the lift to avoid two guards she recognised as Blain's flunkies. They all travelled four flights up the length of the Tower together until the guards exited and Julie found herself able to breathe again.

Greene was sat at his desk, but jumped up as he saw her enter the outer office.

"Ms Martin!" Greene said. "You've left Island Two by yourself?"

"Just temporarily," she said. "Guardsman Travers is escorting Steven Doy and me. I've just stepped away from them to speak to the Governor, if he can spare me some time."

Greene hesitated, looking reluctant, then nodded. "Wait here," he told her.

Julie watched as he stepped into the Governor's office and closed the door. She wished she could hear what Greene was saying to May, and how the Governor was taking it. Before she could speculate, the door opened again and Greene emerged.

"Go in, Julie," he said. "The Governor will see you."

"Julie!" May exclaimed as she crossed the room and sat in the chair he pointed at. "You're certainly the escapologist. This wasn't quite what I expected you to do when I lowered the suppression field."

Julie smiled. "I was brought over in a shuttle," she explained. "Guardsman Travers can't be in two places at once, and we felt Doy needed more guarding in the recreation centre than I did here with you."

May shook his head as he laughed. "Well, I'd agree with you there," he said. "Actually, I'm glad you're here. We have a slight problem; Blain is getting … wound up very tightly, especially with my decision to lower the suppression field. We need results, Julie, and we need them urgently. By tomorrow, if you can."

Julie's eyebrows rose. "There's nothing like working to a short timeframe, is there?" she said wearily. "Well, I'll certainly do what I can, Governor. We're actually working on a very interesting lead right now."

She quickly summarised everything that they had learnt so far, up to discovering Legion's 'name', and the fact it was now hiding inside Fibbens' head.

"How is Legion not controlling this man's body then?" May asked. "He found it apparently very easy with Reg."

"Albinos have a lot more mental strength than other humans," Julie reminded him. "Many also have access to the same powers as we do in the Institute. If it wasn't for the unfounded dislike, we'd have probably recruited them all centuries ago."

"What do we do now? How do you get that being out of his head? Can you question it if you do?"

"I hope so," Julie replied. "But I need something first."

To his credit, May was very quick on the uptake; he immediately shook his head and held up a hand to protest. "No way," he retorted. "I *can't* give you your amulet back, Julie – not when I've got Commander Blain nipping at my heels, trying to find a way to stop this investigation from even happening. He's already reported me once today; can you imagine who he'd report me to if he got wind of the fact that you got *that* back?"

Julie leaned forward and rested her hands on the table. "I thought that was the point," she said. "I thought we were here to circumvent Blain's authority."

"We *are*," May insisted, "but not in order to make him go running to the Empress. We don't need that level of political interference in our work. There's only so many ways I can defend us, Julie, and certainly not against Guinevere."

Julie fought hard to hide her frustration; she could understand what the Governor was saying, but that didn't make it an easier pill to swallow. Her amulet would have made it so much more straightforward. Logically, however, she had to concede it would have made the overall situation so much harder. She nodded, reluctantly, and stood.

"Very well," she said. "I'll just have to do my best."

"Thank you," May say emphatically. "I need you to."

"Governor," she said carefully as another thought struck her, "do you remember telling me earlier about Commander Blain's particular research interest?"

May nodded. "Genetic research," he replied.

"Do you know if he ever found practical applications for his work?"

"I ... don't know," he said. "You know, I didn't actually think to ask my contacts. How stupid of me. Why?"

"I ... Give me some more time on that one, would you?" Julie smiled. "I'm still looking into it. But keep an eye out for someone called Rachael."

May frowned, clearly confused, but Julie turned away before he could ask any more questions; she wanted to research the subject a little more first before having a discussion on it. She hoped that she was wrong, but somehow something told her that she wasn't. And the possibilities that the thought opened up terrified her.

✦   ✦   ✦

JULIE SMILED AT Greene as she left the office, but didn't say anything. She knew Greene wouldn't have been listening in – he was too tactful for that – and she didn't have the time to explain. She was lost in thought as she stepped into the lift, trying to decide how best to plumb the depths of her powers without resorting to using her amulet, wherever it was.

She blinked as the lift began to slow– and then stopped on Level 2, a floor earlier than expected. The doors opened, and she drew herself up to her full height as Robert Blain entered. He didn't look in the least bit surprised at seeing her.

"Julie," he said.

"Lovely to see you again, Rob," Julie said calmly, belying the tension she was inwardly feeling. Her eyebrows rose as she watched him press the "HOLD LIFT" button on the controls. "Can I help you with something?"

"What the hell do you think you're doing?" he demanded. "If you're playing at detective, then perhaps I need to remind you that *I'm* the chief of security round here."

"Then perhaps you should act like it," Julie snapped. "Aren't you going to ask how Guardsman Fibbens is?"

Blain scowled at her. "It's fairly obvious, isn't it? He's in a coma."

"Do you actually care about any of them?"

"I care about keeping this planet secure. We keep order amongst the prisoners, we ensure the Rixxians never find us, and we impose the will of the Republic on dissidents and free-thinkers. That's the entirety of my focus, and I will do it with every fibre of my being."

Julie shook her head. She knew she would never get anywhere with the stubborn mule of Blain's anger, so she changed tack.

"Since I've got you here," she said, "I could do with my amulet back. Can you help?"

Blain smiled; humourless, unsympathetic. "Sure. If you can find it, it's yours."

Julie rolled her eyes and wondered if there was anything she could actually say that would get a half-decent answer.

"Rob, I'm here under Governor May's orders, doing the job you *should* be doing."

"Shame about your brother, wasn't it?" he snarled.

The abrupt change in conversation caught Julie off-guard. "What?"

"Your brother," Blain repeated. "He was a teacher at the Merlin Institute's New York academy, wasn't he? I heard that he was involved in some sort of accident. Such a shame you didn't get to say goodbye before he died."

Before she could think about it, Julie slapped Blain across the face; leaving red marks forming on his left cheek. He touched them briefly, but didn't protest; he seemed to accept that he'd crossed some sort of invisible line.

"Am I right in thinking he was the reason you joined the Institute?"

She didn't bother asking Blain how he had learnt all this; as security chief, he could undoubtedly access any personnel files he wanted to.

"So what?" she asked. "It's not a secret. Yes, my brother died when he was teaching at the Institute, and yes, I idolised him."

"You never found out who caused the accident, did you?"

"No, but that was a long time ago," she said, making sure her voice was even and controlled. "A lot of water has passed under the bridge since then. The Institute conducted a full enquiry, but never released the names to the family. That's part of their system. A mage taking matters into their own hands would bring harm, not justice."

"Liar," Blain shot back. "I know you're as desperate now as you were back then. Well, the Institute *did* find out, but only recently. The Institute captured the killer, Julie. Did no-one tell you?"

"Don't joke about that, Blain. No-one's told *me*."

"Why would they? You're a prisoner. A killer. Oh by the way, has Steven Doy told you *when* he was expelled from the Institute?"

A chill ran through Julie's body; she shook her head, not trusting herself to speak.

"He was expelled at the end of his third year," Blain went on, "in the same year that your brother died."

Julie's mind immediately protested. *No, the two instances are coincidence. They've got to be.*

"Turns out he was quite the student," Blain continued, looking quite cheerful as he spoke. "He was actually sitting his final exams; he'd finished his studies a whole year early. Even *you* took the full four years to pass your studies, didn't you?"

"I'm not interested in competing," Julie said. Although she couldn't hear it, she knew anger was seeping into her voice. Right now, however, she didn't care. "Stop the lies, Rob. I'm absolutely sick of them."

Blain shook his head. "Every word I've said is true," he said. "According to my sources, it's rare for a student to pass in just three years, and they can usually only do *that* with some help. As I understand it, Mr Doy was fortunate enough to have a mentor in your brother. You never met Doy back then, of course. You were deeply involved in your post-graduate studies at the Los Angeles academy."

Julie wanted to close her eyes and shut it all out; every word cut into her, but she refused to take her eyes from Blain's mouth. She wanted – she *needed* – to know the truth.

"Doy was a good, if somewhat overconfident, student," Blain's face had turned serious again. "It turns out that he made a fatal mistake in one of his final exams. He blew up half the examination hall, by all accounts."

"No …"

"I wouldn't lie, Julie – at least, not about this. Doy's ineptitude killed your brother. The man you hero-worshipped died at Steven Doy's hands."

+ + +

DOY LICKED HIS lips. "I'm asking because I *need* to know, gentlemen. One of your colleagues is in a coma over in the infirmary; we need any information you can give us."

The guardsmen surrounding Doy still looked dubious, but the reference to Fibbens – still lying unconscious just a couple of buildings along from where they were all currently stood in the Rec Centre – seemed to act as a wake-up call.

Albinos may not be popular, Doy thought, *but Fibbens is a guardsman first and an albino second. I admire their code of honour.*

Travers had been nervous about introducing a prisoner to the guards' inner sanctum, but Doy was glad he had acceded; whilst the guards had initially been annoyed at his presumption, he felt like he was getting through at last.

"It's all just rumour," one of the guards – Smith – said slowly. "We've got no proof." He shot a look at the rest of the group, seeming to dare any of them to correct him, but they didn't; instead, they shifted awkwardly. They were obviously willing to share rumour and gossip amongst themselves, but it was a different matter to share with outsiders.

"Leave the proof to me," Doy said. "Just tell me what you know."

"You can save Fibbens?" Smith asked.

"I … hope we can," Doy said carefully. He flushed as he remembered Fibbens' emotional plea for death. He hoped it wouldn't come to that. "I can't make you any promises, but you have my word that we're fighting here for his dignity."

That seemed to be the right thing to say, as Smith nodded approvingly. "Commander Blain isn't often in his office," he said. "If you ever need to talk to him, you have to leave a message, and he'll come to find you later."

"Where is he then?" Doy prompted. "Where does he spend all of his time?"

"No-one knows for sure," Smith conceded. "He … Well, in the early days, he spent a lot of time patrolling the mainland. *He* said he was looking for threats, but you wouldn't do that by yourself. He seemed to be looking for something in particular, but we never found out what it was."

"Does he still go out on these patrols now?"

"No, he hasn't done for months," Smith replied. "But he's still not in his office. He just disappears somewhere."

"What makes you say that?"

"Because a few months ago, I needed a decision on something fairly urgent, so I went looking for him. The commander wasn't answering the comm, so I searched everywhere – and I mean everywhere – on Island One. It's not exactly big, so it didn't take me long."

Doy frowned. "Maybe he was over on Island Two at

the time."

"No," Smith replied, shaking his head emphatically. "I checked with them. He wasn't there either. He wasn't *anywhere*. And then, all of a sudden, he was. He just appeared out of nowhere, like he'd been hiding somewhere with a shimmer suit."

"Or somewhere underground?"

Smith nodded, looking relieved to be getting it off his chest, and having someone believe him. Doy licked his lips. Now he just needed to understand how it all fitted together.

THE SOUND OF the lift doors opening again made May pause mid-sentence to Greene, who stood in the doorway to the office. He frowned; it had only been a few minutes since Julie had left. Whoever it was, May didn't want to be disturbed. Catching Greene's eye, he shook his head, and the young assistant seemed to catch his meaning. He turned back, but May saw him hesitate.

"Julie?" he said, a strange note of caution mingled with the surprise in his voice. It sounded off, and May immediately stood in a sort of primal response.

"Get out of my way."

Julie didn't even wait for an answer; she simply barged her way past Greene and into May's office. The door slammed shut behind her, blocking Greene from view. Her eyes were blazing, and her hands were bunched into fists.

"What's wrong?" May asked her, now properly on edge.

"Give me my amulet," she replied. Every word was icy calm, and yet anger radiated from her. Her shoulders were hunched, her eyes were narrowed, and she was almost shaking.

"I won't do that."

"I need to access to Fibbens' memories, and I can't do it without my amulet."

"Why do you *really* want it?" May retorted.

Julie shook her head. She seemed to realise that May wasn't going to respond to her lies. "Did you know that Steven Doy was the man who killed my brother?"

May didn't even hesitate. "Yes," he said. "He made a terrible mistake, and went on the run as a result. But the two of you were getting along, and I didn't want to ruin a potential friendship, as well as a productive relationship." He scowled. "I assume that Mr Blain disagreed with me."

Julie nodded. "I appreciate your honesty," she replied. "You have my word that I won't hold it against you. Now give me my amulet."

"No. I don't trust your judgement."

Julie's eyes bored into his. He knew she was an intelligent woman; he watched as her eyes surveyed the room. Suddenly, a look of realisation dawned on her face, and she looked back at the governor.

She knows.

He stood and walked across the office to get between her and the landscape painting hanging on one of the walls.

"I really don't want to hurt you," she said.

"That's nice to know," May replied. "I don't want you to either. I –"

Julie barged past May, and he was too slow to stop her; she was at the picture in a few quick strides; she clicked her fingers, and both the picture and frame flew off the wall, despite being securely fixed just a moment or two before. A large, square safe sat behind it; it lacked both fingerprint and DNA scanners. Elysium really *was* at the back end of technology, May thought for a second, before that thought was pushed away. Julie placed her hand over the lock, and May heard the familiar *click click click* sound of the locks being opened.

She reached into the safe; a few seconds later, her hand re-emerged with the amulet; a gold-chained necklace with a diamond stone surrounded by a stylised platinum Celtic design. She spun on her heels, looking triumphant.

"How *dare* you keep this from me," she seethed through clenched teeth. "This is *my* property. I can use this now for –"

"For another death?" May snapped. "Julie, one person has died at your hands already. Surely that's enough?"

"My brother *is dead!*" Julie barked. "He deserves vengeance! How could *you* ever understand that?"

May didn't say anything; he didn't need to. A vision of Sara flashed before his eyes, and he suspected that Julie was thinking something similar; a flicker of a different emotion crossed her face, but she didn't say anything. Instead, she growled deep in her throat and waved a hand.

"My amulet stays with *me!*" she said. "You will *not*

take it away again."

Without saying another word, she left the office with long strides. Neither May nor Greene tried to stop her; what would be the point? Her amulet had just magnified her powers ten-fold.

"What now?" Greene asked as he stepped into his superior's office.

May shook his head. "Now we're in serious trouble."

"Do we re-activate the suppression field?"

"We're going to have to," May said wearily. "Go down to –"

An alert chimed on his desk, and he looked down at his computer. He snorted with savage humour, and found that he wasn't actually that surprised.

"Looks like we *can't* reactivate the suppression field," he said. "That's a message from the control room. One of the components has just fried. They can replace it, but it's going to take an hour. Looks like Julie can reach further afield than we imagined. So that's out; now we see the carnage that elemental physics brings to the real world."

DOY STARED AT the screen on one of the tables in the Rec Centre. The colour had drained from his face, and his legs were buckling; they wanted to collapse, and he had to force them not to. He wasn't going to show weakness right now, dammit.

"Are you sure?" he asked. "You didn't mishear?"

Joshua Greene, his head and shoulders visible on the

screen, shook his head. *"I heard perfectly,"* he said. *"So did the Governor. He's on his way, but Julie will get there first."*

"Any suggestions?"

"Don't bother trying to run. However fast you can move, she can move faster."

Doy rolled his eyes. "Thanks for the advice."

The comm link terminated and Doy licked his lips; the guards in the ward room were all staring at him nervously. Whilst they didn't know the reasons behind Julie coming here – Greene had been tactful on the comm, although Doy had worked it out almost instantly – they knew that she had her amulet back, and that she was angry.

"I'm going to contact Commander Blain," Smith said. "He'll know what to do."

"No!" Doy protested. "He won't help us. No-one will. I just need some time to think."

But he only had a few scant seconds before the main door to the Rec Centre suddenly disintegrated, and Julie stepped inside. She looked around coolly until her eyes found Doy, and then her jaw tensed into an even angrier line than it had been a moment before.

"All of you, get out," she commanded.

If it had been anyone else, the guards would have just laughed. With Julie in front of them, her eyes blazing and her amulet around her neck, they didn't even try to argue. Within a few seconds, they had all gone, and the door had returned to its original, solid state.

Doy suddenly felt incredibly alone. He didn't dare move or speak as Julie's eyes studied him carefully. If looks could kill, Doy knew he would be dead already. She lightly touched her amulet, and Doy sagged.

With an abrupt turn of speed, Julie crossed the floor, and suddenly she was stood right in front of him. He tried to suck in a deep breath, but his lungs wouldn't work properly, and he found himself frozen to the spot.

She reached out and touched his face. She was surprisingly gentle, given the fury burning in her eyes, and she was clearly thinking very carefully. He felt a sudden movement inside his head. Julie had begun pushing against his meagre mental defences; she was trying to sift through his thoughts, and he winced at the force of it. He fell to his knees, but Julie maintained the connection; she sank to her own knees, her eyes boring into his.

I won't let you just strip my mind bare! he bellowed his thought at her. *You gave me your word – you swore you'd never read my mind without my permission!*

Julie's mind-sift attempts faltered as she was reminded of her promise. She seemed to go through a brief internal struggle, torn between her anger and her oath. After a few seconds, when Doy's forehead had broken out in a sweat as he tried to resist her, she growled and turned away.

Doy gasped in relief as the pressure lifted, and he collapsed fully onto the floor. His limbs shook as the redness in his cheeks began to fade.

"You killed my brother." It was a statement rather than a question.

Doy's breathing began to slow and, after a few moments, he'd regained enough energy to push himself up off the floor and sit upright. Still wheezing, he knew that he needed to sign to be understood.

It was an accident. I promise.

"You were responsible for a death."

Eight.

Julie blinked in confusion. *What?* she signed.

"Eight deaths," Doy repeated out loud, angling his face so she could see his lips. "That's how many deaths I was responsible for."

His cheeks flushed again, but this time with guilt. He felt hot, stinging tears form; although he'd never forgotten the true depth of what he had done, he'd managed to form a scab over the emotional wound. Now that the wound was re-opened, he let the tears fall.

I messed up my practical exam and caused an explosion. It killed my teacher, two of my friends, your brother, my girlfriend and three civilians visiting the campus. When my girlfriend's father found out what I'd done, he vowed to kill me. I wish he'd succeeded.

Julie crossed her legs, and he watched her cautiously, like she were a coiled spring ready to leap at any moment. She gently touched the amulet as her eyes unfocused.

I idolised my brother, she signed. *He was five years older than me, and we were so close. He'd always play with me when I was a kid, or talk to me if I had a problem ... and never got embarrassed with his younger sister hanging around.*

Doy didn't interrupt; he knew that Julie wanted – needed – to talk about it. Besides, it felt right to hear about the people he'd killed and share the families' pain.

After he died, I stayed with the Institute. My parents didn't approve. They had just lost one child to the Merlins;

they didn't want to lose another, and they had always wondered if a child who was losing her hearing even then could make it in the world of elemental physics. You know, we lose so much of who we are when we become practitioners; we even stop referring to ourselves as humans, and somehow divorce ourselves from the rest of humanity. Somehow we forget that we're just as human as the next person, albeit with extra abilities. My parents were worried I'd forget that. They wanted me to come home.

But you stayed, Doy signed.

I stayed, she agreed. *It took my parents some time to understand why, though.*

Doy fought a brief internal struggle before he ask; *Why* did *you stay?*

Because I wanted to make my brother proud of me, she signed. *I still do.*

He was my mentor, Doy said, *and Matt talked about you so often that I kept forgetting that we'd never actually met. He was proud of you. I made a terrible mistake– one that I can never take back, but I'm not a liar.*

A loud bang made Doy jump and look over Julie's shoulder; she looked round, curious to see what Doy had reacted to. She stood and activated the small view screen next to the Rec Centre door; a guard was rubbing his shoulder where he'd just collided with the door, clearly trying to break it down.

As he lined up for another run, Julie touched the control panel with the tips of her fingers. Sparks shot across it and the door opened. At the same moment, the guard reached the door, shoulder-first. He rolled to a stop on the floor before quickly jumping up and smoothing down his uniform.

He was quickly followed by Governor May, who surveyed the scene, and seemed surprised that everything was comparatively calm. Julie raised an eyebrow.

"It would seem that ..." She hesitated for a moment and glanced at Doy before continuing. "It would seem that I am not as keen to kill Mr Doy as I was a moment ago."

Doy's stomach lurched; *I would have deserved that*, he thought, *but it doesn't mean I wanted it, not any more. I've started to find my place in the universe again. Ironic, that it's inside a prison.*

"I'm glad," May replied. "Mr Doy is punishing himself far more effectively than you ever could. He's shouldering the guilt of what he did every day. Isn't that so, Mr Doy?"

Doy nodded. "Yes."

"I won't be giving back my amulet," Julie said stiffly. "I give you my word that I won't harm anyone. Steve can guarantee that my word means something."

Nodding, Doy added; "I'll vouch for her, Governor. She gave her word to me and she kept it under very ... difficult circumstances."

And she's started calling me Steve rather than Mr Doy, he realised. *That's got to mean something.*

"Can you keep working together?" May asked.

Doy glanced nervously at Julie; now that he'd started working with her on this case, he wanted to see it through. That decision entirely depended on how Julie felt.

"I ... think so," she conceded, "if only because I know it'll annoy Commander Blain."

May looked relieved. "I need results, Julie, and I need them *now*. I'm going to start getting questions from HQ as to why I've turned the suppression field off. I've not told anyone as yet, but it won't stay like that forever. I need to give them something."

"You'll have results," Julie said. "I guarantee it."

BEFORE LEAVING HIS office at a run, May had shouted an instruction at Greene; Blain was to be on the 11th floor, waiting for him when the Governor got back. As the lift doors opened and deposited May back there, he saw Blain, standing tall and smug, by Greene's desk; his assistant didn't look impressed that the chief of security was looming over him.

Yes, May thought, *I want a word with you. Or several words, to be precise.*

"Governor May," Blain said impassively, with an imperceptible nod of his head.

Ignoring him – but slightly surprised that Blain had finally decided to start using his title – May walked straight past him and into his office. He didn't wait to see if Blain followed him, but could hear by the other man's footsteps that he had.

"Josh," May called over his shoulder, "Commander Blain and I aren't to be disturbed."

"Yes, sir."

May heard Greene shut the door quietly behind them just as he sat behind his desk. Only then did he finally glare, with narrowed, intense eyes, at Blain.

"You bastard," he snapped. "You did that deliberately."

"Of course," Blain said. "You don't think I'd do something like that by accident, do you? Granted, it didn't work as I expected, but it still spread a sliver of doubt between two Merlins."

"We need to resolve yesterday's attack and *find* the energy being, rather than sweep it all under the carpet. The only reason I can think as to why you're not cooperating is because you're in some way involved." May sighed. "I want to work with you, not against you. You're meant to be someone I can trust."

"Trust has to be earned," Blain said without expression. "You've done nothing to earn it – except go against my recommendation that we *not* investigate Reg's momentary lapse of good judgement."

May frowned. "Why are you so desperate for me not to investigate? Why don't you want to find out the truth?"

"What's the point? No-one cares about the prisoners here. They're all scum!"

May was taken aback by the sudden ferocity of Blain's venom, and remained silent as the security chief continued. "I have been on this rock since our directorate took over these buildings," he growled. "We house and feed these scum, and for what? It makes me so *angry*; they are nothing but stupid, ignorant dissidents and a drain on resources."

"Then why the hell are you still here? If you *hate* them so much, why not just resign your commission and go?"

"Because there's work I need to finish. The military never managed it, and neither did anyone aboard the *Ulysses*, so *I* have to shoulder the burden. I need to be here. *You* don't."

"We can't go on like this," May said. "You're at my throat all the time and I'm biting. You want my job, and I want a chief of security I can work with."

"What are you saying?"

May pressed his lips together; he'd said it now, and he couldn't take it back.

"I'm suspending you from active duty until further notice. I'll be contacting Director Wood to request a new chief of security. There'll be a guard permanently stationed outside your quarters, where you'll remain until further notice."

Blain's jaw set in a tense, angry line, and May wondered if he was about to let rip, but instead he just turned on his heel and marched out without saying another word. May turned towards the window and looked out over the island, trying to calm himself.

How the hell did it get this bad in less than a day?

Something that had been niggling away at him finally threw itself into his conscious mind. *Did he used to know my sister then?* he wondered. *Elysium's in the back of beyond; why would the Praetorian Guard be interested in an unimportant world this far out? Unless that was precisely the point, and they were working on something they didn't want anyone else to know about.*

He couldn't work out his sister's connection. All Jon knew was that Sara and the *Ulysses* – and Blain, if they

served together as the security chief had just intimated –
had discovered this world. What else had they done here?

What am I not being told?

"WELL, THIS CERTAINLY makes things awkward."

"You're telling me," May replied. He grimaced. "I was
angry."

"You should think before you speak," Wood chastised
him. *"This is precisely what we didn't need right now, Jon.
Who knows what Blain is going to do? We needed
something more concrete against him that we could have
taken to the Sicarii or the press; then Guinevere couldn't
have overridden his suspension."*

"I know, I know, it was stupid of me." May sighed. He
still couldn't quite believe that he'd done it. He'd been so
angry at the security chief that he hadn't stopped to think
about the consequences. Now, he just felt stupid, and yet
oddly fulfilled at the same time.

"So what do we do?" he asked.

"You *don't do anything,"* Wood said. *"I need to report
this very carefully up the line. I'll get McIntyre to help; she's
been removed as personal aide by one of Guinevere's
favourites, but she's still in the personal office and knows
how things work there. This will need some careful
handling. Blain's secure, I assume?"*

"Yes, sir. Commander Blain is en route to his quarters
as we speak."

BLAIN SAT DOWN behind his office desk. He didn't give the
guard a single thought; he was already unconscious and

hidden away. The security protocols Emperor Edgardo had given him wouldn't work any more, but they *would* get the attention of the right people. Right now, every second counted before May locked him out of the network. The codes sped through the communications network that criss-crossed Republic space. Soon, a young woman's face appeared on the screen.

"The codes you have are out of date," she said bluntly. Blain liked her already.

"I know, but I was hoping they would attract the Empress' attention."

"I am the Empress' personal aide. You have my attention … for the moment. Those codes belonged to Emperor Edgardo, so you must have meant something to him. I will decide whether or not you get an audience with the Empress. Speak quickly; you have two minutes."

MAY PACED THE length of his office; thinking about his next step and wishing that his brain would work faster. He stopped by the large bay window and stared out across the compound for a moment, then turned round as a noise behind him attracted his attention. He gasped and took a step back in shock, banging his elbow against the glass as a figure came into view in the middle of his office. May gaped; she was winged and green, for heaven's sake, and she'd managed to get into his office without setting off any alarms.

"Governor May?" she said.

May's mouth opened and closed uselessly for a moment until his brain kicked into gear. Something Julie had said earlier made him frown with the effort of recall.

"Rachael?"

"Do you know who … or rather, *what* – I am?"

"I … I have absolutely no idea. Are you native to this world?"

"Yes, although I am the only one with this level of intelligence … now. A select few were also upgraded some time ago, but they are all dead. I was made more recently."

"By Commander Blain, by any chance?"

Rachael winced and closed her eyes. From the look on her face, May wondered whether or not she might be sick at any moment. She seemed to contain the urge, and forced her eyes open with what looked like a monumental effort as she leant against the wall. The pain was clearly overwhelming, and May immediately took a step forward to see if he could help, but Rachael held up a hand to stop him.

"No, don't come any closer," she said. "My behaviour has been programmed."

May nodded, and took a step back. "Rachael," he said cautiously. "These 'upgrades'; did they include your wings?"

"Yes." She blinked and shook her head, the pain clearly easing. "My wings are a more recent addition."

May stared at her intently, intrigued. "I think you'd better come with me," he said. "We're going to find Julie Martin."

"Why?"

"Because she may well be able to help you get that thing out of your head," May explained, "and you're the smoking gun we need to stop Blain before he does any more damage to this world."

IN THE PRIVACY of his office, Blain had finished speaking.

"*Very well,*" the Empress' aide said tersely. "*Wait by this comm unit.*"

The screen went blank, and Blain smiled; he wasn't offended by the bluntness of the reply. It just meant that he had captured her interest – and, if he could capture *hers*, then why couldn't he capture the Empress' as well?

Blain tapped his chin thoughtfully and smiled; it was clearly time to try the chip he had installed in his creation's head. It was past noon, and he hadn't seen Rachael for some time.

If Guinevere does call, I think it's time I show off my creation.

He pressed a button on his computer –

– AND RACHAEL SCREAMED. May jumped back from her in shock. They had just travelled down from his office, and were about to walk the short distance to the infirmary.

"Rachael!" May exclaimed, kneeling beside her. He looked frantically round, but no-one was visible; everyone was either inside or on Island Two. "Dammit," he muttered, and turned back to the green-skinned being. "What can I do to help you?"

"Nothing," Rachael groaned. She pushed herself to her feet and looked back to the Tower. "I … I need to go," she said. "I can't fight it. It hurts too much. I will come back to you when I can."

SHE THEN TOOK off, her magnificent wings beating hard and propelling her upwards. She disappeared as she rounded the other side of the Tower.

May ground his teeth: things had suddenly become a lot more difficult. Should he go straight to Blain? With what? He now only had the evidence of his eyes, and Blain could easily deny the governor's accusations – and without proof May would just look mad, especially if his security chief tied it in with his mention of the energy field. No. Now wasn't the right time; he needed to continue getting answers, and then go over the ex-chief's head.

4.30pm, 17th April 418

Island One, Elysium

JULIE AND DOY had walked the short distance to the infirmary in an uneasy silence; at least, it was uneasy from Doy's point of view.

Julie's used to silence, but I bet she's noticed the tension now.

Whilst he was glad that Julie had changed her mind about harming him, he was conscious that they hadn't fully resolved the issues between them.

I'd value a friendship with Julie, he thought, *although I might bide my time in bringing that up.*

They reached Fibbens' room, and Julie paused at the door.

"Wait here," she said. "I need to focus. With my amulet, I'm more sensitive to other minds."

Doy nodded, relief showing on his face before he had a chance to control it – which Julie, as she entered the private room, tactfully ignored. She'd been truthful with why she wanted Doy to wait outside, but had omitted that she was still conflicted with her own emotions, and didn't need to be reminded of her leniency – and heightened grief – while she was trying to shift through Fibbens' intermingled thoughts again.

She closed the door for an entirely different reason; *Mages work best when some of the mystique is maintained*, she recited in her head. She could remember those words by rote; they had been said by Matsuyama, one of her favourite professors at the Institute.

The nurses had been unable to tell Julie why – or how – Fibbens had come round for those few seconds and then gone so quickly back into his comatose state. He hadn't moved or reacted since, although a strange echo was now appearing on the brainwave monitor.

Julie looked at the albino, lying motionless in his bed. *You're craving death*, she thought. *What are you going through that's so painful? I just hope I can convince you otherwise. Life is too precious.*

Alone with him now, Julie closed her eyes and began to meditate; she needed to find her centre of calm, which wasn't helped by a sudden flash of thought: Doy. She swallowed and pushed away the conflicting thoughts.

She reached out and touched Fibbens' face, each finger finding the pressure points she needed. With her left hand, she grasped her amulet; instantly, she began to feel a tingling sensation crawling up both arms. She suppressed the inevitable swell of excitement; she had to remain aloof while she guided the energy. It was immediately a lot easier to plough through the layers of random thoughts until she began to get a flavour of his mind.

Fear. Rage. Confusion.

"Why can't I wake up / Where am I?"

Julie frowned in confusion as two distinct, separate voices overlapped.

What the …? Digging a little deeper, she thought back: *Legion?*

She tested the limits of the two minds, trying to see where one ended and the other began. It was difficult to judge, as the fear of one mingled with the anger of the other.

Her head began to throb as she struggled to follow them. Once she could begin to tell the difference between them, she decided to try and force them apart. She tried to target Legion, but it was shifting all the time, trying to avoid Julie's focus so that it could continue to drain Fibbens' life force.

Don't resist me, she thought. *Who are you?*

You are powerful! Submit to me!

Julie was taken aback by its determination, and pushed against it. Her resistance only seemed to make it angrier, and it began fighting back. She was confused by the abrupt increase in its power until she realised that he was trying to feed off *her* energy to make himself stronger. She pulled back; her stomach churned when the entity followed her.

It can't escape without help! she realised.

She tried to stretch away from its tendrils, but this only seemed to make the entity stronger. Just at the point when she was succeeding in getting free, the creature made one final push and tried to launch itself into *her* mind.

Julie cried out as she fell backwards onto the hard floor. Something ripped from her mind and she shivered as a cold wave flooded through her. As she opened her eyes, she blinked in surprise; the ceiling was *distorted*.

Her head's impact with the floor jarred her vision for a moment, but it quickly cleared. The distortion, however, didn't. She blinked again, trying to focus on it, but couldn't fully make the shape out; the translucent field shifted in the artificial light. It was about the size of a football and hovering just above her head. Julie gritted her teeth and channelled all her energy, grimacing with effort as she 'pushed' the distortion field further away.

She felt herself begin to lose consciousness just as she saw Doy bursting through the door – and then everything went black.

✦ ✦ ✦

LEGION'S ABRUPT FREEDOM from Their prison of flesh and bone disoriented Them. They was ashamed and embarrassed that They had been captured by someone small and inferior; the albino had been surprisingly strong, and kept all of Their attention occupied.

But now Legion was free again to search for another body that They could subsume and control, to continue Their revenge – and, as more bodies entered the room, They could take Their pick, although the mind They wanted was perhaps too strong for the moment. They needed to build up to that one. So a lesser mind would have to do for now, one that They could manipulate.

5.30pm, 17th April 418

Earth

WOOD SCOWLED AS the door to his office chimed. "Come," he said abruptly.

He relaxed only marginally when he saw that his visitor was McIntyre. Whilst the personal aide – *ex*-personal aide, he corrected himself – wouldn't be paying him a social call at a time like this, Wood knew that he could speak openly with her.

"Any news?" McIntyre asked.

"None yet." Wood sighed. "I just hope that Jon knows what he's doing."

McIntyre grimaced. "So do I, especially as my usefulness is completely over now."

"What are you talking about?"

"My new posting," McIntyre explained. "It's been decided. I'm being transferred to the Praetorian Guard Operations Division, as civilian liaison. Talk about a non-job."

Wood didn't say anything; he would have just been

mouthing empty platitudes.

"When do you leave?" he asked.

"Tomorrow," McIntyre said with a heavy sigh. "I'll be stationed on Mars."

Wood nodded. "There are other options, of course," he said. "If you want to get out of this system entirely, and if you do feel that your usefulness really *has* come to an end."

"That's very kind, thank you. But I think I'm going to try and make the job work. Who knows; I might still get some occasional nuggets for you. But before I go, I need to confess something, though."

"What is it?" The director's stomach churned; whilst the young woman had always been loyal – and Wood himself had interviewed her – had he been wrong?

"I've been reckless," McIntyre said. "I planted a bug in Tyne Pallachi's computer, just before she arrived. I've been able to monitor all of her communications."

Wood swallowed. "That's an incredibly ..." He hesitated for a moment. "I'm not sure whether to call you reckless or brave."

"Maybe I'm both. I know it was stupid, Director, I really do, but there was one conversation I wanted you to know about it. It's really rather important."

"Who was Tyne speaking to?"

"Commander Blain," McIntyre replied. "About twenty minutes ago. Tyne's gone straight to Guinevere."

Wood stabbed the comm link. "Get me Governor May!" he bellowed. "Now!"

2.30pm, 17th April 418

Island One, Elysium

"COMMANDER BLAIN."

Blain nodded. He wasn't sure whether he should be standing for this introduction, even though it was over the comm link, but it was too late now.

"Empress," he said. "It's an honour to meet you."

Guinevere – a tall, statuesque blonde with pale skin and a piercing, angry expression – inclined her head, as if to say, 'Yes, it is, isn't it?'

"*Tyne has spoken to me,*" she said. "*I had no idea my father was so inventive.*"

"He was –" Blain cut himself off; he had been about to say "a clever man", but decided against that; after all, Guinevere's hatred of her father was well-known. He settled for saying; "– willing to consider *all* forms of science, your majesty."

"*As am I,*" Guinevere said. "*I understand you have a specimen. I would very much to see her for myself.*"

Blain swallowed. "She is on a mission for me right

now, Empress," he lied smoothly. "My apologies. I have instructed her to return soon."

A single eyebrow rose in response to that, and Blain shifted in his seat; he felt, in that instant, like he belonged back at school, in the local comprehensive with the severe teachers who could stop you in your tracks with a glare. He cleared his throat. Guinevere's reputation preceded her, and her propensity for cruelty and violence towards those that displeased her was already legendary. However, today seemed to be his lucky day.

"Very well," she said. *"I shall have to be patient in meeting this famed creature you have created. I look forward to it. In the meantime, Commander, I expect you to continue with your research. Take more creatures from the mainland. Begin the production process. I will send a science team to your location soon to augment your existing resources."*

"Thank you, your majesty. I'm grateful. Any resources will be gratefully received."

"Tyne informs me that you have been experiencing some local difficulties with your new Governor," she said. *"I assume you mentioned it to her because it is somehow relevant to the situation?"*

Blain nodded. "Yes, your majesty, it certainly *is* important. May's not cooperating as he should. In fact, he's actively blocking my research. It's becoming awkward."

"Then consider him dealt with. I will have him removed immediately. You are now Governor of Elysium in his place. I trust this will adequately remove the obstacles."

Blain smiled. "Yes, Empress, it will. Thank you. I'm very –"

"*I wish to see this being before the end of the day,*" Guinevere interrupted. "*Get her back from her mission and present her to me. Your ability to continue with this project depends on me seeing your success so far. If I am not happy, then it will be discontinued and you … will be recalled to Earth.*"

"Recalled to Earth." Blain understood what that meant without needing to ask. He wouldn't be alive beyond the time it took to step foot inside the Imperial Palace.

Blain remained impassive and nodded. "Yes, your majesty."

The comm channel closed; Guinevere wasn't one for small talk, and Blain wasn't going to push it. Not that he needed to, of course. He ran a hand through his thinning hair as he absorbed what had just happened; pending his successful parade of Rachael past Guinevere's sharp eyes, he had been given everything he wanted; the Governorship, authority to continue with his research and the ear of the Empress. Pleasure roared through him as he smiled wildly; things were going to change around here, starting *now* as he got his creation under control.

He stood and looked over his desk to where Rachael lay in a heap, twitching as she sobbed quietly to herself. The chip had worked perfectly, of course; she had returned straight to her creator – to her father – and Blain had made her reveal everything about her travels throughout the morning. Now, Blain needed to re-educate this creature that had been on the verge of betraying him; *I need to teach her the meaning of being truly loyal,* he thought. *If she doesn't get it, then fine; there are plenty more specimens I can choose from the mainland.*

He knelt in front of Rachael and waited until the being turned to face him.

"You've betrayed me," he said simply.

"I was curious," Rachael said, breathing slowly. Blain had set the chip to produce a low level of constant pain. "I will not apologise for what I've done."

"You won't apologise …?" Blain repeated incredulously. "*I created you!*"

"I am evolving from your original design."

"You disappoint me," Blain went on. "I thought I could trust you."

Blain reached into a pocket and pulled out a small remote control; rectangular and tiny – nestling into the palm of the security chief's hand – it was covered in black plastic and had a touch-screen control. The security chief knelt, his shoulders hunched, and rocked backwards and forward on the balls of his feet as he studied her.

"I didn't want to do this, Rachael," he said. "Believe me, I really didn't."

He swiped the screen, and Rachael screamed. Blain watched her impassively; the office was noise-proof, after all, and he saw her cat-like eyes roll into the back of her head.

LIFTING HER HEAD off the pillow – *Pillow?–* Julic abruptly

realised that she was still in the infirmary, although now occupying her own bed. She pushed herself up onto her elbows and looked around. Aside from her aching head, she felt fine; she wasn't a patient woman at the best of times, and lying still was not in her nature. As she swung her legs off the bed, she saw May and Doy heading straight for her.

"Governor," she said by way of greeting. "What are you doing here?"

"I've just met Rachael," he replied. "She's got a chip inside her head that's preventing her from being disloyal to Blain. Can you remove it, do you think?"

Julie considered it, then nodded. "It won't be easy," she admitted, "but she'll be useful as evidence against Blain. Where's Rachael now?"

"Well, there's the thing," May replied. "She was called away; the chip compelled her to go somewhere. I'll order a full search, starting with Blain's quarters, then bring her to you. There are only so many places she can go."

Julie nodded. "Fine," she said. "Governor, can I ask you something?"

"Of course," May replied, looking intrigued.

"How did you not know that your sister discovered Elysium? Did you not talk?"

"We talked a lot," May replied, a nostalgic smile spreading across his face. "She was very proud of her work. But she was also very *good* at her job. She barely spoke about some parts of it. She didn't want to breach imperial security."

Julie looked at Doy. "Did you find out anything in the

Rec Centre earlier?"

"Only that Blain's rumoured to have some sort of hidden facility somewhere on Island One," the failed wizard said. "Somewhere that he would disappear to for days at a time."

Julie and May exchanged a glance. "A laboratory, perhaps?" Julie speculated. "For genetically enhancing local life-forms? I never noticed him disappearing, though. I was rather glad when I didn't see him for a while, and always assumed he was just staying out of my way. But judging by Rachael's abilities, and her inability to tell us where she's come from, then maybe Blain *does* have a lab somewhere."

"It's entirely possible, if somewhat un-inventive," May conceded. "But where would *Blain* have learnt the skills for that? He's a military officer."

Julie shook her head. "He's a scientist first. He only transferred into security when he moved to the Prisons Directorate. In fact, I heard a rumour that he served aboard a Praetorian Guard vessel for a while, here in the Outmarches."

May frowned. "There's only been *one* Praetorian Guard science vessel to have studied the Outmarches in the last hundred years. My sister's ship." The muscles in his jaw tightened as a few of Blain's comments fell into place with a *click*.

"Blain obviously transferred off before the ship was destroyed, but he would have known that Sara was my sister."

"But why would Blain go from being a scientist to a

security officer?" Doy asked. When no-one offered an answer, he continued. "Could Blain have created Legion as well?"

"I don't know, that doesn't feel right to me. But he was obviously doing *something* here on Elysium before the prison was founded."

Julie needed some fresh air; she felt uncomfortable discussing all this in earshot of anyone else, patient or doctor, and needed to get out from the infirmary's sterile environment.

It's coming to something when I feel most comfortable around Noble's successor and the man who killed – albeit accidentally – my brother.

THEY MOVED INTO the meditation garden at the back of the infirmary; it was one of the few innovations Noble had made during his tenure that Julie agreed with, although it had been designed for *him* after he'd spent a couple of days in the infirmary with a case of gastroenteritis. Noble had declared that he couldn't just lie in a bed and stare at the clinically-white ceiling whenever it flared up again as the doctors suspected it might, so the meditation garden had been the result. The mage and May sat down side-by-side on a stone bench at the edge of the pond, while Doy was sat opposite them on another bench. Julie stared at the energy bar Doy had thrust into her hand as they had left; she had lost track of when she'd last eaten, and knew she should try now. Her stomach rumbled, and she sighed; peeling the wrapper from the bar, she bit a tiny corner off and forced herself to swallow.

"There were two distinct minds in Fibbens' body," Julie said. "One was Legion, feeding on Fibbens' mental energy and trying to take over his body. That's why he was in the coma; his brain had shut down all non-essential functions to fight it off. He was losing."

Doy shuddered. "Where did Legion go after it left Fibbens?"

"I don't know," she conceded. "It could have gone anywhere."

"But what do you *suspect*?" he demanded. "I know you have an opinion."

"Just before I lost consciousness, I felt his thoughts. He was seeking revenge for something, and wanted another powerful body to use."

"Or a body senior enough?" May asked.

"I don't understand."

"It was just something I heard Reg Patterson say before he died. He wanted someone 'senior' to him in order to ... well, to do whatever it was he wanted."

"Then we need to make sure you're protected at all times, Governor," Doy noted. "You're the most senior person here."

"There were five people in that room," May said thoughtfully. "You, Fibbens, Mr Doy here, a nurse and a guard. Any of you could be the host."

"That's comforting," Doy muttered. "I've only got a one in five chance of being possessed. Wouldn't we *know* if we were possessed?"

His foot began tapping with nervous energy against the seat leg; Julie had to turn away to avoid being distracted.

"He could be lying dormant," she explained. "Legion had a nasty shock when it was ripped from Fibbens' mind. He probably needs time to recover."

"This wasn't how I was expecting my first day on the job to go," May said with a humourless smile. "I've just sacked my chief of security who's been experimenting on an alien being, my most powerful prisoner is now reunited with her amulet – and I'm not about to remove it from her," he added quickly as he saw Julie's shoulders tense, "and I'm facing an attack from a disembodied intelligence."

Julie nodded. "Sounds like a reasonable summary to me. Time for dinner?"

"I'll be working through, thanks," May said dryly. He waved his own energy bar in front of his face; it was practically all gone, whilst Julie had barely eaten through a quarter of hers; she *hated* them at the best of times. "What's our next step?"

"Well, we need to speak to Commander Blain, that much is certain," Julie said. "He clearly knows far more than he's told any of us. We should all be in on the questioning."

"Agreed," May said. "Do we have a scientist on Island Two who can help us?"

Doy frowned. "Why do you want a scientist?" he asked.

"Because we need to learn what questions to ask and, knowing Blain, he'll try to make the answers as complicated as possible."

"Good point," Julie said. "There are a couple of people we could speak to. Steve, would you accompany me back to Island Two to do some recruitment?"

Doy smiled; he seemed relieved to have been given a task, and one with Julie that didn't involve them pussyfooting around each other.

"I'd be delighted," he replied.

"In the meantime," May said, "I'll go back to the Tower and check in on Blain."

"Governor," Julie interjected, "one of the guards should really be assigned to you on a permanent basis. If Legion is searching for you –"

"If Legion is searching for me," he interjected, "then I doubt that a single guard will be able to make much difference. I'll be fine. I'm still Governor, and I need to set an example."

Julie shook her head at his back as he left.

"I can't work out if he's a bloody idiot or a bloody hero."

"It's a fine line," Doy said. "There's nothing to stop someone being both, of course."

As May made his way back across the compound, the data padd he'd slipped into his pocket before leaving his office made a light chime to indicate a waiting message.

"Governor, I'm so glad you're answering!" Greene's voice said through the comm. *"I have Director Wood on the line for you,"* he said. *"He's rather insistent."*

That was disturbing in itself; Wood was always firm and authoritative, but insistent? That didn't seem far from panic, and that wasn't like Wood at *all*.

"Very well," May said. "Thanks Josh, put him through."

There was a brief pause, then Wood's voice came through loud and clear.

"Jon? Are you there?"

"Yes, I'm here, Richard," May replied. "I've just been having a very interesting conversation with Julie Martin. Blain was serving on the *Ulysses* with my sister for a while. In fact, they were both here on Elysium *before* the prison planet was founded. I'm confident that we'll find out what he's been doing, especially when we find his latest creation."

"Sounds like you've been doing sterling work, Jon, but you're too late."

May frowned at the unaccountable lilt in Wood's voice. He was breathing heavily, like he was walking fast, and he sound panicked.

"What do you mean?" he asked.

"Blain's spoken to Guinevere," Wood explained. *"She knows everything. You've been sacked, Jon. I'm sorry, I had no choice; there's no appeal when the order comes straight from her. Blain's taken over."*

"No," May croaked. "I had him arrested. He was confined to quarters!"

"He's nothing if not creative," Wood retorted. *"If there's anywhere you can hide, Jon, then do it. I'll see what I can do to get you out of there."*

May laughed humourlessly. "I doubt the Republic will send a ship to pick me up for anything less than my execution."

"*I'm not talking about the Republic, Jon, I'm talking about the Sicarii.*"

May froze; had Wood *really* just said that over an open comm link?

"Richard?" he said quietly. "Where are you?"

"*In one of the underground service corridors in HQ,*" Wood replied. "*Jon, McIntyre put a bug into Guinevere's aide's computer. They've just discovered it.*"

"My gods," May whispered. "Is McIntyre with you?"

"*She's dead. It won't take them long to realise where McIntyre was just before Tyne found her – with me. They'll put two and two together and get four.*"

"They'll think you made McIntyre put the bug into the computer."

"*Precisely, so I'm getting out while I can. I don't know how quickly I can get you out of there, Jon, so you'll need to lay low for a while.*"

"Sure," said May, suddenly feeling numb. "I wish you well."

"*And to you.*"

The comm channel deactivated.

7.30pm, 17th April 418

Island One, Elysium

T HE LIFT DOORS opened onto the eleventh floor, and May hesitated. Something didn't feel right. He had become used to the sound of Josh Greene in his office, providing the governor with some gentle background noise. May knew that Greene wouldn't have stepped away from his desk without letting his superior know through the comm link.

He frowned; this hesitation was unlike him. *You won't find out what's going on by loitering in the lift.*

A wave of nausea hit him almost at once as he saw Greene, slumped on the floor and leaning against the desk, staring blankly at the opposite wall with wide eyes. His face was contorted in shock and, as May moved towards him to get a better view, he saw the ripped-open chest cavity properly for the first time.

He knelt down and gently closed Greene's eyes. A familiar voice then interrupted his thoughts, coming from inside his office.

"Do come in, Mr May. We've got a lot to talk about."

May tensed. *I should have guessed.*

He did as Blain instructed, however, and entered the office. The sight of his security chief sat in *his* chair made him clench his fists.

"Get out of there," May growled.

When Blain didn't move, May strode across the office to wrench Blain out of the chair. Before he could even get half-way, an apparition appeared before him, catching him completely off-guard, and blocking his way. Rachael's face coalesced in front of the governor, snarling and baring her teeth. May took a step back and gasped sharply; Rachael looked so *different.*

Is this how you used to be? May thought with a sudden lurch of his stomach. *Has Blain changed you back?*

"I assume you found Rachael's handiwork outside?" Blain asked, his tone not changing from the same cheerful lilt he had used when he'd called the governor in. Without taking his eyes off the alien, May nodded; he was convinced that the green-skinned being would attack him any minute, and was so far relieved by the creature's restraint.

"How could I miss him?" he snapped. "What did he ever do to you?"

"He got in my way. Rachael's my bodyguard, and won't allow anyone to harm me."

May knew he needed to tread carefully, given Rachael's changed personality and the less than subtle hint in Blain's answer. He paused for a moment to consider his next words, and he directed him towards Rachael.

"What's Rob done to you?" he whispered.

"She told me all about your meeting," Blain said casually. He sounded completely relaxed, although May suspected that his current behaviour was more for show than actual feeling. "I realised her loyalty to me was wavering due to some unexpected evolutionary turns. I had no choice; I activated her combat programming, which is designed to increase her savagery and violence by an astounding amount. The only thing holding her back right now is my subtle and kind nature."

"You cruel bastard," May snapped. He looked away from Rachael, taking a chance that a vestige of her humanity – or whatever equivalent she possessed – was still there.

The security chief grinned and, for a second, he looked almost as feral as Rachael. He waved his hand and Rachael stepped away from May, suddenly docile. She sloped silently over to a corner and stayed there, staring blankly into the middle of the room.

"You *bastard*," May snarled. "This is *my* office!"

"Not any more it isn't," Blain retorted. "Guinevere learnt about you giving Julie the investigation. That was enough to convince her you weren't fit to maintain command. When she found out you'd shut off the suppression field too … well, be prepared for a nice, comfortable stay in a padded cell."

"You've warped everything! I can't imagine I was well-represented in this discussion with Guinevere. There's a few facts I need to make sure she knows about."

"Like?" Blain seemed genuinely intrigued.

"Like the fact that Julie Martin was appointed to run the investigation because my chief of security didn't want to."

Blain sat bolt upright in the chair – *My chair*, May thought stubbornly. "It was an investigation no-one wanted except you!" he snarled. "You arrogant, stupid man; you thought you knew better than our superiors? Well, you know *nothing*. This investigation wasn't wanted, *or* needed."

"Were you ever going to tell me that you worked with my sister?"

"How did you know that?" Blain snapped, although May saw the other man's eyes widen momentarily in surprise. Or alarm. "Tell me!"

I've clearly touched a nerve, May thought. *Interesting. May my mother forgive me for the lie I'm about to tell.*

"She told me," he lied. He was blagging it entirely, curious to see if he could get any further information. "I know everything, Rob. I've known since the beginning."

Blain leaned back in his chair, looking thoughtful. His eyes flicked over to Rachael, and he seemed to be studying the alien carefully for a moment.

"That's … unfortunate," he said. "I'd hoped you wouldn't discover their existence. It would have been better if you'd have believed that Rachael was the only one of her kind. I wanted to keep them secret until I could upgrade them all."

There's more of her? May thought, askance. *My god, is Blain trying to build an army?*

"Where are they all?" he asked. "The rest of them? Are

they down in the lab?"

He instantly knew that he'd said too much – and, indeed, said the wrong thing, as Blain's eyes were immediately focused again on May, blazing with anger.

"You're bluffing," he said in realisation, and chuckled. "Congratulations, Mr May, you had me believing you for a minute there. Well done."

May rankled at being called "Mr", but ignored it. For now.

"So if the rest of Rachael's species aren't in your lab," he went on, determined to push the point, "then where are they? On Island Two somewhere? You wouldn't have been stupid enough to set up a lab on the mainland, it's far too dangerous."

"If you get the opportunity," Blain said, "you should explore the mainland. To be precise, there's a small inlet you can reach easily if you travel in a straight line from here to the beach that's nearest to us. You would likely find it enlightening. Before the local wildlife got to you, of course."

"Thanks for the tourist tip," May replied, pleased to hear that his voice was cool and calm, despite his inner turmoil. "I'll go there someday. I've always liked the beach."

Blain seemed disappointed; he'd clearly expected – or hoped? – more of a reaction.

"You've locked out the suppression field," he said. "I can't reactivate it."

May nodded. "I did that this morning when I switched it off," he said. "What can I say, Rob? I just didn't trust you."

"I could set Rachael on you until you give up the code."

"Nothing she can do will make me give you that code. The suppression field stays down. Julie keeps her powers."

Blain looked suddenly thoughtful, and rubbed his chin as he considered the ex-governor. "Can I ask you something?" he said abruptly.

May shrugged again. "Why not; it's not as if I've got anything else to do right now."

"Why?" Blain asked. He sounded genuinely curious for the first time since they had met. "You seem to actually *care* about these prisoners and guards and whatever else. You're obviously not a member of the Sicarii – you don't have the imagination for it, so why?"

"Because someone has to!"

Blain blinked in the face of May's sudden, abrupt frustration.

"It's *you* who's arrogant, not me," May went on. "You believe that you're right just because you've the ear of someone senior to you, and it hasn't for one second occurred to you that *they* might be wrong as well! This whole Republic is corrupt, Rob, if it genuinely believes that liberal, open-minded people have to be imprisoned so their opinions can be suppressed and ignored. The truth always deserves to be exposed!"

Blain raised an eyebrow. "Always?"

"Yes," May retorted, "even if that relates to my sister. Whatever you were doing on this island with Sara and the *Ulysses,* I *will* find out, and I *will* expose you."

"Brave words," Blain said, leaning forward to emphasise the point, "and I'm looking forward to seeing you try. In the meantime – well, we'll see what happens to you. A ship's on its way to pick you up. Until then, you can spend some time with the people you profess to love so much. It's over, Jon. You've lost."

+ + +

JULIE RAISED AN eyebrow and smiled. "You know, I always thought that members of the Sicarii had three heads and breathed fire. I'm disappointed to see how normal you are."

Jan Otto chuckled. "Hey, I resent that," she joked. "I've spent a many years cultivating this veneer of eccentricity. I've never been normal in my entire life."

Julie found herself liking this scientist – in her early sixties, with greying hair and a thoughtful (and yes, eccentric) air – and found it a shame that this was the first opportunity they'd had to talk. Other prisoners had spoken about Otto as being one of the most intelligent members of the prison, and that was exactly what Julie wanted right now.

The two of them were sat in a quiet corner of the prison yard, on one of the benches, with Doy and Luke Edwards – another prisoner, twenty years younger than Otto and ex-editor of the Sicarii' *Reform* newspaper – sat on the next bench along.

"Dr Otto—" Julie began, but the other woman raised a hand.

"Please," she said, "call me Jan."

"Jan, can you tell me why you were arrested?"

"Because I spoke out against Edgardo, of course!" the scientist exclaimed. She looked surprised that Julie even needed to ask. "I criticised the fact that he only invested in nine science vessels for the Praetorian Guard. I think I might have criticised his lack of a coherent science policy as well."

"Ah, well, that would do it."

"And then the Sicarii approached me," Jan went on. "This was about … three years ago, when I was working at the University of London. They wanted more scientists as members, and were passionate about science for science's sake, so how could I possibly say no? I joined up and helped direct their research; cloaking technology, better ship designs, finding places they could work from in secret, that sort of thing."

Julie frowned intently as she tried to phrase her next question more delicately than she was thinking it – but couldn't come up with a way, so she decided to just be blunt; she rather suspected that the doctor would appreciate it.

"Tell me," she said. "What do you know about genetic engineering?"

Jan looked instantly intrigued. "The last great taboo in modern science," she said. "It was Emperor Victor the Second that caused the taboo, of course, when he tried to create a race of super soldiers under his own personal command. The science was very inexact, barely in its infancy back then, and the subjects were left horribly mutilated and disfigured. Ironic."

"What do you mean?"

"Well, before that incident became public, Victor was one of the most popular Emperors ever. He introduced some minor reforms to the Republic – a small free press, public courts and so on – and he was well-loved by the people for it. When this research and butchery came out, public opinion swung almost 180 degrees away from him."

Edwards leaned over from the other bench and attracted Julie's attention. "Bread and circuses," he said.

Julie hesitated. "I'm sorry, Mr Edwards, but I don't follow."

"Call me Luke," the editor said with a disarming smile. "I said 'bread and circuses.' The Romans, centuries and centuries ago, had public games, festivals and various feast days, known collectively as 'bread and circuses,' in order to detract away from the fact that the citizenry weren't, in fact, free – and to distract them from revolting. It sadly worked for a very long time."

"You know about *Edgardo's* attempts at introducing similar reforms to his predecessor?" Julie asked the pair of them. "A free press and so on?"

"Julie," Luke said, "haven't you ever wondered who Edgardo's hero was?"

Julie fell silent as she considered this; was Edgardo using similar techniques to an Emperor from a few centuries before to distract from something *he* was doing?

"He wouldn't be stupid enough to copy Victor, would he?" she asked.

"Julie," Jan said sombrely, "in the world of politics,

people are *precisely* that stupid."

JULIE SAT ON the laundry roof and looked out over the prison yard. *I have to admit, I can understand why Doy likes this spot.*

Even now, in the rapidly dimming evening light, Julie was shocked to realise that it was nearly 8pm; she hadn't been aware of the time, and adrenaline was keeping her going easily enough.

Jan and Luke had agreed to compile a list of things to ask Blain, and they had gone off to make some quick enquiries amongst the compound's other Sicarii residents. Julie liked their dedication, and welcomed the opportunity to have five minutes downtime. She was currently thinking about … not very much, actually. Her brain was fried after the encounter with the entity, and she welcomed the chance for it to be in neutral for a moment.

The rumour mill's started already, though, and you don't have to be hearing to hear it.

Julie's encounter with the disembodied being had morphed into everything from her expelling demons, through to Doy and Julie combining forces to create a new consciousness out of thin air.

I could probably escape right now, and the guards would be too terrified to do anything.

Tempting as that was, she was reluctant; now that she had started this investigation, she wanted to see it through.

Did Blain somehow engineer Legion like he engineered Rachael? she wondered. *But for what purpose?*

A stone hit her squarely on the arm and she scowled;

only one person would be *stupid* enough to interrupt her meditation. Looking over the edge of the roof, she had a moment of pleasure when she realised that she was right. She stepped off the roof and lowered herself gently to the ground, savouring the sensation of power running through her as she did. It was always a struggle to release the energy when it was no longer needed, but she knew that she had to. Every professional knew stories of mages who hadn't been able to ever let their powers fade into the background. They were constantly switched "on" at full capacity. None of those stories ever ended well. Most practitioners could push the "tap" of boundless energy to the background for the time it wasn't needed.

"Mr Doy," she said, "when I said I wanted five minutes alone to meditate before returning to Island One, I don't recall *then* telling you that you could throw stones at me."

You're right, Doy signed. *I like to live dangerously.*

Clearly, Julie retorted, slipping back into sign language as she smiled at his courage. *Actually, I'm glad you're here, as I've been thinking.*

Doy's facial expression changed; he looked suddenly nervous.

What about?

You tried to save me.

Did I? When?

In the Infirmary. Just before I lost consciousness, I saw you run into the room with your powers fully charged, despite the risks. You were willing to fight for me, irrespective of my earlier threats. I'm curious – why?

Because it was the right thing to do.

He had signed it so quickly, so awkwardly, that Julie knew it was the truth.

Were you searching for forgiveness? she signed back.

Doy hesitated – and then nodded. *The thought did cross my mind*, he conceded, and swallowed hard, looking as though he was waiting for Julie to erupt with anger, but she was too impressed with him for that. She gave him an appraising look.

"I appreciate your honesty." Julie relaxed. They seemed to have reached a rapprochement, and it felt good. Doy suddenly frowned, and his eyes unfocused.

"What do you hear?" Julie asked.

People are shouting. It sounds like an argument.

He moved to cut through the buildings, but Julie grabbed hold of his wrist.

"Don't think so two-dimensionally," she told him. "I've been practising; I can do this now even with the scattering field."

Doy's eyes widened as the vista around them *shifted* – and they found themselves, without warning, in the middle of the yard. Side-stepping, whereby someone could move between two points without crossing the intervening space, was advanced power – and not everyone could manage it. The scattering field was displacing Julie and Doy's internal compass, but she was learning to compensate – and, over small distances at least, Julie was relieved to note that she hadn't lost her touch.

She'd used side-stepping frequently, but Doy was clearly more ill-at-ease, with the appropriate word being "ill." In the space of a few seconds he'd gone deathly pale with a green tinge; he had to bend over and lean on his knees to recover.

They had their backs against one of the library's outer walls, surrounded by a semi-circle of prisoners.

She was relieved that she couldn't hear the jeering and cat-calling from the twenty or so prisoners surrounding them; their facial expressions were contorted into enough ugly hatred for her liking. She stamped a foot on the rough ground; the concrete shook and cracked, causing the mob to stumble, and many fell to the floor.

The quake only lasted about two seconds, but it was long enough to stop the mob's bellowing and shouting. Everyone's attention was now fixed on Julie, who hadn't otherwise moved; her shoulders were squared, eyes blazing with fury, and her fingers so tightly wrapped around her amulet that her knuckles were white.

"I'm surprised at all of you," she said, her voice cold with rage. "We shouldn't be fighting. We *need* each other."

Her eyes fixed on a prisoner she recognised, Thaddeus Hills, who was one of those who had managed to remain standing. In his mid-fifties, he cut an imposing figure – and yet, as Julie looked at him, he shrunk back from her. In truth, she liked him for his clear, precise lip pattern and his natural, intelligent thinking – up until now.

You seem frightened of me, Julie thought, *and right now I'm fine with that. Fear can be healthy from time to time.*

"Thaddeus," she said, "I'm surprised at you most of all. You're a professor of philosophy, and yet you're leading a mob against a fellow prisoner."

Hills' long, thoughtful face looked confused.

"Julie …" he said slowly. "He only just arrived … and we thought … well, after Noble, we thought that he was here to take some of us away." He shrugged.

Noble? Julie thought. *Why were they thinking of him?*

She turned to face Island Two's newest prisoner, keen to get some answers – and raised her eyebrows in surprise.

"Governor May?"

May rolled his eyes. "It's *Mr* May now, Julie, but thanks for one last reminder."

+ + +

JULIE AND DOY decided to introduce ex-Governor May to the laundry roof; it had seemed the most appropriate, and private, spot to go to. Whilst the angry mob had dispersed after Julie's intervention, none of the three had wanted to risk May being too visible and exposed; he was clearly the focus of their displeasure and represented everything they wanted to complain about in the Republic. Whilst May had broad shoulders, he didn't want to take responsibility for everything that Guinevere was currently enacting.

The *ex*-governor had just finished telling Julie and Doy about his encounter with Blain. Neither of them looked particularly surprised at his betrayal.

"How has no-one else discovered this spot?" he asked as he finished his story.

He surveyed the scene in amazement. When Julie and Doy had first brought him here, he had imagined that it would be a matter of minutes before some of the prisoners had found them, but so far no-one had. They hadn't followed the trio as they had led May away from them, either – they were too scared of Julie, it would seem – and the laundry wasn't as easily accessible as he had imagined In the end, Julie had needed to give him a little boost, to get him up to the top.

RIGHT NOW, THEY had all the privacy they needed, and that suited May. He looked to his right and saw Doy translating his words into sign for Julie. He flushed with embarrassment; he hadn't given that any thought as he'd asked his question into the ether. As Julie turned to face him, he gave a wan smile.

"Sorry," he said. "I didn't think."

"It's fine," she replied. "I'm used to it."

It occurred to May then that it *shouldn't* be fine; after all, she was having to speak aloud so he could communicate with her, and he'd not given her needs any thought. He resolved to do better.

"As to your question," Julie went on, looking thoughtful, "I can't entirely answer it. We've just been very fortunate, and the guards have a wary respect for our now-unsuppressed powers that both Mr Doy and I have been careful to exploit."

She smiled and looked at Doy. "Given our altercation earlier today, I suspect that level of respect will go up dramatically. Two Merlins had a fight, and both have come out of it alive. We'll be dining out on this for months."

"Yes," Doy replied. He didn't even smile at her attempt at humour. "We should talk about that at some point, Julie."

Julie shook her head. "No," she said, "there's nothing to talk about. At least, not for the moment." She offered him a wan smile, which he returned. "And now," she said, "you will have to excuse me. I need to go and deal with something."

Without a second glance, she vanished into thin air.

"What the hell?" May said, sitting up straight. "The scattering field –"

"Julie's learning to work round it," Doy said. "She's very powerful."

"Clearly."

May looked out over the rooftops; the sun was setting rapidly now, and he felt exhausted. His day had started early, being woken abruptly from a dream, and the close of the same day was tormenting him like a nightmare.

"I don't suppose you've got any aspirin on you?" he asked.

Doy shook his head. "A lot on your mind?"

"You could say that."

Doy chuckled. "You and me both, Governor."

"I'm not governor any more, Steve."

"Well, I can't exactly call you Jon, can I?"

With a wry smile, May raised an eyebrow. "You just did," he said. "And on that note, I think I'll turn in. Do you reckon you can help me down from here?" He peered over the edge of the laundry roof. "I'll break my neck if I jump down."

4.30am, 18ᵗʰ April 418

Island Two, Elysium

MAY HAD BEEN tempted to wait for Julie to return, but he didn't know how long she would be. He and Doy had been sat there uselessly – and he didn't like feeling useless. The sleep he'd got in the dormitory was equally unsatisfying, however; he kept waking at every little sound.

So, at 4.30 in the morning, he was lying on his back, staring up at the dark ceiling, waiting for the morning alarm call and thinking about what would happen today. He'd heard people grumbling as they had come to bed last night, but had pretended to be asleep so that he could ignore them. Would they feel the same today?

A sudden, abrupt movement by the side of his bed made him jump; Julie reappeared in the blink of an eye, and it was all he could do not to scream. He pushed himself up onto his shoulders and gaped at her.

"Where have you been?" he gasped.

"Making some enquiries," she said enigmatically. "Get

dressed; I'm going to wake up Doy, and I'll meet you by the entrance in five minutes."

JULIE VANISHED BEFORE he could ask her anything else, and a couple of minutes later, he was by the dormitory's front doors. Guards were posted outside, but the trio were at least away from the sleeping forms of their fellow prisoners.

Julie and Doy appeared from inside the main room, through the double doors that separated the sleeping quarters from this small anteroom and the front doors to the courtyard. Doy was yawning, and his hair was tousled and sticking up everywhere; May smiled. Julie, however, looked as focused and as serious as she had the previous evening, and May's smile faded; the lack of sleep was clearly not affecting her in the slightest. At least not yet.

"I've found out something very interesting," she said without preamble. "After the *Ulysses* discovered Elysium, the official story is that this world languished on our records as a 'planet of interest' until the Prisons Directorate took it over."

May couldn't help himself. "Well, if it's in the Republic history books, then it must be true." He rolled his eyes. "So can you fill in the gaps? What happened between the *Ulysses* discovering Elysium and the prison being built?"

Julie nodded. "The *Science* Directorate had first dibs on this world; they were here for just under two years, and had a Praetorian Guard science vessel assigned to support it. I think you can guess which ship that was."

"The *Ulysses*."

Julie nodded. "Yes. Your sister led up the military team who protected the scientists from the indigenous fauna. Dr Blain was head of the science mission."

"What were they doing here?"

"I don't entirely know," Julie admitted. "However, Luke Edwards from *Reform* knew more than he was letting on. Edgardo wasn't as liberally-minded and reform-driven as everyone thought he was. He had a secret agenda, and the research – the genetic research – on Elysium was a part of it. Exactly what, I don't know, but if his hero was indeed Emperor Victor II, then we can safely assume that it was something to do with developing a warrior race. We were getting on a war footing at the time, half-planning to launch an offensive against the Rixxians, but Edgardo needed shock troops – lots of them."

"Blain said something odd to me before he had me unceremoniously transported here," May said thoughtfully. "He indicated that there were more beings like Rachael on the mainland, and that we'd find out something interesting – presumably about them – near the coast in a little inlet."

Julie frowned for a moment; she didn't seem to be following his unspoken proposal. Doy, however, was quicker on the uptake.

"No way!" he exclaimed. "You're proposing that the three of us travel to the mainland to find these aliens. Are you crazy? Pangaea is dangerous. Even *we* wouldn't be safe there!"

May glanced at Julie. "Well, I have far more faith in

Ms Martin here than I do any creature on the mainland."

Doy shook his head. "This is madness," he said. He suddenly grinned. "But I do like getting involved in the occasional piece of madness. Life's more fun that way, isn't it?"

Julie nodded approvingly. "In that case," she said, "there's no time like the present. I've been studying this world for the past two years; I can get us there."

Before either man could react, she touched her amulet, closed her eyes – and then, without any warning, they were stood on a deserted, windswept beach. May gasped from the shock of the move; he stumbled and tripped, falling onto his backside. His hands reached out to help cushion the blow and, as he landed, they gripped handfuls of dry sand. He breathed heavily and tried to suppress a sense of nausea as he looked at his surroundings. It was still dark, given the early hour, but a sliver of sunlight had begun to emerge from the horizon.

"It's normal to feel disconcerted by a large move," Julie said. "Especially the first time; non-Merlins struggle with the abruptness."

May looked further along the beach. "What about Steve? He's had the same training as you, hasn't it?"

"Side-stepping is post-graduate study," Julie replied. "In any case, some people aren't natural travellers."

As Julie helped him up, he looked around with a mixture of fear and excitement. The beach was barren and more of a vague scar that separated the sea to the right from the tall, expansive forest to his left; the sand disappeared off into the distance in either direction, further than his eyes could see, and the sea was lapping up onto the shore.

"I was actually aiming for the forest," she said with a sigh. "The scattering field pushed me off-kilter."

"I've heard so much about Pangaea that I half-expected there to be danger from the minute we arrived. This beach is dead."

"But the forest is alive." Julie glanced at the trees and her mouth set in a strong, serious line. "Someone's watching us from in there."

Intrigued, May looked towards the forest and peered at the first line of trees that ran into the far distance, just like the beach. Some primal fear made the hairs on the back of his neck rise up; he couldn't see very much, given the pre-dawn darkness, but the line of trees looked cold and forbidding.

May took a step forward, but Julie grabbed hold of his wrist; when he looked round, she shook her head.

"I wouldn't advise it," she said. "Look again."

May turned back to the line of trees and froze; had he just seen, despite the gloom, a flash of movement between a small grouping of trees? If so, he quickly lost sight of it again. Before he could react, another quick movement caught his eye further up the forest line, but then it vanished. He could hear feet running through the forest, and the hint of bodies brushing against tree branches that then sprang back into shape.

"What was that?" he said urgently. "What did I just see?"

"The one thing that Blain never truly expected us to

see," Julie said. "He never thought we'd make it here. Look; they're coming out now."

May looked back and blanched. A group of twenty or thirty humanoids, looking very much like Rachael, walked slowly and deliberately out of the trees. Even from this distance, May could see that their red eyes were focused entirely on the three visitors.

"Oh shit."

5.15am, 18th April 418

Island One, Elysium

B Y NOW, RACHAEL had lost all track of time. Had it been a night? Two? A week? She didn't have any idea, but she *did* know that the pain had consumed her. Blain had napped occasionally, but resumed his torture each time he'd awoken.

She had screamed until her throat was raw; now all she could manage were half-hearted groans as the shocks continued to pulse through her body. She remained on the floor of the governor's office, unable to stop the convulsive shakes that coursed through her, while Blain looked on, his face unchanging and impassive.

"You will *never* disobey me again," he hissed. "I *must* have your loyalty."

Suddenly, Rachael felt a presence touching her mind; not the one she had felt before, but a *new* one, calmer, from a greater distance away – on the mainland. The mind touched hers and, for a moment, her intelligence took control. Her chip-enhanced emotions weren't overstimulated any more, and it felt glorious. It reminded Rachael how much she appreciated her intellect. Her eyes snapped open, the redness in them intensified by the pain she was trying to control.

Blain is hurting me, she realised. *He's not my friend or my master any more.*

5.30am, 18th April 418

Pangaea, Elysium

JULIE WASN'T OFTEN wrong, but had always been willing to admit when she was.

Now is one of those times, she thought.

She'd assumed that the beings who'd emerged from the forest were exactly like Rachael. They were *virtually* the same, but differed in two respects; they didn't have wings, or the same level of intellect. They were instinctive, clever creatures, but lacked the spark that Rachael possessed.

Rachael's fellow beings, who were now on the beach staring at the three humans as the sun finally dragged itself over the horizon and added some light to the proceedings, reminded Julie of the Neanderthals back on Earth, the species who had died out as humanity began its rule over the planet.

And the cosmos, she thought. *We've always been the same, though. We've taken what we wanted and forgotten the rights of others.*

The word "tyrannical" lodged itself in her mind and refused to leave. She didn't care; any vestigial loyalty to the Republic was fading as she realised that Blain's behaviour was supported by people at the very highest levels. She had always been loyal to the Institute more than the Republic, but had started questioning *all* authority of late. Things were clearly not as simple as they appeared.

"They won't understand us," Doy said, without taking his eyes off the green-skinned beings. "How are we going to communicate with them?"

The group of twenty-six – mostly male, but with a couple of females dotted amongst the crowd – watched Doy carefully as he spoke. They seemed curious about the noises he was making, although made no move to emulate him.

"Is this what Blain wanted us to see?" Julie wondered. The Neanderthals' attention turned to her. It was vaguely unsettling to see so many pairs of red eyes focused entirely on her, but she tried to ignore it. "These beings?"

"Maybe," May said with a shrug. "But I'm not sure. He was clearly grandstanding, telling me to visit something that he never thought I'd actually get to see. It's obvious that Rachael is an off-shoot of this species, but there's got to be something more."

They stopped talking as a ripple of activity amongst the group made them pay attention; one of the women was elbowing her way to the front and no-one was stopping her. In fact, the others seemed to be subtly deferring to her, bowing their heads respectfully and allowing her through. She soon arrived at the front of her fellows and glared at each of the three visitors in turn, clearly trying to show how little she was intimidated by them. She was five foot six or so, wearing leathers that protected her chest and legs, but very little else, and had tight, powerful muscles all over her body.

If I didn't have my power, Julie thought, *I'm not sure I'd be able to defend myself.*

"Do you think she's their leader?" Doy asked out of the corner of his mouth – and signed it at the same time to make sure Julie understood.

"Maybe," Julie replied. She couldn't help but add; "Or perhaps they're matriarchal."

"Don't push it," May muttered, but there was no humour in his voice, just tension. He stopped himself saying anything more as the woman stepped forward and pointed at Julie. Doy and May tensed and stepped forward – and the woman stopped abruptly, then half-crouched like she was prepared to leap towards them, and hissed in fury.

"Wait!" Julie said quickly, holding up her free hand to stop May and Doy doing anything else. "Back off. Let her approach."

"Julie –" Doy started to protest, but Julie just glared at him and he got the message. He nodded once and stepped back; May had already done so.

"I trust you, Julie," he said. "Just don't do anything stupid."

Julie inclined her head and looked back at the alien woman, still half-crouched. She had been watching the encounter closely and, as the two men backed away, some of the tension seemed to disappear. Standing up straight – almost regally so – she made eye contact with Julie, and the Mage was convinced that she could see an intelligence in them.

Has Blain experimented on them, too? she wondered.

The woman now stood directly in front of Julie; her eyes rested on the amulet hanging round her neck, and she reached out to touch it. Julie shook her head.

"No!" she said in a firm voice. Although she knew the woman wouldn't understand the word, Julie hoped she would at least understand the tone.

The woman seemed to; she jerked her hand away from the amulet like it had burned her, and glanced to the rest of her group behind her, who silently backed away a few steps.

Julie became aware of something at the back of her mind, just touching the edges of her thoughts, and it took her a moment to realise what it was.

"My god," she muttered. "They're telepathic! She's trying to get into my mind!"

Before she could react, May was by her side; he grabbed her face and turned it so she could see his mouth. "I can feel one of them trying to root around in my head as well. Let's get back to Island Two!"

Julie winced as someone tried to stab into her mind again, but she was able to force the woman out. She wanted to try and communicate with them, but she felt ill at ease; she'd been caught off-guard, and May was right; they needed to get away.

"Dammit!" she cursed.

She gripped her amulet and they all disappeared.

5.45am, 18th April 418

Island One, Elysium

BLAIN WAS INTRIGUED; the chip in Rachael's mind was working – he'd checked the diagnostics three times, just to be sure – but his creation wasn't responding to the pain any more.

He sat behind the governor's desk – *his desk* – and watched the alien carefully. Blain had implanted the pain receptors as an emergency device, he didn't take any particular pleasure it, but needed to teach his adopted offspring a lesson.

The autonomic physical symptoms were still there, of course – the shakes and shivers throughout her body whenever Blain pressed the button on the small device – but there was absolutely zero verbal or psychological response.

Something wasn't right; Blain couldn't help but wonder if he'd gone too far and pushed her into some sort of catatonic state.

If I have, then I'll need to dispose of her carefully, he

realised – but then smiled. *No great loss. I'll just select a new body from the mainland and upgrade it. After all, I've perfected the physical part of the process now. But I'll have to push her in front of Guinevere somehow first. I can be … creative, I'm sure I can. Maybe a hologram?*

He chuckled. As he thought about all the possibilities that lay before him with his below-ground laboratory, he realised that life wasn't all bad.

Perhaps I can realise Edgardo's vision after all, just a few years later than he wanted.

5.50am, 18th April 418

Island Two, Elysium

THE TWO MEN reacted far better to the side-stepping this time; they were more prepared for the shift through the intervening space, and the adrenaline pumping through their systems as a result of the unexpected attack had distracted them.

"What in the seven hells was that all about?" May demanded. They were back on top of the laundry building, with May pacing along the flat roof, except that – this early – no-one was around. Even the guards seemed to be back in their tower in the middle of the yard. "Those beings have got telepathic abilities, for god's sake! Has Rachael got that sort of power and we don't know about it?"

"I've never heard of that before," Doy said.

"Could they have had their intelligence taken away from them?" May asked.

"Possibly," Julie said, "but we're getting into the realms of the wildly speculative. I'd suggest reining in the theories until have a better idea of what's going on."

May swallowed. Julie was right, of course. The more he looked, the murkier this whole world became.

"Agreed," he said, "and that's why I won't let Rob get away with whatever he's doing, and I can't do it from here."

"I'll get you back there," Julie said, smiling with a confidence that buoyed him. "You have my word."

May relaxed. The tension ebbed out of his shoulders; with Julie on his side, he felt a hundred times stronger. He took her outstretched hand and gripped it tightly, then glanced to his right where Doy was stood, looking thoughtful.

"How about you, Mr Doy?" he asked. "Will you help me?"

"Why not?" the failed wizard. "I seem to have a window in my calendar."

May returned the smile, and only then did he realise that Julie hadn't yet let go of his hand. He frowned and turned back to face her; she was looking at him quizzically.

"Why do you have mental shields?" she asked. "They're not natural."

"I can explain –" he choked out, caught off-guard. "I ..."

He hesitated. Julie was looking *intrigued* rather than angry.

"The Sicarii train all their members to develop their mental defences," he said. "To protect us from interrogation by the Praetorian Guard or their ... specialist inquisitors."

The Sicarii worked on a cell-by-cell basis, so an operative like May wouldn't know many other members – Wood, however, would, and had taken May into his confidence.

The Merlins were silent for a moment as they absorbed the news – their faces were pictures of shock – so May continued. "I joined up after Sara died. I couldn't live with myself knowing that she had faithfully served the Republic and got precisely *nothing* in return; no medals, no pension rights to her family, nothing. I saw the Republic for what it truly was. A bastardised pastiche of a corrupt, cruel Empire."

"My god," Julie whispered. "How have you avoided detection?"

"Because I'm very good," May replied without false modesty. "I'm trusting you here, to show my faith in the pair of you. I don't expect it to be misplaced. Richard Wood has revolutionised the leadership in the last few years; it's become a lot more dynamic. He's the deputy director-general of the Sicarii."

Julie nodded. "I'll keep your confidence," she said. "I appreciate you trusting us. But the Sicarii have been accused of being a terrorist cell. You can't deny that, surely?"

May winced. "I take the point," he said. "A few rogue elements have gone too far, and I would have them locked up tomorrow if I could. The rest of us – and we're bigger now than even I know – are determined to make a difference."

Doy folded his arms across his chest. "Did Wood

recruit you??"

"Yes," May replied, "and … well, I know he has plans for some pretty audacious raids in the next few weeks. That is, if he survives the day." He bit his lip nervously. "He's been discovered. I don't know if he made it out, and McIntyre might had been forced to give my name to the intelligence services – and then I might as well be dead. Blain will be ordered to make it happen and he'll do it with pleasure."

"He'll have to go through me first," Doy said quickly, and Julie nodded.

"Me too," she added, and smiled at May. "You see, Jon, you've made friends in the right places. We'll make sure you're okay; as long as the suppression field is off, our powers are more than a match for the Black Watch."

"Whatever happens," May said, touched by their rallying words, "if Richard survives, he'll be looking for a safe haven to hide from the Republic. We should offer him a place to stay, for as long as this world is safe."

Julie nodded. "I have no problem with that," she said, "although we need to *make* Elysium safe again. It won't be as long as Blain's in power."

"Then we need to move quickly," Doy said. "Can I make a suggestion?"

"Speak your mind," May urged him.

"We still need to discover the whereabouts of Legion," Doy said. "I'm convinced all of this is related… somehow."

"What are you suggesting?"

"You both go to Island One and do whatever you need to do to evict Blain from the governor's office. I'll and go and speak to the guard in the control tower. He was the one from Island One when Julie was attacked earlier. When I was in the recreation room yesterday, I managed to take a look at their rota; that's where he's working this morning. He may well know something, or have seen something that we missed."

"Be careful," May told him, then turned to Julie. "Let's go. I'm fine with this side-stepping business now. It's surprisingly easy when you learn to ignore the nausea."

Julie shook her head. "We're not going to side-step into the Tower," she replied. "We'll need to get creative."

"Why can't we just side-step to level ten and walk up the final level?"

"Because Blain will have undoubtedly increased the security around your office, and there's a separately-controlled suppression field around his office."

"So what do we do now?" May asked. Sarcastically, he added; "Fly over?"

"Yes," she replied simply.

THE TOWER ON Island Two wasn't nearly as tall its counterpart over on Island One. It was four floors high and half the floorspace, with the top level set aside as an observation platform. This enabled the guards on duty to look out over the prison yard and coordinate any response needed as a result of prisoner unrest.

Doy huffed and puffed as he climbed the final few steps – there wasn't a working lift inside the tower – into the control room. Through the large, 360 degree window panorama, he could immediately see the tall, thick wall all the way round the yard, and the guards patrolling along its length.

Trust our paranoid culture, Doy thought as he sucked in another breath. *Everyone watches everyone else … even in a prison.*

There wasn't much in the room; two chairs, both facing away from Doy, with a long computer terminal in front of them. Aside from the wall, Doy could see out over the yard – although, he was pleased to note, not the laundry building, which was hidden behind the prisoner's infirmary – and over the wall. He could see all the way towards the harbour and ocean. It was a beautiful vista, all things considered.

Only one of the chairs was occupied; Doy he could see the top of a guard's head.

"Mr Kent?"

Guardsman Kent didn't react.

Something felt wrong. Doy moved forward and put a hand on the man's shoulder. The pressure pushed Kent's body to his left and it fell awkwardly to the floor.

Doy stared at Kent's body, in case he suddenly came back to life, but he realised that was being stupid. Kneeling beside him, Doy felt his wrist.

There's no pulse – but he's still warm.

A memory suddenly rushed into his mind, unbidden, and he couldn't hold it back. It was the last time he had seen a dead body up close; when he'd woken from the explosion that had been entirely his fault, Doy had hazily realised that the lab – or what was left of it – was seriously unstable, and that he had to get out. On auto-pilot, he had begun crawling on hands and knees over rubble, broken glass, splintered wood … and bodies.

Most had looked like they were sleeping at first. Matt, though – he was dead, there was no mistaking it, what with the large shard of glass buried in his stomach. It had been the first time in his life Doy had seen a dead body, and to know that *he* had been the cause created a crushing pain in his chest that he knew wouldn't ever leave him.

"Stop it," he told himself in the present day. "For god's sake, a man's dead and you're feeling sorry for yourself."

Looking round to check that no-one had followed him in, he began to panic.

He leapt to his feet, his eyes darting everywhere, but there was no distortion, no sudden movements, nothing. Adrenaline raced through his system and his heart pounded against his rib cage as he suddenly realised that he wasn't thinking three-dimensionally. He looked *up* – and there it was, a strange effect hovering in mid-air that was distorting the creamy-white ceiling behind it.

It wants me! He realised, *Stupid, stupid – I was so stupid, coming here by myself!*

Doy pulled himself together and made a bolt for the exit, to draw the entity out into the open and nearer to Julie – *She'll know what to do!* – but Legion was quicker. The being slammed into him before he was half-way across the room, and the surprisingly solid impact sent him flying to the floor. After a few moments, he sat up, paused, then stood – and smiled awkwardly. His eyes burned red as he scanned his surroundings.

"This one has power," They said, a distorted quality to his voice. "I can use it."

*   *   *

"YOU SHOULDN'T HAVE defied me, Rachael," Blain said wearily. "I gave you security. I gave you a *mind*, and you repay me by betraying those gifts."

Blain had stopped torturing the alien now, since there didn't seem to be any further need; she was still unresponsive and dormant.

But I've made my point. I think.

After a few minutes, Rachael had recovered enough to move. She dragged herself to the corner of the governor's office. She was a beaten, pathetic creature – *and I can't even bear to look at her any more.*

Blain crossed to the sprawling windows behind the governor's desk. He was going to have to start again, and risk Guinevere's wrath by explaining what happened.

Island One was calm and ordered, with a few administrative staff crossing the courtyard below him. As his eyes scanned the landscape, however, something caught his eye that, abruptly, had appeared in front of the building, down on the ground.

"What the hells?" he exclaimed. *"Dammit!"*

He was about to press the alarm, but he froze as he watched Julie and May look up at him; the Merlin grabbed May's wrist and they began rising up into the air.

"How are you doing that?" Blain muttered to himself.

"You should be feeling the leakage from this floor's suppression field even from there."

May was looking around as they rose, grinning at the sight of them moving steadily into the air. Julie was looking straight up, however, at Blain; she was smiling too, but the security chief knew her well enough to recognise the slight strain behind it. She was clearly struggling with her powers as the two of them got closer and closer to the 11th floor. To her credit, however, she kept rising, until they were level with Blain. The chief backed up, shocked at Julie's ability to continue using her powers despite the field extending four feet out from the office. He realised that he had backed into the middle of the room, away from the alarm under the desk that enabled him to contact his guards.

He made eye contact with Julie, who seemed to have come to the same realisation. There was a faint sheen of sweat on Julie's forehead and May – being supported entirely by Julie – was casting nervous glances in her direction, clearly thinking the same as Blain; *How long before her powers cut out?*

Blain was about to make a run for the desk when it happened; the thing Blain had been frightened of. The glass in the large, landscape window began to warp and twist into impossible shapes. It then twisted like *so*, turned *that* way, and there suddenly was a gap in the glass wide enough for both Julie and May to step through, which they did silently, and landed on the carpeted floor. The glass snapped shut again behind them, like it had never been anything other than completely solid.

Julie slowly released her breath and wiped her forehead. She looked completely relieved not to be fighting the field any more.

Blain glared at May; he looked relieved that they were on solid ground again. "I assume you've come to reclaim your office?"

"Of course."

Blain shook his head. "Give me the codes to the suppression field," he said, "and I'll be lenient on both of you. You must realise that you're both under a death sentence. I'll commute that if you release the codes to me."

May grinned. "You mean the Empress hasn't given you all the codes yet?" he asked. "Surely she trusts you?"

Blain snarled. "Just give me the damn codes!"

"No. Why would I? You don't *deserve* the codes."

"You're *nobody* now," Blain snarled. "I don't have to answer to you again."

"Want to bet?"

It was only then that Blain realised May wasn't looking at him. Blain span and gasped as he saw Rachael standing up from her position in the corner, her red eyes alert and angrily focused on the security chief. He reached to his belt, to activate the pain monitor, but Julie, moving with surprising swiftness, grabbed a book off the desk and slammed it into the back of his head. Blain's eyes rolled upwards and he collapsed in an unconscious heap on the floor.

May looked between the book and Julie for a moment, his eyes wide in shock. Catching his eye, Julie glanced at the book before looking back at the governor.

"What?" she asked.

"That's the complete works of Shakespeare. It's a family heirloom, and you've just used it to knock *him* out."

"You're on an alien world, thousands of light-years from home," Julie retorted. "If Shakespeare knew his collection was here, I doubt what I've just done would factor first in his list of priorities."

May opened his mouth to retort, but couldn't come up with an effective argument, so shook his head. He glanced at Rachael; the green-skinned alien was staring at the prone body of her creator.

"What's Blain done to her?" he asked.

"The intelligent part of her is still there," Julie said, "but it's struggling to regain control. The pain that Rob inflicted has pushed her consciousness deep into her psyche. The anger and rage of her natural state seem to be in control right now."

May eyed Rachael carefully. "How can you tell the intelligence is still in there?"

"Because she hasn't attacked us yet. Something's holding Rachael back. *That's* her intelligence. We just need her to get that part of her consciousness back in control, but she needs our help. Maybe my amulet will help punch though the suppression field round this bloody office so I can *do* something."

She grabbed hold of Rachael's shoulder; she snarled at the mage, but Julie refused to be swayed – and then, all of a sudden, Rachael's face softened.

"You're in there," Julie said. "Come on, Rachael. Fight your programming."

She watched a flurry of emotions cross Rachael's features.

I'm frightened.

Julie heart skipped a beat; there she was! *I know you are,* she thought back. *I would be too. This isn't natural.*

I'm not natural at all! Rachael protested. *I was engineered by Robert Blain! Nothing about me is natural. I am not used to these intense emotions. Take them away!*

No, Julie insisted. *You're not thinking straight; you're just overwhelmed. Blain's not helped you learn to properly control your emotions. I can – if you'll let me.*

I cannot fight this, Rachael though. *The emotions hurt. I do not want them!*

Let me help. Trust me. I can guide you.

Julie quickly found what she was looking for; she visualised it as a black blot in the rainbow of Rachael's emotions. In reality, she knew it was a small metallic implant inside Rachael's brain that was still stimulating her emotions far beyond what she could cope with.

What are you doing? Rachael demanded.

She tried to fight against Julie's touch, but the mage was able to calm her down. Julie didn't respond to her question; she reached the blackness and wrenched it away from the rainbow. Julie crunched it in her mind's eye, rendering the chip useless. She felt Rachael cry out in pain, but knew she had succeeded as she withdrew from Rachael's mind. The being drew herself up to her full height; the intelligence had reappeared behind her eyes.

"Thank you," she croaked. "I am myself again."

She looked down at Blain, still unconscious on the

floor. "H betrayed me. I evaded him when he kidnapped my clan the first time, but he captured me when he came here again, and now I am almost grateful to him for giving me intelligence. Humanity is … confusing."

"*You're* confused?" May muttered, but was urged into silence by a glare from Doy before Julie could see. He swallowed and looked at Rachael. "So Blain was experimenting on more of your kind before you?"

"Yes," Rachael replied, "but he failed, in the end. What will happen to my father?"

"He'll be arrested," May said.

Rachael nodded. "Yes," she said. "That is just. He must pay for what he has done."

"The Republic won't ever put him on trial," Julie noted.

"But the Sicarii will," Jon said.

Julie thought about that for a moment, then nodded. It felt right somehow.

"Rachael," she said suddenly. "Who's Legion?"

"I think it is one of my siblings. We were all given intelligence and, somehow, one of them freed himself from his body. Our culture is…was…based largely on absolutes. I suspect Mr Blain caused his death, but it won't stop until it has killed everyone associated with this world's history." She considered what she had just said, and added, "I suspect it will not even stop then. Your entire species is in danger."

7am, 18th April 418

Island One, Elysium

LEGION HAD NEVER *experienced a body attuned to the forces around them, and They didn't know – and certainly didn't care – about the regulations forbidding failed wizards from using those powers. It was such a strong sensation that They never wanted to let it go.*

The small portion of Doy that was still just *him* cried out. It *hurt*, to be suppressed into a minute portion of his consciousness, and he was trying with all his might to force his way out, but Legion was powerful. He also cried out in fear and humiliation; not just for the fact that his consciousness was imprisoned and that another entity was controlling his body, but also for the all-consuming power that was flooding through him. He wasn't used to channelling energy of this magnitude, and was terrified to see what this strange being was going to do with it all.

They were aware of the annoying, gnat-like presence of the body's original owner itching away at the back of his consciousness, but couldn't do anything about that – at least, not yet. They weren't strong enough to fully expunge it, but They were was doing Their best to suppress it.

Doy couldn't allow Legion to take control and destroy everything he had worked so hard for – his new-found friendships, a pride in himself and others, and a desire to contribute something useful to his world, at last. He pulled himself together – refusing to allow this being to strip his pride away from him as well – and began to fight back.

✦ ✦ ✦

BLAIN GROANED AS he awoke; his head *throbbed.* No blood matted his salt and pepper hair, as far as he could tell, but he guessed that a good-sized lump was already forming on the tender spot. It bloody hurt.

I knew I should have gotten rid of that stupid book when I had the chance.

Two figures came into gradual focus.

"Jon May," he said. "Oh, and look – Julie Martin. How wonderful."

Julie rolled her eyes. "I can see that the collision between Shakespeare and your head clearly hasn't affected your personality. More's the pity."

Blain blinked a few times to clear his eyes; he tried to raise a hand, but a metallic pressure on each wrist told him that he'd been handcuffed to a chair.

"You still don't trust me, I see."

"Give me one good reason why we should."

"Rob," May interjected, "we need information."

Blain looked at the governor with a mixture of

surprise and contempt. "Are you honestly expecting me to help you?"

"We've been to the mainland."

Rob snorted. "I didn't think you'd honestly do it," he said thoughtfully. "I'm impressed you got out alive. They don't usually take prisoners."

"I imagine they just root around in your head until they've taken anything of value."

"They're feral," Blain snapped. "What do you expect?"

"No they're not," Julie retorted. "They're telepathic. And who are we to say they're so primitive just because they don't choke their planet with politics and waste their time collecting trinkets of no real value?"

"Why should we afford such lesser creatures any *consideration?!"*

Julie was taken aback by the anger on Blain's face; she had struggled to read his lips as he snarled that last sentence, but had followed enough of it to get his point – and, judging by May's look of surprise as well, she had interpreted his tone clearly.

"Because genetic engineering is illegal," she said, forcing herself to stay calm. "But I don't need to tell you that. It's why you've been doing this in secret. The last time this happened, people were crippled and beyond help. It was cruel and oppressive, even by our standards, and we were rightly ashamed."

"We don't have any right to interfere with their natural development." May added, folding his arms.

Blain grinned. "Neither Edgardo nor Guinevere agreed with you."

"Stop all these games, Rob!" May snapped. "Just tell us the goddamn truth! What the hell were you working on? It's clearly not linked to just Rachael. What were you doing to the others? If it wasn't against everything I knew the Institute believed in, I would be encouraging Julie to root around in your head right now."

Blain shook his head. "You and your moral stands," he snarled. "It's pathetic. You're so weak; morals should be made to serve us, not the other way around. I want to protect this Republic against scum like the prisoners on this backward world. We need to find ways to defend ourselves against degenerates. *That's* what we were developing here on Elysium."

"You were developing weapons?" Julie said.

"Of course," Blain replied, looking surprised that Julie had to even ask. "There are dangerous elements out there – including the Merlin Institute. I respect your power, but we should also fear it and, if we can, control it."

"What were the weapons?" May demanded. "What were you developing?"

"Shame you can't ask your sister," Blain said. "Did you know that Sara *died* here? These green-skinned freaks that you're so fascinated by; they killed her, after she betrayed her own kind. She deserved a slower, more painful death than she got."

Julie watched Jon May, impressed with his self-control. She would have reacted far more impulsively, but Jon remained still, his eyes boring into Blain's.

"My sister was an honourable woman," he said, "and you won't drive a wedge between us. Tell us what we need to know. Tell us about the weapons. I want to know what you were developing."

Blain's jaw worked furiously for a moment; he clearly resented being spoken to like this, but he also seemed to realise that he had no choice any more; Julie had flexed her fingers and moved her hand towards his face; the intimation was clear – speak, or I'll take the information from your mind.

"We were initially developing biological and chemical weapons," Blain said in a low, angry growl, "but aside from some limited success at the start, those tests went nowhere."

"Those types of weapons are banned under practically every interstellar accord in existence," May said. He looked at Julie. "Did you know about this?"

"I knew there was a science colony," she conceded. She felt sick at the thought of what had been done in the name of the Republic. "I also knew that it was being supplemented by a science vessel. I didn't know anything else. Records were restricted by the Emperor."

"I'm not surprised." May said. "Rob, when did you start genetic research instead?"

Blain rolled his eyes. "What does it matter now?" he snapped. "Guinevere will support me the same way Edgardo did. She's already said so. None of this questioning will make any *difference.*"

"Except you'll be able to brag," Julie replied, surprisingly softly, given the rage she felt. "You *want* to brag about what you've done, don't you? And I want to know exactly what's been done in the name of the

Republic. I think I have a right, we all do. We all live here; this is our home as much as yours. Just tell us the truth."

Blain considered her levelly. He wasn't smirking or looking angry for a change, but rather stared at her impassively. His scrutiny unnerved her for a moment. She wasn't used to this level of intensity from Blain.

"You're very persuasive when you want to be," Blain replied. "Maybe I *do* want to brag, but I want you know how much you've failed … and how I've won."

Julie gave a tired smile; now *there* was the Blain she knew and loathed.

"So tell me," she said. "When did you begin genetic research?"

"About four months after we set up," Blain replied. His voice was calm and measured now, and he seemed completely unconcerned by the line of questioning. "The weapons weren't panning out as we expected – we were struggling to get the mix of chemical agents right – and Edgardo was pushing for results. We had discovered a race of Neanderthals living here. Edgardo gave us his blessing, so we went ahead with certain enhancements to their physical and mental capabilities." He made a face. "That knowledge was partly lost when we evacuated the planet. I had to practically start from scratch with Rachael."

May breathed out and shook his head. "What part did you play in this?"

"What else?" Blain replied, his chest puffing out with warped pride. "I was the chief scientist on Elysium for two years, and I developed the genetic engineering machinery for the entire planet. And you know what? I loved every second of it."

"You bastard," May snapped.

Blain pulled against the handcuffs that chained him to the chair. "It was all done for the greater good of the Republic. When Edgardo realised what Elysium's potential was, he was completely behind us!"

The governor replied, shaking his head in disgust. "It wasn't your fault, you were just following orders. That's a repugnant defence, Rob, and you know it."

"You sound just like your sister," Blain retorted wearily. "She and I had this argument, and I won then as well."

Julie laughed; although she had been struggling to follow the to-and-fro between the two men, she had caught that last sentence from Blain very clearly.

"That's a very subjective term, isn't it?" she asked. "'Won.' Wasn't the science colony closed down after a major incident?"

Blain clenched his jaw and looked back over at May. "A major incident that wouldn't have happened if your sister hadn't suddenly discovered a conscience."

"She *always* had a conscience."

Both May and Blain winced suddenly. Julie looked between them, before something out the corner of her eye caught her attention; the large bay window that she had been able to manipulate a few minutes before was warping and twisting again, but clearly by a far less skilled practitioner – the twisting and bending in the glass was more out of control than she would ever have allowed.

The window abruptly shattered into hundreds of

pieces; she turned her face away from the tiny shards that flew towards her, but she could still feel glass colliding with her body, pricking at her through her lightweight clothing. She tried her best not to wince or cry out, but she was sure she didn't entirely succeed.

As the last shards fell to the floor, she turned to face the newest visitor – and immediately knew something was badly wrong. Steven Doy stood amidst the wreckage, seemingly unconcerned by the destruction he had just caused. He looked confused, however, as he brought his hands up and flexed his fingers, clearly trying to access his powers.

But he knows about the suppression field, Julie thought.

"Steve?" she said. "What's wrong?"

"I …" he began. "I felt your power. You are more powerful. I wish it for myself."

Julie noticed, for the first time, Doy's red eyes. She glanced over her shoulder at Rachael, who was staring intently at Doy with her matching scarlet gaze.

"Rachael," she said in what she hoped was a softer tone of voice, "can you help us? Are you telepathic like the others? Do you know who's taken over Steve's mind?"

"Legion," Rachael replied immediately. "Legion has taken over your friend's mind."

"What have you done with Steven?" Julie demanded of Doy – or, rather, of the being that possessed him.

"He is here," the entity said through Doy's mouth. "He is fighting me for control."

"Why are you taking over people's bodies?" May asked.

The entity ignored the governor; instead, it remained entirely focused on Julie.

"You are like this one," it said. "You have power, but far more. Submit to me."

"Go to hell!" Julie snapped. "If you think I'll give up my mind – and my powers – to you, then you're deluded. You've already discovered it, but I'll spell it out if I have to; you have no power in this room."

"I will find a way."

"You'll use my power over my dead body."

"That is a reasonable proposition."

Doy's face contorted in pain and *shimmered*.

I'm the most powerful battery here, she realised. *It could use me to destroy everything.*

Doy collapsed as the energy released him and began moving towards Julie; she saw May dart forward to check Doy's pulse.

"I don't fear you," she said. "But you should fear me."

She was distracted for a moment by Rachael, who became a streak of green as she darted across the room. For a moment, Julie thought she was planning to attack the parasite, but she was wrong; Rachael jumped straight through the smashed window, beat her wings hard and fast, and headed off into the distance without so much as a farewell.

What the hells? Julie wondered, but dismissed it, though she was disappointed. She hadn't taken the alien for a coward.

It was frustrating; the suppression field stopped her from channelling the power she needed to properly defend herself. If she had been just a few feet away from this office, she would have had far more control – and could have undoubtedly fought and won against this being in a matter of minutes. She'd had the opportunity to consider it more after the encounter yesterday, and was confident her powers would be a match for it, as long as she wasn't caught completely off-guard like she had been earlier. Without her abilities however, they were at an impasse. It was only then that she felt an odd, niggling feeling at the back of her head.

It's you! she thought at the energy being, confident that it could hear her. *You're trying to access my thoughts.*

It felt for a moment like the energy form was trying to tell her something. It was an odd sensation, to have someone – or some*thing*, in this case – trying to enter her mind. She was distracted by a touch on her arm; she flinched for a moment, but realised that it was May, a sheen of sweat on his face.

"It's trying to do the same to me," he said. "Let me help."

"It seems particularly fascinated with me. For as long as it is, let's go with it. I need you to do something for me; lower the suppression field around this room. I fried the circuits earlier, but I know they've been repaired. I haven't got the energy to do that again. Now that it knows I can't use my powers in here, I doubt it will let me leave until it's taken over my body. With my powers back, I can get rid of this creature once and for all."

The governor hesitated; he looked like he wanted to argue with her, but acquiesced as he saw the determined look in her eyes. He nodded, cast a nervous glance at the energy being, and darted back over to Doy, who was beginning to regain consciousness.

"What happened?" Doy asked. He pushed himself up onto his side and rubbed his eyes clear. "How did I get here? What ..." He hesitated as memories started to return, and he glanced up to the ceiling. "That thing invaded my mind."

His eyes lost focus and a faint glow appeared around his hands; he was channelling elemental power, and his eyes – flashing anger – turned towards the entity.

"*Don't!*" May said quickly. "The suppression field in here wouldn't let you make anything more than a faint mist, I reckon. Come on, we need to get the field shut down."

Reluctantly, Doy nodded. He pushed himself awkwardly to his feet; he briefly stumbled, but grabbed Julie's arm to steady himself and then caught sight of Blain, chained to the chair, and Julie, who was staring intently at Legion.

Looking confused, but realising that this wasn't the time for questions, Doy followed May towards the exit. May hesitated, and looked back at Blain.

"Planning to gloat before you save your own skins?" the security chief snarled.

For a moment, May considered doing just that.

But I won't, he told himself. *He knows the control system for the suppression field better than I do. I've got it locked, but he can help me turn it off properly. We can't wait for the usual shut down process.*

"No," he said quietly. "I'm not one to gloat."

May removed Blain's manacles, and watched as the security chief rubbed his wrists.

"I assume you want me to help you shut the suppression field down?" he said.

May nodded.

"Rob, if we don't give Julie her powers back so she can stop Legion, it will just keep on killing, using Julie as its vehicle. I don't know about you, but that thought terrifies me."

Blain nodded. "Okay," he said. "Let's go."

Doy followed him closely out of the governor's office. May paused and looked back at Julie, who hadn't seen his and Blain's exchange; they had been out of her eye-line.

Be well, Julie, he thought. *Keep fighting. We'll get you your full power back.*

+   +   +

RACHAEL HADN'T WANTED to leave the fight, but she needed answers; that being had a history, and in its history laid the secret of how to defeat it. She had become convinced, as soon as she had seen Doy's eyes, that she was missing something.

She flew high above Island One, and hovered for a moment as she reached the harbour, her wings keeping her carefully in place. She looked back at the Tower, and felt an odd mix of emotions.

I owe these humans nothing, she told herself. *They created me, then imprisoned me and manipulated my emotions to convince me that I should do their bidding. I could just leave now and never come back.*

That thought died a quick death. Something about it didn't sit right with her; despite her best attempt to convince herself to the contrary, she *did* feel a debt of gratitude to the humans – or, at least, to the ones that opposed Blain.

He is my father, she remembered, but then shook her head as anger surged. *No father should treat their child in such a way.*

She turned and beat her wings harder, now flying directly towards the mainland.

THE UNLIKELY TRIO travelled in the lift. May was glad that Doy had stood between him and Blain; *Although I can't imagine Doy's particularly pleased about it.* He didn't like being so close to this monster, but knew that he didn't have much choice.

May had visited the basement earlier that day, to enter the long, randomly generated prefix code that had prevented Blain from hacking into the controls for the suppression field.

I just hope Blain can remember his own prefix code as easily. If he can't – or he won't release it – then we're screwed.

As the doors opened, Blain barged past the other two then stopped in his tracks and looked round.

"My word," he said in amazement, "You're actually

going to do it. I assumed you were just pretending to help Julie in order to get away from the alien."

"You think I would leave Julie behind? What sort of man do you take me for?"

"A stupid one, clearly," Blain retorted. He scowled at the governor. "We need to *escape*, not give one of our delightful *magicians* control over the *entire* planet." He glanced at Doy and smiled insincerely. "No offence."

Doy shrugged. "It's not hard to ignore everything you say, especially when you can't even get our name right."

"You're as human as the rest of us!" Blain growled. "Why do *you* have those powers and we don't?"

"Because it's deeper than that, Blain, and I suspect you already know that. We deal with the fundamental forces of the universe, not cheap magic tricks. And as for being human, I'm proud of that, but I'm also enhanced. It's a natural part of human evolution. It's been happening for generations; you're just trying to push things along with your experiments."

"Enough!" May interjected. Time was running away from them, and they all needed to concentrate. "We need to stop Legion *now!*"

"You've really not thought this through, have you?" Blain snapped.

"What do you mean?"

"Between the *Ulysses* and my laboratories, there were nigh on one hundred and fifty creatures being upgraded. That's not including the thirty or so failed experiments that we exiled to Pangaea."

"So are you saying that there could be upwards of a

hundred *more* of these beings floating around Elysium somewhere, all wanting to kill us?"

"Something like that," Blain said. "You're clearly better at maths than you are at critical thinking." He spread his arms wide. "So come on then, Mr Governor. Shut down the suppression field. I'm not sure I'm feeling inclined to help now that I know you're homicidally suicidal and willing to let a Mage get full control of her powers."

You bastard. I should have guessed.

He looked around; the room was small, windowless and airless, and brimmed with technology. Three desks sat in a semi-circle facing away from the lift entrance, screens with complex displays on the wall in front of the desks, and four free-standing units against the walls either side of the lift. The technicians had undoubtedly fled when they had heard – or followed on the internal comms channels – that the governor's office had been compromised. News like that would have travelled incredibly fast, and no-one in their right mind would surely want to hang around … aside from the three men in the basement, who now had no technical support to call on.

Fantastic, May thought with a sigh. *No technicians to point me to the terminal I need.*

He smiled as a plan of action suddenly occurred to him; it wasn't by any means technical or clever, but it had the element of surprise, and he couldn't wait to see Blain's face when he tried it.

✦ ✦ ✦

RACHAEL LANDED ON a strip of beach that cut along a stretch of the mainland like a scar; it looked peaceful and calm, but she knew it held its own secrets. Vague memories of a time before her current intelligence made her shudder. She could already feel a pressure against her mind, and recognised the shape of it.

They're still here, she realised with a sense of relief. *I was right. They would never leave the graves of their ancestors unattended. They're still capable of compassion and kindness, even without a higher level of intelligence.*

A wave of loneliness overwhelmed her, and a sob erupted from deep within her chest; *These are my people*, she thought, *but I do not belong here.*

She knew exactly where she was going, despite all the time she had been away. The forest was calling to her. She could *feel* their minds in there, returned to what they once were.

HER WINGS FOLDED close to her back; some primal instinct made her recognise the folly in flying over the canopy of trees. She could remember the dangerous birds that flew high above Pangaea, attacking anything that dared to share the same space.

I'll remain on the ground, she thought. *I can move more safely there.*

She was soon in the forest, moving on autopilot; despite her heightened intelligence, the deeper, instinctual part of her brain knew exactly where to go, and she went with it. Strangely, she didn't feel frightened or nervous, just sad that she had forgotten so much about her old life so quickly. That sadness was temporarily forgotten – or just pushed to the back of her mind – as she entered a part of the forest which was smashed apart.

Not much was left of the offending shuttle; the nose was buried deep in the ground, almost up to the cockpit, and both wings had been sheared off. Weeds and creeping vegetation had grown over the body and into the cockpit through the smashed windscreen; obviously no-one had thought – or bothered – to collect it after its crash.

She studied the words down the side of the craft, barely visible under the greenery that was slowly taking over. *Ulysses-1*. Rachael's mind immediately made the connection; *Sara May's ship. I'm closer than I realised.*

She continued through the forest. It was peaceful, but eerie – a word she had heard from Blain. She had never experienced the emotion behind it until now, and she winced as she continued to walk. This whole area was familiar, and a flash of memory assaulted her; she had run through this part of the forest as a younger woman, playing with her friends and laughing over the pleasures of a good meal that evening. There was something ahead – a gathering place.

Soon she found it; a clearing. It was their meeting place, their communal eating place, their venue to socialise and be together. She would go out to hunt, but would always return here – to her home. Life had been different back then; it was still dangerous, there were so many natural predators, but they had survived, generation upon generation. And then the humans came.

And then the humans came.

She could remember fighting; the first wave of humans that had come down from their ship had carried strange artefacts. Rachael's kind had learned to kill or be killed, and that was exactly what they had done with the first wave of pink-skinned aliens.

Then a second wave had arrived, this time with weapons, and Rachael and the others had again seen them off – but not without casualties of their own. Seven of their extended clan had died, and those that had remained had grieved. When yet more humans came, the clan had fought back with greater ferocity because of their grief and anger. Eventually, they had been overwhelmed.

I escaped.

Rachael was gasping for breath, tears rolling down her cheeks as she experienced the force and weight of the memories.

I escaped, she remembered. *I was afraid of the pink-skins coming towards us with weapons, cutting us down in droves.*

She had to fight hard to push the memories away; she was conscious that she was no longer alone in the clearing. Others were emerging from the darkness cast by the tall trees. Rachael realised then that she had sunk to her knees, and she forced herself up again. She almost laughed, suddenly overjoyed to see her brothers and sisters again after so long. Her loneliness ebbed.

She wiped her eyes clear, and the smile fell as she

concentrated on their faces.

What's happened to you? she wondered – and tried to project the question to them with her mind. *What happened to your intelligence?*

She felt their curiosity through the fledgling mental link, but no words formed; they clearly hadn't understood her question. For a moment, she despaired, unsure how she would be able to communicate with them – but then realised that she wasn't thinking about the problem in the right way.

I'm thinking like a human, she realised with surprise, *not like my own species.*

She closed her eyes and fully opened her mind to the mental link. She took a breath and connected to her siblings.

I feel your pain. Share it with me.

+ + +

"Stop it! You're destroying everything, you idiot!"

May moved to smash the metal pipe down against another console, but it was wrenched out of his hand. He heard it clang against the floor, the loud noise ringing round the small room.

"Temper, Robert," May said lightly. He was rather enjoying himself – both in destroying the machinery and at how much it was clearly upsetting Blain. "Anyone would think you actually cared about something other than yourself."

He glanced at the computer console he'd damaged.

Crude but effective, he thought. *At least it got a rise out of my delightful security chief.*

"I trust Julie implicitly," he said coolly, "and she may be our only hope."

"Because he hates Mages," Doy said, "and his bigoted views don't allow him to think that our powers could ever be used for good."

"You're just a prisoner," Blain said dismissively. "Why should I bother listening to you? You couldn't even qualify as a full wizard."

"I managed to channel enough power to scare you earlier," Doy said calmly. "I might have been possessed at the time, but the power was *there*, surrounding me, and I can still remember how to use it, now we're free of the suppression field again."

"Do you *want* me to destroy these generators as well?" May growled.

"I don't trust that sort of power," Blain said, "but I *do* trust technology. If you destroy the equipment in this room, the colony will collapse. Security systems, suppression fields, medical equipment would all fail instantly – and it would be your fault. If this room and its generators are destroyed, everything shuts down. There are no more fail-safes."

"The colony could well collapse *without* any damage to this room," May noted.

A loud *boom* sounded far above their heads; all three men looked up, but the ceiling was as solid as ever – and gave no clues as to what had just happened.

"What the hells was that?" May muttered.

Another *boom*, slightly closer this time, made the ceiling shudder. Alarmed, May looked at Doy. "Steve, what's happening?"

Doy swallowed. "Blain thought she would be too dangerous without the suppression field in place," he replied. Looking at the security chief, Doy addressed him directly; "You were wrong. She's more dangerous now than she ever was because she's no longer in control. She's lost, and Legion is coming for us."

"What happens now?" May asked, his stomach churning.

"We're in the shit, Governor," Doy replied, "and that's just the start."

+ + +

RACHAEL WAS ALONE now in the clearing. She had learnt all she needed to from her siblings, including one thing she'd been afraid to admit before now.

She had continued to develop and grow, her different intelligences increasing leaps and bounds with every day, and yet her siblings had been driven insane with the mere memories of the minds they'd once possessed.

A part of her wanted to stay here and help this group, who were focused now on tending their sick. So they were wandering aimlessly through life now with no other purpose. Her species were dying, slowly and painfully, but she knew there was nothing she could do here, not really. Everything they had shown her through their mental link had also told her something else; that they no longer wanted help.

They are too badly damaged. They just want to die.

✦   ✦   ✦

LEGION WAS SURPRISED to have overcome the human's resistance. Julie's strength and power was incredible, but she had suddenly collapsed, completely overwhelmed by the ferocity of Their attack.

My authority is now complete, They thought. *I will punish this world for their crimes – and then I will seek their superiors and punish* them *as well.*

They felt wonderful, with the Merlin's powers flowing through Julie's body, but it had been like trying to swim through treacle at first, especially up on the eleventh floor. Even with the amulet, They were barely able to channel anything. However, he'd been able to make full use of that trickle of power, forcing a hole in the floor to escape its effects. It would, of course, have been simple enough to walk out the door, but They needed to practice this new skill. As They dropped through each floor, more power flowed into Their new body, and Their confidence grew.

They could feel Julie's consciousness fighting at every step of the way; she was screaming and pushing all her anger and frustration and hatred towards Them to force Them from her body. But They were stronger than she could possibly know. Julie was trapped inside her prison, and soon she would die.

+ + +

ALL THREE MEN remained exactly where they stood; May and Doy had both agreed that Julie would inevitably track them down, wherever they went, and so would rather meet their fate head on. Blain, too, had stayed behind, although he wouldn't say why, and May didn't bother asking; he knew lies and misdirection came out of Blain's mouth came just as easy to him as breathing.

"She's getting closer," Doy said. "Only a few levels to go."

"How is she doing this?" Blain demanded. "The suppression field—"

"Clearly doesn't mean anything," Doy interjected, "so just shut up about it!"

Blain opened and closed his mouth a couple of times, looking dumbstruck. May struggled – and failed – to hide a smile.

"Even with the best suppression field in the world," Doy went on, "there's a tiny portion that it *can't* suppress. A good wizard or witch can force some of their powers through this small gap." He cleared his throat and glanced nervously at the ceiling again. "Julie – or, rather, this entity that's controlling her – has already found that out."

"Then we won't stand a hope in hell."

Another loud *boom* and crack of masonry sounded above their hands.

Blain shot May a look of venom. "If only I could have kept my weapon," he growled.

"What would you have done?" May snapped. "You wouldn't get the time to use it."

"What should we do when she gets here?" Doy asked.

May shrugged. "That depends on what she's looking for," he replied. "She might just wish to shut the suppression field off."

"I doubt it," Blain said. "If she'd have wanted to escape its effects, she could have just left the building."

The ceiling was beginning to splinter; three large uneven cracks appeared from the centre. Without speaking, the three men moved back into the relative safety of the lift.

"I'm not sure this is such a good idea," Blain muttered. "From a security perspective, this is the worst place we could be standing."

"You mean, aside from under half a tonne of falling masonry?"

"A part of me is wishing we'd made a run for it."

"Good luck," Doy retorted. "Maybe that'll distract Julie from attacking the governor and me." He brightened up at that thought. "Actually," he went on, "that's not such a bad idea. Go for it, Commander."

Whatever retort Blain had been planning died on his lips as the ceiling collapsed under the weight of Julie's attack. The cracks opened and connected, and several large pieces of masonry fell to the floor. Large clouds of dust curled up into the room, causing all three men to cough and splutter and close their eyes tightly to protect them from the dust.

When the dust had cleared, May was the first to open

his eyes again and, despite expecting the sight before him, he stepped further back into the lift. Julie Martin stood in the middle of the room, looking cool, calm and collected – and possessed. Her eyes blazed red, unaffected by the chaos around her. They flicked between the three of them until they eventually settled on Blain.

"You are the one I recognise," she said. "*You … you were here before.*"

Blain pulled himself up to his full height.

"I think I know who you are now," he said, "but even if I'm right, what's done is done, and we can't change the past."

"Who do you think I am?"

"You're one of the creatures from this world that my team and I attempted our first upgrades on. We didn't realise until too late that you were telepathic. When you were all freed from our laboratories, I wondered if any part of you had survived. I was clearly right. How did you manage to free your mind from your body? I assume your body died?"

He's pushing too much, May thought. *The scientist in him is coming out now, and this isn't the right time. He needs to stop talking and think about what he's saying – although, to be honest, I'd be happy just with him shutting up.*

"I am impressed … yet surprised," Julie said. "You have a deductive mind and a good memory, although you have not understood everything. I survived because I seek revenge. That much you deserve to know."

"You want revenge for what we did to you?" Blain

snorted with savage humour. "I can understand that. I'd probably feel the same in your position. But do you honestly think you'll get revenge against *everyone* who was possibly involved? The galaxy's a big place, and there are some powerful people out there."

Julie smiled. "There are some powerful people down here as well," she replied. "Would you not agree with that, Mr Doy?"

Doy swallowed and nodded; he'd felt Legion's force of will and lust for revenge.

"What are you searching for?" Blain went on, drawing Julie's attention back to him with a wave of his hand. "Me to atone for my sins? Or do you want to try and change the past by getting blood on those borrowed hands of yours?

"I do not wish to change the past," Julie replied. "Your moral certainty would be rather less repugnant if you didn't already have a lot of blood on *your* hands."

"Then what are you waiting for? Kill me now!"

"What's he doing?" May said, sotto voce, to Doy.

The failed wizard shrugged. "I have absolutely no idea," he replied.

Julie's head cocked to one side as she considered Blain. She seemed tempted by the stupidly brave offer Blain had just made. For a moment, there was the merest hint of golden-green energy floating round her left hand, but it disappeared just as quickly as it arrived.

"Tempting," she said. "But no. Not yet. I have a job for you."

"What do you want me to do?" Blain asked. "We could

be allies, you know."

"You expect me to form an alliance with *you*?" she said. "You destroy our culture and maim our souls, and then you expect me to befriend you? You are a self-serving, arrogant and insidious individual. Once I have used you I will cast you aside, like *you* cast aside my species."

✦   ✦   ✦

LEGION FORCED THEM outside into the bright sunlight; the sun was high above them – it was *hot* today, and Blain wondered if that was why Legion had brought them outside. The security chief had to squint against the sun to look at Julie; she had deliberately manoeuvred them so they were staring in its direction.

Something at his back forced him down, his knees hitting the groung with some force. He glanced around; the others were being forced down as well, and as Blain turned, he just about saw the red flash in Julie's eyes. Legion was keeping them pressed down. His hands pushed out in front of his torso to protect him from the hard ground, and they were cut by the sharp gravel.

Island One should have been properly paved years ago

He refused to cry out in pain; he wouldn't give anyone here the satisfaction that he was hurt.

Both May and Doy fell to their knees on either side of him, and he got a small sense of satisfaction when he heard them both grunt at the impact.

It's the small things in life.

271

Julie had taken them to the courtyard immediately outside the entrance to the tower. All the other staff had fled to the harbour, as per the standard evacuation procedure that Blain himself had put in place from the very beginning, leaving the four of them alone.

He looked up; Julie was looking at the humans, a menacing – and highly unusual – smile on her face. She made eye contact with him.

"You have managed to disrupt my hearing in some way. How have you done this?"

Blain was thrown for a moment, but then it clicked.

"Legion is relying on Julie's speech reading to talk to us, but if she's fighting him, then he can't follow us as easily as Julie would. How can we use this against her?"

May looked round, confusion on his face.

"We haven't –" he began, but Blain cut him off.

"We won't tell you," he said, "unless you give us some guarantees in return."

Julie frowned. "No," she replied, "no deals. What have you done?"

"We've suppressed your hearing," Blain said, inventing wildly, "and we won't return it to you until you give us certain assurances."

"What are these … assurances?" she asked with evident distaste.

"Leave Julie's body," Blain said, "and return to the mainland."

Julie laughed, hard, as she watched Blain's lips move and, as Blain had predicted, shook her head. He glanced to his fellows, who were looking between him and Julie with open astonishment.

"Do you honestly think I will give into those demands?" she asked. "Or were you asking for your own amusement?"

Blain smiled as he gave a half-shrug. "You can't blame a man for trying," he replied. "I didn't think you *would* go for those proposals, but I had to ask, just in case hell had frozen over. Now I can make a more realistic proposal."

The humour in Julie's face faded as she looked carefully at Blain.

"You led the teams on this world when humans first arrived here," she said.

It was a statement of fact rather than a question, but Blain nodded nonetheless.

"Yes," he said, "I was in charge of over one hundred science personnel on Elysium. For a very short time, I was in command of the *Ulysses* as well."

Out the corner of his eye, he caught May's head snapping round to look at him; *Ah, so he didn't know that either*, Blain thought with a certain degree of satisfaction. *The security protocols around his sister's betrayal have held. It's a pity. I would have liked Jon to know how severely Sara betrayed the Republic before she died. Another time, perhaps.*

"Then why should I listen to a single word you say?" Julie asked, drawing Blain out of his memories. "I wish nothing more than your complete and utter annihilation, but only after I have made you betray your kind and give me the secrets I need to destroy everyone else who was complicit in the butchery of my people."

"You have absolutely no reason to trust me," Blain conceded, "except for one thing. You want to see me humiliated. Killing me here, in the dirt of Elysium, isn't enough for you. You want me humiliated in a far wider, more public arena, alongside the Empress."

"Perhaps I just wish to torture you for information instead, as you once tortured us."

"As soon as you lay a single finger on me," Blain retorted, "I *will* kill myself."

"You are negotiating from an incredibly feeble position."

Blain smiled. "And yet you're very interested in my argument."

"I am," she conceded. "You think I should take you prisoner and make you escort me to the empress personally."

"No," he replied, "I'm proposing an alliance."

"You believe that we would seek an alliance with you, the murderer of our people?"

"I didn't murder them; yes, I kept them prisoner and altered them for the service of the emperor, but I didn't kill them."

"Then who did?"

"The sister of this man," Blain replied, nodding towards May.

"*What?*" May exploded. "How dare you! Sara was honourable and decent!"

"I remember a woman ..." Julie said slowly, her eyes now unfocused and distant. "She came to visit us in our prison on the ship. She didn't know what had happened to us before. Her intentions were pure."

LEGION DIDN'T LIKE to admit it, but They were struggling to contain Julie's personality; she was fighting back with the most passion They had ever experienced.

If I could use all of her strength rather than a scant portion of it, I would be powerful beyond belief. But she is resisting me at every step.

This resistance had made Legion strongly consider the torturer Blain's proposal; otherwise, They would have dismissed it in a heartbeat.

I have waited for too long to act, They thought. *Blain could lead me to the source of this corruption. With a stroke, I could decapitate their leader and leave their Republic rudderless. Perhaps, in time, I could destroy it from within.*

They felt a savage sense of pride; there was so much potential for destruction, and a temporary deal with Blain would get Them everything They wanted.

Power comes in many forms.

LEGION DIDN'T LIKE

JULIE FELT THE consciousness leave her body, leaving her fully in charge of it again, and she wanted to scream out with joy. But there was no time. She had seen into Legion's thoughts, and had been able to sense its plans. It had been so focused on its revenge – and had spent so much time alone, plotting and scheming – that it had been driven entirely mad.

Blain is playing him. If Legion had a modicum of sanity, he would recognise that.

Julie blinked a couple of times, and realised she was lying on the floor. She forced herself to her feet, her left hand automatically reaching out and gripping her amulet.

Blain was gone, and both May and Doy were also on the floor, unconscious. She felt a sense of relief as she realised both men were still breathing. Doy was coming round, and as he saw Julie standing over him, his eyes widened in panic – but, surprisingly, seemed to get that under control more quickly than Julie had expected and began channelling energy.

"I'm nowhere near as powerful as you," he said, "but I won't allow you to do anything to us! I'll fight you every step!"

Julie smiled at him – trying to make it as calming and relaxed as possible – and held up her hands in surrender. "It's just me, Steve," she replied. "It's Julie. Legion has left my mind." Doy just stared at her for a moment, his eyes searching her earnest expression, then seemed to relax; the power disappeared from his hands, and he held one up to Julie so she could help him to his feet.

"That's a relief," he said as he straightened his prisoner's uniform.

Julie could think of a number of responses, but all of them were cut off as she saw May shifting slightly and opening his eyes. He reacted similarly to Doy as his eyes focused on Julie, and tried to back away.

"Governor, I'm not—" She sighed, and looked at Doy. "You explain," she went on. "I'm not going through this again."

"Governor, it's Julie," Doy confirmed. "Legion's left her."

"What happened?" he asked as he pushed himself to his feet.

"I decided to allow the being into my mind, because—"

"You *let* it in?!" Doy exclaimed.

Julie held up a hand to forestall any further argument. "At that point," she went on, "I thought it was just a single entity. I was wrong. Legion is the combined consciousness of *all* the Fairfield beings that once lived on the *Ulysses*."

"They merged together?" May asked.

"Yes, and it was thanks to your sister that they were able to do it."

May frowned. "Sara?" he repeated. "How? I don't understand."

"There's time for that later," Julie said. "Suffice to say, she was incredibly brave. I've seen their thoughts. Legion assumed it was a one-way process. They were wrong."

"In that case," Doy said, "do you know why Legion went with Blain?"

"Over the last few years, Legion has just had its own thoughts for company, so it's slowly gone mad. Its desire for revenge has transmogrified into something else: a desire for *power* as well. Now that it's taken over Blain, perhaps it will finally *get* that."

"It's … not quite that simple," Doy explained.

"Then perhaps you need to *make* it simple, Mr Doy," she said, more sharply than she intended, and she pressed her lips closed.

Doy swallowed nervously. "Legion left your body, and clearly had every intention of taking Blain's body like it did with you and me." He shuddered at the thought of it. "But Blain's confident, I'll give him that. As Legion approached him, he held up a hand and told it to stop. The surprising part was that it *did*."

Julie glanced at May for confirmation, and he nodded.

"What happened after that?" she prompted.

"Nothing," May said, picking up the story. "Blain's eyes were closed and they seemed to be communicating telepathically."

Doy waved a hand at Julie to get her attention. "Blain opened his eyes, looked straight at Legion and just said, 'yes,' then he got up and headed towards the harbour. The next thing I know you're looking down at me."

Julie turned to look towards the harbour, which was just about visible in the distance. Despite the warm, sunny day creating a mild heat haze that distorted her view, she could still make out the shuttles.

"He'll travel to the mainland," she said abruptly.

Doy moved into her vision and his hands moved in a flurry.

How do you know that? he asked. *Surely they'll both want to leave the planet?*

"But where will they go?" she answered, speaking for the sake of May, who had joined Doy in front of her. She didn't want to exclude him, although she knew Doy had simply signed out of habit. "A shuttle only has a limited range. Its speed is slow, and it would run out of power before it even left this solar system. They're going to need to hide out until the next supply ship arrives."

"It's in ten days," May said. "The *Agamemnon*."

"Then that's when they'll strike," Julie said confidently. "Blain will be able to supply the codes to get onto the ship without anyone knowing, or maybe he'll find a way to override the central computer."

"I don't propose to wait ten days," May said. "This ends, *today*."

Julie nodded her agreement. "Let's get a security detail together and head over to the mainland," she said. "I'll lead it, with your permission; between my powers and the detail's firepower, we'll secure Blain in no time."

"And what about Legion?" May asked. His face was stoic and impassive. "Do you honestly think he'll just stand by and let you arrest his new-found best friend?"

"I'll fight it again," Julie replied, with a confidence that she didn't entirely feel. "It's been in my head once. I understand it better now."

May shook his head. "I disagree. So far, both you and Steven have been possessed by this entity, and it's been able to access your powers with worrying ease. Do you honestly think you'll be able to do anything different this time?"

Julie bristled, despite herself. She disliked being questioned over her ability, especially when she had a few doubts herself, but didn't want to concede them. She noticed that Doy hadn't seemed to take offence at May's comment; he seemed remarkably sanguine about the level of his own abilities.

"What do you suggest, then?" she asked. "Leaving them until the *Agamemnon* arrives? Perhaps we should wait a bit longer until I can call up an entire squad of Merlins!"

Although she couldn't hear the exact tone of her voice, she was well aware that that it was rising; the intensive speech therapy she'd undergone as a younger woman had taught her how to use her body to detect changes in vibrations that came with a change in her tone. She deliberately paused and took a slow, careful breath to calm herself.

"Governor," she went on, "we can't wait. We need to deal with this *now*."

"I agree."

"And we need to send a security detail for Blain."

"I agree."

"And I should go alone."

"No, Julie. We're going together."

Julie scowled, but turned to start down towards the harbour. They were wasting valuable time, and her stomach churned with anxiety. They'd barely gone six or seven feet before being abruptly stopped by Rachael, who landed softly on the ground in front of them.

"I'm glad I found you," she said. "I apologise for leaving abruptly."

Julie frowned. "Where did you go?"

"To the mainland. I have been looking into the history of my people and the humans who served on the

Ulysses … including Sara May."

May swallowed. "We've learnt some of it already," he said, "from Legion. Some of its memories leaked into Doy and Julie's minds when they were possessed."

"I regret that Legion has done this to you all," Rachael said.

"You know who Legion is, I assume?" Doy asked.

Rachael nodded. "Yes," she confirmed, "I have suspected for some time, but needed proof. When I saw my kin on the mainland, their intelligence stripped away, I knew the truth. My brothers and sisters sacrificed their own higher sentience – the consciousness Blain created for them – to create this entity, and as well as giving it all their minds, they gave it their most intense and prevalent emotions as well; fear, rage, hate."

"You never joined them?" Doy asked.

"I wasn't one of Commander Blain's original experiments," she explained. "Not all of our kind were tested on; many of us escaped his clutches. I was found by Blain after the prison was created; he went on a foray to the mainland to find more of our kind to continue his tests." She spread her arms wide. "I am the result."

Julie tapped her foot anxiously; whilst she was interested in Rachael's news, they really needed to move *now* and pursue Blain before he did anything dangerous down at the harbour, and then disappear onto the mainland.

"Rachael," she said, "we need your help. Blain and Legion have gone to the mainland to remain concealed until the next Republic supply ship arrives. They intend to leave Elysium and get revenge for the crimes against your people – and, I suspect, for Blain to have an opportunity to settle some old scores with people who kept denying him the scientific opportunities he craved."

"That must not happen," Rachael intoned seriously. "Revenge is a dangerous emotion, and Legion must not be allowed to continue. I will help you to track him down."

Julie looked at May and Doy. "I won't argue with either of you," she said. "If you want to come as well, then we should all go together. Take hold of my arm."

They shuffled awkwardly together and held onto Julie's right arm. She closed her eyes, focused, and they all disappeared.

11.15am, 18th April 418

Pangaea, Elysium

THE SHUTTLE TOOK off from the harbour under Blain's control. Given that he was keeping one careful eye on the amorphous energy being currently hovering over the co-pilot's seat, his steady direction of the shuttle impressed him.

But I won't trust Legion, he thought. *In the same way it doesn't trust me, I'm sure.*

He checked the external sensors, but nothing was following them – at least, not yet.

That will change. May wouldn't allow me to get away with this, but with Julie Martin and that pleb, Doy, egging him on, I'm surprised he's not hanging from the undercarriage.

Another thought projected into his mind; *How long?*

Blain had to blink a couple of times as he focused on the controls in front of him. Legion was managing to project directly into his mind and, every time it did, he also caught vestigial images of other things as well;

snippets of the *Ulysses*, the cold laboratory tables the aliens had been operated on, the pain they felt, and a lot more.

Is that deliberate, or is there genuine leakage from its mind?

"We'll be on the mainland shortly," he said. "From there, we'll have to find somewhere to hide from the inevitable search party that May will send out. After that … well, the *Agamemnon* will be here in ten days." He glanced at the entity and broke into a grin. "And then the universe is our oyster."

I hope so, Legion replied. *My desires extend beyond this world.*

Blain couldn't fight the shudder that went down his back at the emotion behind the being's thoughts; it was angry and determined, but also tinged with elements of grief. He hadn't encountered such raw, passionate emotions before, having always been so sure and confident in himself. It almost took his breath away.

For a rare moment in his life, Blain suddenly felt a frisson of fear. He wondered if he had made a terrible mistake, but knew it to be too late for regrets. It was time for decisive action, not for doubt.

It was a quick journey over to the mainland and, before long, the shuttle made its final descent, carrying a not-too-happy security chief and his disembodied companion.

The clearing's too exposed, he thought to himself, and had protested as much to Legion when he had proposed it. *We need to find somewhere else. This shuttle is built for difficult flying and landing, it wouldn't be a problem.*

But Legion had insisted; their landing site *had* to be this clearing. Blain had argued, but conceded the point after a sharp stab of pain across his right temple.

He brought the shuttle to a slow, comfortable landing; thankfully, the ground here was fairly smooth and flat, so Blain had no concerns about getting the shuttle down. Although he *did* have concerns about what he would find if he had to leave the safety of the shuttle.

Although I don't intend to if I can help it. There're enough emergency rations to keep me going until the Agamemnon arrives.

But the forest canopy was so dense in places that he couldn't get a proper reading of the surrounding area. Whilst there were wing-mounted laser pistols on the shuttle, and Blain was skilled in using them, the clearing wasn't *that* big. There wasn't much space around it to give him advanced warning of any attacker, and Blain wasn't convinced that the sensors would pick anything up in time for him to react.

"We shouldn't be here," he said. "I know places where we can defend ourselves."

Don't worry, Legion replied. Its amorphous form, distorting the air around it, remained static above the co-pilot's seat and "spoke" in a toneless note, leaving Blain completely unable to read what he was thinking.

"If we're attacked by any of the local fauna, and I'm killed, then you won't get off this planet to take the revenge you desperately want."

I have considered that.

"Good," Blain went on, satisfied that he had managed

to make Legion see sense. "In that case, I'm taking the shuttle to another location, one that's safer and easier to defend."

No.

Blain's hands froze over the navigational controls; Legion's voice had developed a note of anger and determination that hadn't been there a moment before.

"What?" he asked, surprised by the sudden change. "But I just told you that—"

I know what you said, Legion said into his brain, *but I am not interested.*

"Back on the island, you were willing to do business with me."

No. Back on the island, I was willing to do anything to let you think *that. Now that you are here, I do not need to maintain the pretence any longer.*

Blain looked out the front screen as he heard a dull, metallic thunk; it sounded like something had hit the front end of the shuttle. For a second, Blain assumed it had been some fruit falling from a tree – but then he saw what it actually was, and he realised that he'd been played for a fool.

A tall, green-skinned female, crouched on the shuttle's boxy nose, was staring in at him from outside. She was lithe and muscular and looked like a twin of Rachael, but without the intelligence in her eyes.

Do you not remember her?

"Of course I don't!" Blain snapped. "There were so many of them. How can I possibly be expected to remember *all* of them? You all blurred into one after a while."

He pressed his lips tightly together. He realised that he'd just made a huge tactical error, and all because his emotions had momentarily gotten the better of him.

Dammit.

He froze; he'd been trying to subtly shift in his seat so that he could jump up and move to one of the consoles behind him before either Legion or this unthinking, yet dangerous, woman could react – but he knew now that it was too late.

"You've been reading my thoughts all along," he said in realisation.

Yes, Legion replied anyway. *Our telepathic abilities are more powerful than you considered. We do not need you any longer. We have access to a shuttle, and I am amongst my own kind; I can guide them into piloting it. You are redundant.*

Blain could feel its amusement whirling round his brain. "Get out of my head!" he bellowed, and jumped up to reach the weapons controls. Behind him, he heard a sharp, metallic *chink* as the being smashed her metal-tipped spear against the screen. And then Blain heard an even-worse sound; the screen starting to crack. The screen was meant to be incredibly tough; the shuttle was designed for near-planet orbit, after all, but the spear looked incredibly savage. It was only then that he realised the spear tip was neutronium-coated. It had been upgraded, that simple weapon, with an advanced coating from what could only be a piece of metal from a Republic ship. The alien had clearly found the *Ulysses*; she had even known how to strip a piece of its plating and enhance her spear. Had Legion helped her? Blain grimaced. Of course he had; she was under his control, and Blain was astounded to realise that he hadn't thought of the consequences. Well, now he had to fight back.

He reached forward to the weapons controls and began typing out a command sequence, but suddenly his hands wouldn't work; they were frozen a couple of inches away from the console. He looked round at Legion.

"Are you doing this?" he demanded. "Let me go! Give me control again!"

You speak to me of control? Legion asked, incredulity and amusement rolling off it in waves. *How ironic. Our population is almost extinct, apart from a few isolated pockets.* You *imprisoned us.* You *tortured us.* You *tried to turn us into a race of slaves, and you almost succeeded. Now it is our turn to teach you the ultimate lesson.*

Blain's tried to push his hands forward. When that proved futile, he tried to move away from the console, then realised that his legs were no longer under his control either.

"Let me go!" he demanded.

Do not fear, Commander Blain. You will soon be released from your *prison.*

The screen shattered under the woman's attack; the cracks had spread over the entire screen, and now the toughened glass broke and shattered into thousands of tiny pieces, leaving the interior open to the elements. Blain felt a rush of fresh air blow past his face.

Abruptly, his limbs were back under his direction

again, but it was too little, too late; the woman was now inside the cockpit, her red, angry eyes focused entirely on him. Blain reached urgently for his pistol but, as his fingers curled around the handle and began pulling it from its holster, another sharp stab of pain in his temples made him fall to his knees, clutching either side of his head.

The woman stood in front of him, tensed and ready to attack, but not moving. Her eyes were closed, and she looked for all intents and purposes like she was in some sort of mental commune. Blain realised that that was about right. Legion had undoubtedly taken control of her mind.

Will you accept your death like a man? Legion asked. *Will you stand up to meet your fate, and have at least one honourable moment in your life?*

"I will *not* be lectured on how to act by a … a thing," he said. "I'm better than you. You're nothing but green-skinned pieces of *filth!*"

A pity. I had hoped you would show at least a glimmer of honour in the end. Well, it proves your true self, Mr Blain. You will always be remembered as a despicable excuse for a human being. Just like the rest of your kind.

The woman's eyes snapped open and focused. On Blain. A sharp, feral grin stretched over her face, and she dropped her spear.

"Don't do this," Blain protested, suddenly desperate to do anything to survive. "Please, don't do this. I can make it worth—"

The woman leapt.

✦   ✦   ✦

THE QUARTET APPEARED at the tree line on Pangaea. May looked at Rachael, wondering how the alien would be affected by the side-step, but she didn't seem to be bothered in the slightest.

"Let's go," Julie said. She walked into the tree line, and the others followed.

May swallowed; he was now treading the same path as his sister. A painful knot of emotions threatened to overwhelm him, and he brushed away the unexpected tears.

Stop it! he chastised himself. *You need to focus.*

They walked for a while, moving deeper and deeper into the forest. Julie led the small group confidently and without hesitation. It seemed as though she had some sort of homing device attached to her, as she would occasionally veer left or right through a different – but identical-looking – group of trees.

Abruptly, May stumbled on a tree root just as they emerged into a clearing. He scowled down at it for a moment, then looked back up. He gasped at the sight of the shuttle.

"Blain can't be far," May said. "The shuttle won't have been here long."

"Commander Blain is closer than you realise," Rachael said. "Look."

May peered more closely at the shuttle, They were facing the cockpit, and May had to shield his eyes against the late afternoon sun, harsh in the clearing after the dimness of the forest. He couldn't make out what Rachael was talking about, from this distance; clearly, the alien – *the native*, he corrected himself – had far better eyesight than he did.

He stepped closer to the shuttle and stared into the cockpit through the smashed glass. Immediately, his heart sank and he felt an odd mixture of emotions; a powerful stirring in the pit of his stomach as he realised that Blain would never stand trial.

"Dammit," he muttered. "I didn't want this. What a pointless, stupid death. Blain came all this way to escape, and he's dead, just like that. It doesn't feel … right somehow."

Rachael nodded in apparent understanding. "I know how important justice is to humans," she said thoughtfully. "I can respect that. But there are different forms of justice, and who is to say that the human version is the only way?"

"When the person being given justice is one of ours, then we *are* able to say that," May snapped. "I'm not going to pretend that human justice is the only brand in the universe, but it's *my* brand, and I had every right to pursue it with Blain!"

He took a breath, realising that he been almost shouting, and slowly expelled a breath.

"I'm sorry, Rachael," he went on, "I'm not angry with you, I'm angry at the situation. I wanted Blain to admit to his crime; I wanted him to *understand* exactly what he'd done to an innocent species."

Rachael glanced up at Blain's body, then back at May. "It looks to me like he already *has.*"

May studied Rachael for a moment; her red eyes were wide and focused on the governor, and he could see the intelligence – and the compassion – in them.

Perhaps we can learn things from each other after all.

"What shall we do now?" Julie asked.

"We still need to find Legion," May replied. "He wouldn't have killed Blain without a plan; he undoubtedly still intends to reach the *Agamemnon* in ten days' time, and he's still just as dangerous. Rachael, how many of your people are still alive?"

"I can't be precise," she said. "We were never numerous to begin with; there are too many other predators on this world. There are perhaps three or four thousand of us scattered in small clans across the continent. Most of those clans probably never meet; they will be families of no more than twelve or thirteen."

Julie frowned. "I picked up one memory from Legion that suggested a larger grouping here, around this clearing. Maybe around forty or fifty."

"That was after a group of my kind were given intelligence, but wounded by human scientists during the experimentation procedure beyond Blain's ability to repair them," Rachael explained. "Their early experiments were roughly carried out, and all those who were badly damaged were allocated for destruction. However, it would seem that Captain Mulholland of the *Ulysses* was able to smuggle them back to their natural environment."

"How do you know all that?" Doy asked. "Did Legion

tell you?"

"No. When I travelled here earlier, I came across that group and was able to communicate with them. I wanted evidence of Blain's crimes."

"Did you find any?"

Rachael nodded. "I believe you call them 'black box recorders?' I discovered the one belonging to the *Ulysses*." Her head tilted to one side. "Why are they called black boxes when they are actually orange?"

"No idea; my sister would have known," May said. "Where was it?"

"With the rest of the wreckage."

"From my sister's shuttle?"

"No, from the *Ulysses*. I … assumed you knew."

"You assumed that I knew *what*?"

"That the *Ulysses* crashed here on Elysium."

Interlude

Two Years Ago, RSS *Ulysses*

"**W**ORK, YOU STUPID machine, *work!*"

Sara May slammed her fists against the console in front of her, knowing it wouldn't make much – if any – difference; except for making her feel better.

Only a bit, though, she thought. *Did the engineers misalign something?*

She wasn't enough of an engineer to assess the problem, and there wasn't enough time to run a diagnostic; Blain was on his way by now.

I wish I'd paid more attention in engineering classes.

She glanced around the small anteroom to the medical ward where 137 Fairfields were being held. Two consoles were positioned either side of the entrance from the ship's corridor; directly facing that door was a forcefield, looking into the long room where these beings were imprisoned.

As she had entered the anteroom, a number of them had looked up from whatever they were doing – and then promptly looked away again. They had clearly learnt not to show too much interest in their human captors. Some were sat at tables, reading or playing board games, others were sat cross-legged on the floor and staring, clearly bored, into space. Sara could see some lying on their bunks at the far end of the room.

Well, they may have been conditioned to look away up to now, but I need them to change the habit. If they can't help me, then I'm screwed.

"Hey!" she called through the forcefield. "I need your help over here!"

A number of them looked round, more curious this time, but most just scowled and turned away again. One or two, however, remained staring at her, curiosity and hatred mixed in their gazes.

"Why do *you* need our help?" one of them – a stocky male – challenged her. "Is this the next form of torture you're working on?" He clicked his fingers. "Oh, I'm sorry," he went on, "I meant to say 'medical experiment,' not torture. How careless of me."

"Stop it!" his female chess companion, sat directly opposite him, hissed. "You'll only provoke her!"

"No, he won't," Sara said quickly. "I deserve everything you can throw at me. I didn't know what was going on here before today, but I'm still complicit. We all are."

The male snorted in derision and turned back to the chess game.

"I want to help you," she went on. Her anxiety increased with every minute she wasted. "I want to help you, *and* your friends imprisoned on the surface."

"They're more than friends!" the male snapped, looking up again with hatred in his eyes. "They're family. We're *all* family – and you're ripping us apart!"

"I want to change that, I swear," Sara protested. "I know about the suppression field around the ship. I can lower it with your help."

"Is this psychological warfare?" the man snapped. "Because if it is, I'll bite."

With an almost-casual movement, he swept the game to the floor, the pieces clattering with a drawn-out echo around the long room. As the sound died away, Sara noticed that more of his fellow aliens were starting to pay more attention.

"Garrick, don't!" the woman said sharply, standing and grabbing him by the arm. "She'll only use it against you."

Garrick pulled his arm out of her grip. "I don't care," he replied. "I've had just about enough of this. I *want* them to see us angry. They've raised our intelligence only to brow-beat us down again. I've had enough, and I want them to know it."

He turned back to look at Sara and pointed an accusatory finger at her. "It's people like *you* that put us here in the first place. Even if you *didn't* know about us being here, you represent everything that is rotten about your beloved Republic. Drop dead!"

"No, but only because I want to help you escape first."

Garrick hadn't been expecting such a blunt response; the raw pain Sara felt clearly flowed through her voice, as the alien hesitated for a moment, clearly lost for words.

"I'm proud to belong to the Praetorian Guard," Sara went on, "and I've served it faithfully for a long time. But this isn't right, and I refuse to stand by and allow it."

Garrick scowled. "How can I believe anything you're telling me?"

"Because I'm willing to back up my words with actions."

Sara turned back to the console; she had nothing else to lose now. If the suppression field wasn't going to come down, then she theorised that the sheer numbers of aliens – all of whom looked to be strong, powerful beings, with muscles taut under their skin – could be more than a match for the crew on board the *Ulysses*.

I know I'm betraying my own kind, but we need to make this butchery public.

She manipulated the controls in front of her and heard the familiar hum of the machinery switched off and, when she turned back, the shimmer had gone from around the door. There was nothing between her and the aliens.

"Before you do anything," she said, "all I ask is that you listen to me."

Garrick and the woman with him exchanged a glance pregnant with meaning; they seemed surprised, yet relieved at the same time. The woman smiled.

"If this is true," she said, "then we could be free."

"They could still be testing us," Garrick replied, in a far softer tone than Sara had been expecting, given his anger of a moment ago. "Tread carefully."

She nodded and then looked round at Sara. She'd crossed the separating six feet in an instant, stopping at the doorway. Sara caught her breath at the woman's swiftness, impressed at the compassion and curiosity in her eyes. The alien hesitated before crossing the doorway, but after a couple of seconds, she found the courage to do just that – and smiled to herself as she stepped into the ante room without being harmed.

"I've never been this side of the partition before," she said softly as she looked round.

"You should never have been separated from the rest of your kind."

The alien fixed Sara with a steely gaze. "On that, we agree," she replied. "My name is Yardon. That's the name I gave myself. According to your records, I am Patient 99."

"I'd prefer to call you Yardon," Sara said, trying a small smile – and relaxing slightly when Yardon smiled back. "I assume you would, too."

"You assume correctly," Yardon replied. "Who are you?"

"I'm Sara May," she replied. "I'm the *Ulysses'* executive officer."

"Hah!" One of the other beings, a tall, gangly alien with wavy brown hair and sharp, serrated teeth, hadn't been able to contain his amusement. "You're the second-in-command, and you expect us to believe that you didn't know what was going on down here?"

"Whether you believe it or not, it's the truth," Sara replied, forcing herself to stay calm. "I'm amazed that Captain Mulholland was able to keep it from me, but she did. However, now I know, and I want to do something about it."

Yardon frowned. "What will you do?"

"Lower the suppression field," she answered, "and return your powers."

Yardon's eyes widened in surprise, and Sara heard a number of gasps from the other side of the now-open doorway.

"You know what we could do with those powers?" Yardon asked.

I've experienced a tiny blast of it down on the planet, Sara thought, but decided that it wasn't the right time to mention that.

"Yes," she said. "I know."

Sara nodded. "Can you help me lower the suppression field?"

"I can," Yardon replied. "Many of your colleagues thought we were stupid and deaf, and didn't worry about what we overheard."

"Let me reassure you," Sara noted, "that I am presuming no such thing."

"I like you, Sara," Yardon said. "I wish we'd met under different circumstances."

The hope surging in Sara's chest vanished; she knew how this was going to end.

"Shall we get started?" she said, waving a hand at the console.

"Commander May, please report to the bridge."

She tensed, and saw Yardon doing the same; it had been Blain's command coming through loud and clear on the internal comms, and his voice was clearly as unappealing to the aliens as it was to her. She could hear some mutterings from within their living space, but tactfully decided to ignore it for the moment.

"You should answer it," Yardon counselled. "I'm sure you know what happens if he doesn't get his own way."

Sara grimaced. "Blain doesn't appreciate how *I* can be if *I* don't get my own way."

"I'm sure it will be an interesting meeting of minds."

"I don't intend on going. I'm staying here to help you. Work faster."

Yardon's forehead knitted together in a tight knot. "What do you mean?"

"I'll only be able to make my excuses for a short time before he comes looking for me and finds out what I'm doing."

She brought her wrist communicator to her mouth and activated the two-way speaker.

"This is May," she said. "I'll be there shortly."

She then unclipped the communicator from his wrist, dropped it to the floor and stepped on it. The crunch of electronics momentarily filled the room.

"There's a monitoring chip in it. Anyone can track me. Not any more, I guess."

"Not any longer."

"Blain's not stupid. He'll figure it out. I've brought us a few minutes, no more. The fact that *he* called me to the bridge means he's already deposed the captain. Keep working."

Yardon nodded and returned her focus to the console. Her nimble, long fingers crossed the controls quicker than Sara could keep up.

"Some of the wiring has become misaligned," she said. "It's no-one's fault, but these things happen when a machine is added to existing circuitry and then not checked regularly."

"Can you fix it?"

Yardon smiled at her, revealing sharp, serrated teeth. "Help me with this plating."

They both knelt and reached under the console, where a panel gave access to the inner workings. Between them, they were able to yank it away, and it came clattering to the deck. Yardon immediately began fiddling with the circuitry; Sara watched with fascination.

"Where did you learn all this?" she asked.

"It was programmed," Yardon's muffled voice came back. "Your scientists felt that, as well as brute strength, their new army would need some technical expertise to do the more … fiddly tasks that might come up from time to time."

"You mean espionage."

Yardon emerged from the base of the unit, her green face moist with a sheen of sweat and the smile back across her lips. "Yes."

She stood and pressed a few more controls.

"How much longer?" Sara asked anxiously.

"It's already done."

Sara swallowed. "I was expecting something of a ceremony."

"No need," Yardon said. "It was –"

She didn't finish the sentence however. As the suppression field lowered completely, May glanced into the room where the other beings were waiting, and saw that they all had their eyes closed and their mouths slightly open. Many of them – Garrick included – had tears running down their faces.

Abruptly, the red alert klaxons began blaring, and the light strips around the room flashed red to the same beat. May winced at the sharp, sudden sound, and brought her hands up to her ears in reflex.

Shit! she thought. *This is it – now or never.*

The aliens, however, hadn't reacted; they all seemed entirely focused on the telepathic commune and joy at being able to share their minds again with each other.

"Yardon!" Sara called out over the klaxons which, given the tight space they were in, seemed ten times louder than the occasional times she'd heard them blare out on the bridge. *"A security team will be down here in minutes! Whatever you're going to do, do it now!"*

If Yardon heard her, then she didn't given any indication. Sara glanced towards the door; she'd locked it from the inside, but that wouldn't hold a security detail for very long.

"Bridge to Commander May, come in."

Blain's voice over the internal comm system was tense and angry, but Sara had no intention of replying – there was no point continuing with the façade, not any more.

Why aren't they doing *anything?* she wondered, looking around at the Fairfield beings.

Yardon's red eyes were glowing brighter somehow, almost like they had been lit by an internal fire that had been absent until now.

Is this your natural state? she wondered.

"No," Yardon replied, clearly reading her mind. "We have joined our minds together."

"What do you mean, joined them together?"

"Wee are one single mind," she said. "In your parlance—"

"We are one."

Every alien had spoken that final sentence together, their individual voices merging into a harmonic whole. The hairs on the back of Sara's neck rose as she looked round, and saw row upon row of glowing red eyes staring back at her.

"Oh gods …" she muttered. Her back collided with the bulkhead. She watched as a physical disturbance began to shimmer into the large wardroom. On impulse, she ducked as a tendril snaked out into the anteroom and hovered close to her head for a minute, then moved to Yardon's. A smaller tendril snaked down to touch her head.

"We are Legion," the multitude of voices said in perfect union, "and we are many."

All of a sudden, as if they were controlled by a single switch, all the aliens collapsed to the floor. Sara began to move forward to check on Yardon, but a new voice made her stop.

And I am one.

Sara's head snapped round; there was no-one there. She realised then that the words had formed in her mind without going through her ears.

"Who are you?" she demanded.

I am revenge, the voice said. *I am anger. I am rage. I am the emotions and thoughts and intelligence of each of the beings you see before you. I am their deepest, primal, ancestral fears – and I am their conscious thoughts as well. You have given us intelligence, and they used that intelligence to make* me. *I am Legion, and I am one from many. I will destroy all those who have devastated my people, and I will seek revenge from all those complicit in our pain. No-one will be safe, and this galaxy will quake.*

1.00pm, 18th April 418

Pangaea, Elysium (Present Day)

J ON MAY SAT quietly on a fallen branch, staring into the middle distance. Since he and Rachael had retrieved the black box recorder from part of the wreckage – the huge ship had broken up into various pieces as it had entered the atmosphere – May had listened in fascination to the last moments of the *Ulysses*, as well as the true last moments of his sister's life. He hadn't wanted to look for his sister's body. She could have been in any part of the wreckage, of course, but he wanted to remember her just as she was.

"Did he genuinely believe what he was doing was right?" Rachael asked.

"Hmm?" May said distractedly. "Sorry, what did you say?"

"Apologies, Governor, I didn't mean to divert you from your thoughts."

"No, I welcome it," May replied. "At the moment, my thoughts are just going round and round in circles. What was the question again?"

"I was wondering if Commander Blain actually believed in what he was doing – sacrificing the *Ulysses* for the good of your Republic – or did he do it for selfish reasons?"

"Sometimes, both can be the answer at the same time," May replied. "We're complicated beings, Rachael. Our emotions are never simple."

"I am realising this. I spoke to Blain about it myself, fairly recently."

Doy looked round from his sign language interpretation for Julie. He looked intrigued. "What did he say?"

"He was fairly dismissive of my dilemma," Rachael conceded. "He was distracted by his work, and then, when he discovered that I had revealed myself to other people … well, you are aware of the outcome, of course."

May nodded. It pained him to think of his sister having such a gruesome, savage end. But he felt a surge of pride as well; Sara had been willing to sacrifice her life so that the aliens had a chance.

The thought of Legion brought an image to his mind from the black box recorder.

"Rachael," he said slowly, "how far does your telepathy extend?"

Rachael looked confused, and May clarified. "Is there a point beyond which your telepathic powers can't work? Can you only read minds over a certain radius?"

"My ability is weak over a few hundred feet. I can detect collective surges in emotion – and I can usually detect where my own people are, if not what they're feeling."

"So, the two groups of your people – on the ship and here on Elysium – would have been aware of each other, but wouldn't have been able to communicate. Am I right?"

Rachael contemplated that for a moment, then nodded. "Yes."

Julie cleared her throat, and May looked at her; he hoped she had managed to follow their conversation. "What are you thinking?"

May stood and tapped a finger thoughtfully to his lips. "Rachael, if you're normal for your species, then family who were imprisoned here on the planet wouldn't have been able to give their minds to Legion, would they?"

"I doubt it," Rachael replied. "There would have been too great a distance."

"Then we've been looking at this all wrong," May retorted, speaking faster as his mind worked overtime. "Rachael, *both* groups were working as combined entities, and we've assumed that meant *one* single being; but if they weren't linked together into one single consciousness because of the distance involved, then there's only one logical argument."

"There are two Legions."

"Or there *were*," May noted. "One was aboard the ship when it crashed, don't forget."

"Legion would not die because of a crash," Rachael said confidently. "From the moment my brothers and sisters merged their intelligences into a single entity, Legion could survive independently of a physical body."

May's eyes darted round the forest. For a moment, he had – against all reason – expected to catch sight of the Legion he had already met, or this second Legion that had also been spawned when the suppression field had been lowered.

"Why haven't we met this other Legion?" Julie asked.

"I do not know," Rachael admitted. She looked thoughtful. "But it is the one from my siblings who remained on Elysium."

"How can you know that?" Doy asked. "What's the difference?"

"This second Legion hasn't experienced the death of its physical forms," Rachael said. "There's a special bond we feel between mind and body; experiencing the death of my body would drive *me* insane. The Legion from the *Ulysses* experienced it a hundred-fold."

Rachael paused; she seemed to be listening – or mentally searching – for something.

"She is close," Rachel said. "It has a different voice to the Legion weknow."

"Different how?"

"It is calmer, almost peaceful. It is a myriad of calmer emotions."

May instincts had been right, although he wasn't particularly happy about that.

"So now we have *two* Legions, both on Elysium and both potentially chasing us down. I want to talk to this new Legion."

"That shouldn't be a problem," Doy said.

May hesitated. "It's here, isn't it?"

Julie nodded. "It's behind you right now."

You have made a terrible mistake coming here, the new entity said. *I suggest you go back to where you come from, before my counterpart realises you are on the mainland.*

Four pairs of eyes fixed on this new being; it looked almost identical to Legion, but had different hues in it; purple, green, orange, and occasional, fleeting splashes of others.

And please, the being went on, *call me Myriad.*

"Do you recognise this woman?" May asked, pointing at Rachael.

Of course, Myriad replied. *She is one of us, but wasn't born out of the pain we have experienced. It saddens me to think of so much death and destruction. My people broke free when we were able to feel each others' minds again. We reacted passionately, defending our territory and seeking revenge for what you did.*

"Do you still seek revenge?"

No. Why should I? Collectively, we accomplished it wonderfully at the time. But, in the process, we lost our innocence. We killed indiscriminately. That makes us no better than the ones who killed our kind.

Julie stepped forward. "You're aware of Legion?"

Yes. I have felt his presence often enough, but I doubt They are aware of my existence. They have something of a one-track mind.

"Why didn't you seek him… Them out?" May asked. "Why have you stayed hidden?"

Because I have work to do, Myriad replied. *The beings that gave me their intelligence entrusted me with their minds; they need me to protect them and I do so willingly.*

"So where *is* Legion?" Julie asked. "If he wants to get to the Empress, then he'll still be planning to use the *Agamemnon* to escape."

They will try and manipulate one of our own kind, Myriad said. *Our species are the only ones he is willing to trust.*

"Can Legion do that?" Doy asked. "Possess one of your own kind, I mean?"

Yes, if they have no other choice, Myriad replied, although it sounded disgusted.

"Rachael, wouldn't you be the ideal candidate for Legion to take over?" Julie asked.

"Of course," she said. "I would be an attractive proposition."

"Then we need to attract Legion here," she said. "Rachael, forgive me for asking, but how do you feel about being bait?"

Rachael, however, looked nervous, which made Julie tense. She followed the alien's gaze, which was fixed on a point six feet in the air; a distortion effect visible against the top of the gently-moving trees and close to Myriad. Legion had arrived, out of nowhere, and Julie took a step back reflexively; she could remember how it felt, having her mind compressed by the entity now floating towards them. It sent a cold shiver down her spine.

"It looks like they're squaring up," she said.

"They're curious," May said as Doy signed. "They're studying each other."

"Legion thought he was alone," Rachael noted.

Legion's emotions were leaking and Julie could feel them; rage, anger and desire for vengeance – but it had been surprisingly tempered for a moment by another emotion: curiosity. She felt that emotion shining out almost like a beacon.

Perhaps Myriad can succeed where we've all failed.

She became aware of a communion between the two beings that was subconscious; no thoughts were audible, and she had to strain her mind to detect anything. There seemed to be a flow of thoughts and feelings between them, and their colours and shapes were changing almost moment by moment; from gold to red to green to blue to yellow and round again.

"They're each trying to make the other understand," Julie said.

The colours kept jumbling together, but a few kept taking prominence; Legion's red flashed dark and vivid, but started to fade, swapped for blue and greens, with Myriad taking the red, then disappearing, and then cycling through again.

Myriad's trying to remove some of Legion's hate towards humanity, Doy signed.

All of a sudden, just as Julie was beginning to wonder how long it would take to come to an agreement, a sharp – and painful – emotion stabbed into her head.

NO! I will not be driven from my path! The humans must pay!

Julie looked up just in time to see Legion barrelling towards Jon May, its form contorting in rage. The Governor gasped sharply as Legion entered his mind. Julie hadn't been able to react in time, but gripped her amulet now. A hand steadied her left wrist; Doy held onto her, a determined look in his eye.

"If you try and extract Legion, you'll kill May!" he said firmly as she looked directly at him. "Remember how it felt when Legion was in your head? It wrapped itself around our consciousness and squeezed *hard*. That's exactly what it'll be doing to May, and anything we try with our powers will just make it worse! We only got it out of Fibbens' brain because it *wanted* to be freed!"

"We need to help him!" Julie retorted.

Doy nodded. "I agree, but our powers aren't the way to do it."

"Help our friend!" he barked at Myriad. "Right now, you're the only one that can!"

Myriad was silent for a moment, then noted; *Your kind did terrible things to us.*

"Yes," Julie interjected, "our kind did, and they must pay. Blain already has; it seems that he paid the ultimate price, and I doubt that many people will weep for him. The other scientists who took part in this … horror have also died. Emperor Edgardo is now dead, betrayed by his daughter. Even *innocents* died to free you from us."

My sibling believes that more vengeance is required.

"Then Legion is wrong."

Out the corner of her eye, she was aware of Doy tensing, but she ignored him; she needed to do this *her* way. She pointed to May, still prone on the floor.

"This man's sister sacrificed herself for you," she said. "She had the suppression field controlling your telepathy lowered so that you could do what was necessary. She gave her life so that you could live."

I did not know this.

"Now you do!" Julie said, more forcefully this time. "So help him. Help us all, please. We want to make this right, and we don't all deserve to suffer because of what some of our kind have done and paid for. We want peace. What do *you* want?"

Very well, Myriad thought at Julie and the others. *I will do what I can.*

Myriad slammed into May's body. He drew in a rasping breath and clutched his head.

"Myriad wants to die." He sucked in a deep, rattling breath. "Both of them were born from pain and torture and horror beyond anything we can imagine. Myriad is ready to die; it wants to discover what else is out there. It cares for her brothers and sisters gladly, but it's lonely and restless."

"What about Legion?"

"It ..." May winced as the fight continued behind his eyelids. "I don't think it honestly understands anything beyond its own desire for vengeance. In a sense, that's all it is now: a semi-conscious ball of vengeance. It won't stop for anything, except death. It doesn't want to die, but *needs* to in order to be stopped."

"Then we need to get them out of your mind," Julie said as a moment of understanding passed between her and May. "When they're out, we can do the deed and then seek redemption somehow."

May shook his head. "I've already sought all the

redemption I need," he said.

"Governor –"

"Jon," he interjected. "It's Jon."

"Jon," she corrected herself, "I'm not willing to kill you to get to the others."

"You've got to!" May said, more urgently this time. "I can only contain them for a while, Julie. I can keep them inside my head for a while thanks only to my training with mental shields. They won't be able to escape; they're symbiotic, in a way, and whether they realise it or not, they draw energy from the bodies they inhabit. With both inside me, my death will rebound – they'll lose their power source. If they don't extricate themselves in the right way, they'll die as well."

Julie shook her head; she refused to countenance it. May grabbed her face to get her attention and pulled her to the ground. She gasped as a moment of pure emotion passed through her; they remained frozen in place as they shared a connection.

"What's happening?" Rachael asked.

"I don't know," Doy admitted, "but be ready to run away, very fast."

Abruptly, Julie fell backwards, landing awkwardly, without taking her eyes off May. The governor, on the other hand, winced again, and pressed his eyes closed tightly. Doy pulled Julie up from the ground and made sure she was looking at her.

"What do we do?" he asked. "I'll support you, but I want to hear it from you."

She shook her head, brushing away an escaped tear.

"We do what Jon told us to do," she said. "We have an opportunity to stop this."

Rachael glanced at May, shaking in pain on the floor as the two entities fought in his head, then looked back at the Merlin. "But to take another innocent life …" she muttered.

"He's of sound mind," Julie said simply. "He understands the cost."

"There'll be a reckoning," Doy noted. "We'll have to accept the consequences of what we're doing. The corruption in the Republic goes deeper than we realised."

"I'm taking responsibility for this," Julie said. "I won't ask it of you two."

"You don't have to," Doy said. "I won't have you do this alone."

"I concur," Rachael said. "I won't allow you to shoulder this burden by yourself."

May opened his eyes. "I can feel them," he said, "inside here –" he tapped the side of his head "– and Legion's getting stronger. It's more comfortable with fighting; Myriad won't last much longer. It's time."

Julie nodded. She raised her left hand and aimed it directly at May's chest; golden energy began flowing through her body. Doy placed a hand on her shoulder. Rachael stood off to the side, but still within Julie's eye line. May winced in pain.

"The Republic has always been venal and corrupt; cruel emperors and a toothless Senate for starters. We're *all* responsible for what happened here, Julie, even if it was because we didn't ask enough questions. You know Blain created the scattering field?"

Julie swallowed. "I always wondered," she said, "but I could never prove anything."

"Legion and Myriad knew," he said. "When he stole a shuttle and fled the planet, two and a half years ago, he seeded it to try and stop anyone from finding the *Ulysses*. He didn't want its secrets to be given up easily."

"And then the change of ruler meant that we came back quicker than he had expected," Julie whispered.

"We're all to blame for accepting a corrupt system, Julie. We need to stop. We need to make amends." May gestured between them. "You have the harder job. Make a Republic a better place for everyone to live. Join the Sicarii and support them if that's what it takes."

He winced again and doubled over. Breathing heavily, he rested a hand on the hard, compact ground. "Save the Republic from itself. Fight for it."

"You have my word."

The energy around Julie's hand released and slammed into May's chest, knocking him a couple of feet back along the ground. His body skidded to an unceremonious halt close to the huge trees on the outskirts of the clearing. Julie walked carefully across the clearly and knelt down by him; she felt his pulse, then rested a hand on his forehead.

"It's ended," Doy said when she turned towards him. "It's over."

Julie shook her head. "It's not over, Steve," she said. "Now the hard work begins."

4pm, 18th April 418

Island One, Elysium

"So NOW YOU know everything," Julie said. The intercom in Governor May's office was on broadcast, and she was telling everyone – prisoner and staff alike – what had happened on Elysium over the last few years and, more pertinently, over the last twenty-four hours. "Everything I've seen, you know. More blood has been shed on this world than is decent or humane, and we should be appalled by what's happened.

"There have been a lot of honourable sacrifices too; Captain Mulholland and Commander Sara May of the *Ulysses*. Governor Jon May of Elysium. They gave their lives to fight the corruption that's infected this Republic."

Julie leaned back in the Governor's chair, a seat she was only occupying temporarily whilst she made this announcement. She had spent the last few hours eating and drinking her fill, while debating what to say next with Rachael and Doy, and she knew that what she was about to do was right – albeit still nerve-wracking.

"We now find ourselves in a rather unusual situation," she went on. "We can see the truth shorn of any conspiracies, lies or secrets, and it's now down to us – collectively – to decide what to do.

"Democracy is an alien concept, but one I'm willing to experiment with for a decision of this magnitude. Do you want to ignore all that I've told you, and stay as we are; a part of the Republic? If we do that, a new Governor and executive team will be appointed, and we'll undoubtedly live out the rest of our lives here in the Outmarches. But we'll probably be safe, for a given value of 'safe.'

"Or do we consider an alternative?" Julie took in a breath and released it slowly before continuing. "Many of you are members of the Sicarii, and you performed other jobs alongside that membership. You're used to leading a double life, which put you in some danger should you be discovered. So do we accept some danger now?"

She glanced up at Doy and Rachael, who were standing in the room with her, and they both gave her encouraging nods.

"Should we do something innovative? This prison planet is an aberration in the Republic; we're outside its formal boundaries, and its existence in the neutral zone between us and other empires isn't acknowledged. No-one knows we're here. Would the Republic want to take us by force if we removed ourselves from their control? I doubt it. I doubt that the Empress would be that stupid, to send a military fleet – easily detectable by our enemies – into the Outmarches and risk an all-out conflict. What if – what *if* – we became a free outpost? What if we allied ourselves with the Sicarii? What if we changed the nature of freedom? We could become free."

Julie swallowed. In that moment, she wished that she could be over on Island Two, to listen to what people were saying about her proposal.

"I'm not willing to make this decision by myself, however," she said with finality. "I will not allow an autocratic ruler to make decisions about the fate of this world. What is decided today will affect every life on this planet, so everyone living here will have a say. The majority shall have the say. You have thirty minutes to cast your vote."

She cut the comm link and motioned for her two companions to sit. Doy did so willingly, but Rachael remained standing.

"What's wrong?" Julie asked.

"You offer the residents of Elysium free will?" Rachael asked. "Why?"

The blunt question might have offended some people, but not Julie; she liked the alien's direct way of speaking. *It's refreshing to have someone so shorn of any diplomacy and say what they truly think.*

"Because I don't want to be like the Republic," she replied. "We *need* to show them that there's a different way, no matter the consequences."

Rachael nodded. "I can understand that," she said thoughtfully. "I do not wish to be like Commander Blain, for example."

Julie looked her up and down, studying the six-foot-two-inch green-skinned alien, with muscles everywhere and a set of wings on her back.

"Rachael, I don't think there's *any* chance you will be confused for Robert Blain. I have the feeling you will be your own … person."

"I hope so."

Julie nodded, then turned to Doy. "If the vote goes our way, we'll need to get you verified as a wizard. The Institute will only come after you otherwise; they'll still see you as one of theirs, even out here in the Outmarches. Are you ready to retake your final exams? I would be gratified if you didn't kill anyone this time."

Doy's jaw dropped open; her statement was a bolt out the blue, and said as though it were the most normal thing in the world.

"I would like that very much," he said slowly – and very thoughtfully, as his brain began fizzing with possibilities. "And, for the record, I consider your brother's death as one death too many, especially as he was someone who I trusted and respected very deeply. I will never allow myself to forgive – or forget – what I did."

"Nor would I expect you do," Julie said sharply, bringing Doy up short. She cleared her throat and her features softened. "However, I think we are capable of extraordinary acts. We must never forget, but we can still achieve forgiveness."

They were silent for a moment as they considered each others' words, and were grateful for the understanding that seemed to pass between them. Rachael remained silent, but nodded approvingly.

"One thing to bear in mind, though," Doy added slowly, his eyes unfocused as he seemed to be thinking something through to its conclusion.

"What?"

"The Institute will be after us *anyway*," he noted. "They're still an arm of the Republic, and if this new Chief Warlock is anything to go by, then he'll be Guinevere's pawn before long. They'll send the Hunters after us, don't you think?"

Julie considered it for a moment, then nodded. Doy could well be right.

"Then we'll have to do something about that," she said. "I doubt all Merlins will think the same. Maybe we can exploit that split. I think it's time for the Institute to realise that they don't deserve a monopoly on our powers." She smiled. "Self-determination seems to be catching."

Doy smiled back, but the comm unit flashed, and she looked towards it; the given time hadn't elapsed yet, so she knew the light wasn't the result of that. They would have to consider all this politics later; this was an incoming communication from off-world.

What it is? Doy signed to her when she looked around. *Is it the Empress?*

"I don't think so," she said. "There are six Praetorian Guard vessels heading straight for us. They're on a trajectory straight from the Mars shipyards."

Doy shifted awkwardly in his chair. "Guinevere couldn't have sent them," he said aloud, for Rachael's sake. "But who else would?"

Feeling like she was in a sudden, strange dream, Julie answered the call and recognised the man instantly. Even though they had never met, everyone in the Prisons Directorate would know his face.

"Mr Wood," she said aloud.

Out the corner of her eye, she saw Doy tense and lean across the desk. Even Rachael was intrigued; she, too, knew of Wood, most likely from Blain's instructional downloads.

"Ms Martin," Wood said brightly. *"How very nice to make your acquaintance."*

"Likewise, sir," she said. "I'm glad to see you still alive. Governor May was concerned for your safety after your most recent contact."

"Thank you. And Jon? I hope he's safe too?"

Julie swallowed. This wasn't a conversation she particularly wanted to have, but knew that she couldn't hold off from having it.

"Director ..." she said carefully. "Governor May is dead."

Wood was silent; he didn't move a muscle for a moment, then leaned back in his chair and looked away from the screen. Julie couldn't be sure, but she thought that she saw his eyes redden; he certainly wiped something off his cheek.

"Damn," he said. *"Damn."*

Julie didn't speak; she felt her cheeks redden with sudden emotion.

"How?" Wood asked simply.

"He sacrificed himself," Julie replied. "I ... was forced to kill him under his orders."

"I can imagine he did," Wood replied. *"He clearly knew*

that was the best option. Thank you for being the one to do it."

Julie nodded, but didn't want to say anything else on the subject; she was still processing what she had done. Wood seemed to pick up on her emotions; he leaned forward again and gave a weak smile.

"We'll grieve later," he said. *"Right now, I need to bring you up to speed. As you probably know by now, I'm a member of the Sicarii. In fact, I'm one of the directors leading it, and have been for some years."*

"Yes," Julie replied, "and you're in a Guard vessel, heading straight for us."

"Almost correct, Julie. I'm actually in a Sicarii vessel heading straight for you."

Julie *knew* that she hadn't mis-lip read that. "You've stolen the ship?"

"We've stolen six of them. We've been planning this for months. Now just seemed like the right time. I had to flee anyway, so why not kill two birds with one stone?"

"Well … quite."

Julie was impressed with Wood's audacity. He was clearly a good actor as well as a daring soul; to bring the rebellion's plans forward and steal six ships right out from under the nose of the Republic's ship builders was phenomenal, to say the least.

"We're survivors, Julie. The Sicarii ensures. You're a survivor too."

"I like to think so."

"Then why not join us?" Wood said. *"Become a part of the Sicarii. Elysium could become our base. It's outside of*

Republic control and—"

"Mr Wood, let me stop you there," Julie interrupted. "I absolutely agree with you, and know precisely what you're thinking. The rest of Elysium's population are currently thinking the same thing."

Wood frowned. *"How?"*

"Because I told them. I told them everything, and I've put the future of Elysium in their hands. They're currently voting on proposals to cede from the Republic and become a base for the Sicarii. Or, if you would prefer, their home world."

Wood's mouth opened and closed a couple of times. *"You've put it to the vote?"* he stuttered finally. *"My word, what a … novel approach."*

"I will honour the result. If they don't agree…"

Wood nodded; he seemed to understand.

"Jon wanted me to make a difference, and make his death mean something." She smiled. "I think I'm doing just that, don't you?"

The computer flashed. The deadline was up.

And yet I don't want to check, Julie thought. *I'm scared of both outcomes. I want to be free, but I'm wary of it too. Freedom means hard choices.*

She clicked to a different screen – Wood's face still visible in the corner – and she swallowed. The vote was unanimous.

"Well?" Doy prompted as she turned to face him. "Julie? What's the result?"

Julie smiled. "We're free."

Another silence rolled round the room, but this was a different kind; pregnant with meaning, and full of heavy, intense emotion. Julie looked at the group in front of her, two human, one alien, who all carried the same look of intensity and relief.

"We have to honour the vote," she said. "But I want everyone's agreement first. I'm going to be relying on you all to make this a place worth fighting for. Steve?"

Doy didn't even hesitate. "Of course," she said. "I welcome the fight, if only to prove that I'm more than what the Republic *thinks* I am. I want to do this."

"Rachael?" Julie said, turning to the green-skinned alien. "What about you? This isn't your fight. You could just walk away without anyone thinking anything less of you."

"*I* would think less of me. I wish to stay and undo the damage my creator did to so many. I belong here now, and I am content to be a rebel."

For a moment, Julie caught a hint of sorrow behind Rachael's words, like she had been forced to leave another life entirely behind, but the emotion quickly evaporated. She seemed determined again, and that was all Julie could ask for.

She looked back at the screen. "Mr Wood," she said more formally, "your fleet is welcome here. We hereby apply for membership to the Sicarii."

A shiver ran down her spine as she spoke the words aloud. It was excitement, she knew, from breaking free of the chains – mentally as well as physically – that had surrounded her. She could now do something new with her life.

"*Your membership is approved,*" Wood replied, a huge smile on his face. "*Permission to approach?*"

Julie frowned. "I'm not sure I can give you that permission," she said.

"*I'm making you Governor of Elysium, effective as of now. Only you can give permission.*"

Governor? Of an ex-Republic prison planet? That was a responsibility and then some. Julie looked out through the bay windows. She didn't know what she was looking for, but there were so many new challenges out there. Ceding from the Republic wasn't going to be easy, but it *would* be done. *She* could be the one to do it, and honour Jon's sacrifice.

She felt suddenly – and oddly – relaxed. *Time for things to change around here.* She looked back to the screen, where Wood was waiting for her response. She smiled.

"Welcome to Elysium."

Legend tells us that Elysium is the place where souls of heroes go after death, to lead a blessed and happy afterlife.

Whether it really exists is a debate for another day.

There *is* an Elysium in the real world, however, and it *is* the place for heroes … if only the residents realised their potential.

This is just the beginning.

Acknowledgements

Starting a new series can be hard, especially when I was so fond of the characters in the last one. However, I've had the chance to start again with new characters, and grown to love them just as much – if not more. These characters have got so much mileage in them; I'm excited to be at the start of a journey with them. They're becoming my friends.

Who do I thank for this? So many people, I have fantastic, supportive friends who have understood the occasional cancelled meeting if it meant needing to work on an idea that had sprung into my head.

Diana, Barbara, Kirk, Chelby, Jon, Lynda, Richard, Julie, Heather, Lisa, Helen, Paul, Kani, Jayne, and so many others. These folks deserve honourable mentions; I think they're brilliant people, and I'm glad to have been able to rely on them in so many ways.

To my friends who allowed me to use their names for characters; it's made them more rounded and alive.

Sara-Jayne, you have taken me into Inspired Quill's stable a third time and let me explore the beginnings of a new world – no, a new *universe*. Thank you for giving the book thorough edits and improving the quality inside these pages.

Mum & Dad. What can I say? You've given me love,

understanding, and a passion for literature without ever suggesting I couldn't do what I set my mind to. You're truly inspirational, and I'm honoured and thankful to have you as my parents.

So many readers have got in touch after the success of Fall From Grace and Leap of Faith, and said nice things to me about them. Some of you have even said you were looking forward to reading my next book; well, here it is. I hope I've done you proud.

To everyone here, and to everyone I've not mentioned; don't ever think I underestimate your value to me. I am the richer for you.

About the Author

Matthew lives in Broadstairs on the north Kent coast, a town that counts Charles Dickens, Oliver Postgate and Charles Hamilton as just three of its denizens.

Matthew is an epic fan of science fiction and fantasy; he loves everything from Terry Pratchett and Joe Abercrombie through to Arthur C Clarke and China Mieville – and plenty in between. His first two titles, *Fall From Grace* and *Leap of Faith*, are a duology, focused on a trio of friends living in Broadstairs, and is focused on themes of friendship, life, death, war, and humanity.

When not writing, Matthew works in the charitable sector. He's also a disability advocate, focusing specifically on "invisible" disorders such as autism and developmental control disorders. He writes and speaks on the subject personally and through T2D, the company he co-founded.

Find the author via his website:
www.matthewmunson.co.uk
Or tweet at him: @mnwjm1981

More From This Author

Fall From Grace

"It's time for Heaven to become a democracy."

Since leaving his calling in the priesthood and saying goodbye to the church, Paul's life has gone from bad to worse. But now, his inability to hold down a job is the least of his problems.

He and his friends, sceptic extraordinaire Joseph and academic psychologist Lauren, are thrown headfirst into a celestial war that has raged on for two millennia. As a secret plot begins to unravel, the fate of thousands lies in their hands.

To put things right, the three of them must venture into the Heavenly Ruling Chamber alongside those who started the rebellion two thousand years ago – and survive coming face to face with the Almighty himself.

Fall from Grace speaks about faith, loss, friendship and the truths we all seek.

Paperback ISBN: 978-1-908600-00-4
eBook ISBN: 978-1-908600-01-1

Available from all major online and offline outlets.

www.ingramcontent.com/pod-product-compliance
Lightning Source LLC
Chambersburg PA
CBHW032057180726
48284CB00002B/323